They walked down Preston's crowded main street. . . . There was no sidewalk and the women had to pick their way carefully through dung and ruts. The fading light of day made way for chandeliered illumination through the saloons' big windows and batwing doors, casting their artificial glow onto the dusty street. . . .

Blanche reached down and took Teresa's suitcase from her hand. "Thanks," she said gratefully, and bumped into a man just coming through a pair of batwing doors.

The bearded cowboy staggered when he righted himself and said drunkenly, "Well, what have we got here?" Clumsily, he reached for Teresa.

Wanting only to lie down on a real bed and not move until tomorrow, she pulled away angrily. "Lay off, cowboy."

"Hey," he growled. "Don't get so goddamn uppity."

"Lord, how trite," she said to Blanche. "I'll bet I've heard that line a thousand times."

Carefully, Blanche set down their suitcases. The cowboy again foolishly reached for Teresa and in a quiet deadly tone Blanche warned, "Let her go."

"Don't," Teresa said quickly to her protector. "Let me handle him."

"I'll handle him," Blanche roared, and stepped past Teresa to grab him. . .

The Long Trail

The Long Trail

PENNY HAYES

The Naiad Press Inc.
1986

Printed in the United States of America
First Edition

Cover design by The Women's Graphic Center
Typesetting by Sandi Stancil
Editor: Katherine V. Forrest

Library of Congress Cataloging in Publication Data

Hayes, Penny, 1940–
   The long trail.

   I. Title.
PS3558.A835.L66 1986   813'.54   85-32016
ISBN 0-930044-76-2 (pbk.)

ABOUT THE AUTHOR

Penny Hayes was born in Johnson City, N.Y. February 10, 1940. As a child she lived on a farm near Binghamton, N.Y. She later went to school in Utica and Buffalo, graduating with degrees in art and special education. She has made her living teaching most of her adult life, in both West Virginia and New York State.

A resident of Ithaca, N.Y., she lives with her lover of five years. Her interests include backpacking, mountain climbing, canoeing, traveling and early American history.

She has been published in *I Know You Know* and various backpacking magazines. THE LONG TRAIL is her first novel and she is hard at work on her second.

To Karen

PART ONE

THE TEXAN

CHAPTER ONE

In the spring of 1869, the sun beat down relentlessly and mercilessly on the eastern Texas town of Starcross. It curled the mid-spring grasses striving to survive in tiny spots of shade along dusty streets and near empty water troughs and in narrow alleyways where it was seldom sunny at all. Nothing moved unless it had to or was designed by nature to bear up under the excessive heat. Everything else hid in buildings or under rocks or in holes dug deep into the earth to escape the stifling air. In the distance, a thin scrawny dog yelped in pain as an angry cowboy kicked it out of his path on his way into a saloon for a tepid beer.

The old pendulum clock hanging on the rear wall of the school house would strike three-thirty in five more minutes. Blanche Irene Bartholomew saw the time stretching immeasurably before her. She could live ten thousand lives in the next five minutes, so slowly would the minutes drag. She sat uncomfortably, with aching back and stomach, behind a large heavy oak desk stained a deep dark brown and adding to the already depressing atmosphere of the combination one-room church and school house.

The building, a small rectangular affair constructed of slab lumber inside and clapboard on its exterior, had once been painted white. The interior had yellowed ages ago, and through harsh Texas sandstorms and snowy blizzards the clapboards had lost their paint except for an occasional fleck or two. Four big windows on either side of the structure allowed for as much light — and heat — as possible. Behind Blanche's desk a large slate board attached to the wall listed reading, writing, ciphering, and spelling lessons throughout the week. On Sundays it announced the hymns to be sung for services. In the rear and off to one side sat a large pot-bellied stove. Also in the rear and to the right of the door, the room's only exit, hung two pictures, one of Sam Houston, the other of George Washington. Beside each was a small American flag, even though Texas, which had seceded during the Civil War, hadn't yet been readmitted to the Union and wouldn't be before next year. Beneath the windows were nailed crude pegs for the children's wraps in inclement weather. On the same raised platform on which sat Blanche's desk was a small church organ, played faithfully and well by Blanche every Sunday morning. Ten five-foot long straight-backed wood benches faced Blanche, aligned in two rigidly neat rows and severely designed to keep young minds and old bottoms awake during learning and worship. Atop the building's gabled roof a small steeple housed the bell that

4

clearly rang the beginning and end of each school day and the start of Sunday services.

Seventeen children, damp hair plastered against their foreheads, were seated on the benches. Nine boys, ages eight to seventeen, sweltered in long-sleeved linen shirts rolled up to the elbow and opened at the neck, and long dark pants held up with wide black or red suspenders and worn tucked into heavy leather boots reaching half way up the calf. The younger lads wore ankle-high shoes laced tightly to their feet. Eight girls, ages seven to sixteen, wore dresses, some printed, some plain, fastened tightly at the neck and reaching to midcalf. Underneath were long-legged panties, one or two petticoats, thick white stockings and high-buttoned shoes. A few of the younger children wore white bib aprons.

With glazed, sweating faces and watchful eyes the children waited, as did Blanche, for the big hand to touch the six and so to free them all for another day.

Blanche pressed together heavy fat thighs in a futile attempt to staunch the flow of blood she was sure was seeping into her petticoat through the rags she wore during this wretched time. She prayed fervently that she could make it home without incident and that Matthew would come peaceably and not delay her a second longer than necessary.

Blanche stole yet another quick glance at the clock ticking loudly in the silent room in competition with the sleepy sounds of buzzing flies flitting in and out of the opened windows. The minute hand clawed its way toward the six. Three more minutes and, thankfully, she could release her charges. She had given out homework assignments earlier in the day, knowing no one would listen during the last five minutes in this baking oven. James, her oldest student, would open up first thing tomorrow morning to air out the place from this day's boiling temperatures.

In the last row Blanche watched James sitting quietly beside Caroline. Until last fall when Caroline had moved to

5

Starcross, James had been an uncontrollable beast, sassing Blanche year after year, never doing his homework, putting the younger children up to endless pranks, and driving Blanche into rages of near-hatred for him. Caroline had been an absolute stroke of luck, and Blanche, without realizing her own ingenuity, had seated her on the bench next to James. After that he had been a different person, thoughtful and kind, offering to help Blanche, even bringing in the firewood throughout the winter months without having to be asked.

The strong attraction between James and Caroline was a thing Blanche at twenty-eight had still never experienced. Even so, she knew how powerful it could be; how almost mindless one could become in the grip of passion. Last fall, very late one night, she had awakened unable to wait for morning to relieve herself. She could have used her chamber pot, but if the weather was at least bearable she always used the backhouse — far more inconvenient but much more acceptable to her natural fastidiousness. A pot full of urine under the bed repelled her.

Because of her father's expansive way of doing things, even as children Blanche, her younger brother Matthew, and her sister Mable, were able to have their own rooms upstairs in a handsome two-floor home. Downstairs slept their parents.

As Blanche passed by their bedroom on the way to the backhouse with only moonlight for guidance, she heard an unusual noise coming from inside their room — almost like the sound of pain. Recognizing her father's voice, she stepped to the door, opening it only a couple of inches.

The full moon cast just enough light through the window to show the large shadowy form of her father as he stood nude before her mother on the further side of the bed. His head was thrown back as he moaned out his ecstasy, his hands on his wife's shoulders and hers around his waist. Blanche hadn't dared make a move for fear of attracting

6

attention. Nor did she think she could have if she'd wanted to.

Hypnotized, she continued to watch her parents in their play as her mother drove her father wild with her mouth. He finally gasped, "Wait," and crawled around her to lie flat on his back. She hardly allowed him to get comfortable before she straddled him, impaling herself, letting him thrust himself into her until she, too, had begun to echo the sounds he was making.

It was her mother's turn then to say "Wait." Together they rolled over until he was above her, her legs locked around his waist in a death grip. They moved as one body then, faster and faster and at the height of their passion when it would have been impossible for anything to interrupt them, Blanche had stolen silently away from the door, her face burning with shame from witnessing such intimacy.

She forced her mind away from her parents' bedroom and turned her thoughts instead to her sister and brother. Mable and Matthew, as alike as crows, were blessed with their mother's red hair, green eyes and fair skin. Outspoken and well liked, they were slim and graceful, a condition causing Blanche to continuously pray for humility and acceptance. Both were able to eat tons of food and never show an ounce.

Blanche, on the other hand, was very much like her father, tall and dark and swarthy with almost black eyes. She was given to obesity, a hated thing about herself. Something she hated even worse than her obesity was the hair growth on her body. In ways she had never noticed on other women, her hair grew thick and matty under her arms and lay fine and soft but noticeably dark on her cheeks, flowing down from the sides of her face to her jaw-bone. Her eyebrows were thick and black and if she didn't bleach the hair on her upper lip every day or so, she could nearly be taken for a man. She thought her arms so repulsive in their furriness that no matter what the heat she never rolled up her sleeves in

7

public. And as uncomfortable as she might be in this torridity, she was grateful for long dresses and high-buttoned shoes and dark stockings to hide her legs. She even had a deep voice.

As the final minute slowly ticked itself to death, Blanche continued watching James and Caroline, knowing what was ahead for the young girl, wondering how Caroline could ever allow it to happen. Without wanting to, Blanche again vividly saw in her mind's eye the scene she had inadvertently stumbled onto between her mother and father that night.

Never had it occurred to her that her parents indulged in sexual play. It was certainly reasonable to believe they did and stupid of her not to have ever thought about it before then. She was here. And so were Mable and Matthew. But to be conceived in such wild animal behavior was more than her mind could grasp.

She had made it to the backhouse that night just in time to vomit her supper. She remembered staggering back to bed to spend the rest of the night alternating between time on her knees for forgiveness for snooping and desperate attempts at sleep, to shut out the unacceptable private lives of her parents.

The following morning at breakfast her parents behaved as if nothing had occurred the night before. Blanche began to question whether she had actually seen anything at all. And then her mother placed before her a heaping plate of eggs and sausage.

Sausage was one of her favorite foods. Her father made them from pigs he raised. The sausages were big, thick, juicy things stuffed in gut casings from the pigs themselves. She stared senselessly at the succulent meat, completely unaware of the cheerful conversation around her. In a desperate attempt to bring the world back into focus, to help deny the evidence of her own eyes, Blanche picked up a sausage with her fork and put one end into her mouth. As the sausage slid past her lips, for a moment she became her mother, and the sausage, her father.

She dropped the fork to her plate, the sausage still impaled upon it, knowing it had been no dream last night after all but something disgusting her parents did to each other. Bringing a hand to her mouth to hold back the bile threatening to overflow her lips, she ran to the backhouse to heave her guts over and over until she was so weak she had to hang onto the sides of the walls to keep from fainting.

Her mother had followed to stand by, her repeated offers of help waved away by Blanche as she retched a dozen more hurtful times before gasping, "I'll be all right. Go on back to the house. I'll be all right."

But she hadn't been all right. Since that time she had never eaten a sausage nor any other food that raised gruesome memories of that night. And for nights afterward, she had counted numbers into the thousands before falling asleep.

Mercifully the clock let out one deep, mournful gong announcing the half hour. Blanche stood. She didn't dare walk to the front of the room. If she had leaked through and soiled her dress. . . .

"Caroline," she said, enlisting the older girl's aid, "please dismiss the class today."

In seconds the room was empty, a slight rise of dust visible in the sunbeams slashing their way through the opened windows.

Blanche continued to stand motionless with eyes closed, to compose herself. But inactivity was a luxury, and she soon broke the brief moment of repose to grab a handful of cloth from the rear of her dress. Expecting the worst, she tugged impatiently at the material to check the seemingly endless yards of fabric. Looking back and down over her shoulder she saw there was no stain, thank heavens! Lord, how she hated the dress. She would never have made it for herself but

9

for her mother's insistence that dark colors made her look thinner. She doubted that anything could make her look thinner.

The dress was severely designed to fit snugly up to her neck, down to her wrists and firmly against her body, flaring out from her waist to the floor. It had a tremendous capacity to hold in heat, making her entire being want to scream from confinement.

Between being terribly overweight, having to deal with her woman's monthly problem, and the temperature hotter than she ever remembered it at this time of year, she wished she could do something else, be someone else in another way of life. But what other types of lives were there to choose in Starcross other than that which she saw every day — wife and mother, or dancehall girl? What else was left, except teaching?

Fretfully, she opened a desk drawer to retrieve her hat, a useless item which held in more body heat and only served to remind her of some fool bird perched on top of her head. With a long hatpin she anchored the hat onto hair worn parted in the middle and drawn back into a bun at the nape of her neck. She would have liked her hair hanging loose and free, cascading down her back; it would be cooler. But women her age wore their hair as she wore hers. Her most secret personal preference was to cut it off up to her ears.

She picked up from the desktop her parasol, another thing no proper woman traveled without in the sun. Finally, she grabbed her small cloth purse and hung it by its thin straps from her wrist. At two hundred and fifty pounds she felt like a beast of burden.

She slammed the drawer shut, and on her way out closed the windows and locked the door behind her. She walked quickly down the school's three wooden steps noticeably hollowed by thousands of footsteps over the years, and into the bone dry street deeply furrowed from frequent heavy supply wagons supported by big iron-rimmed spoke wheels

10

and pulled by two- and four-horse teams. She was careful not to trip over a rut or step in dung as she walked toward Starcross. She soon reached the main street, some distance from the school itself, and stepped onto a dusty wooden sidewalk. She tried in vain to shake from her hem the dust that puffed up with each step she took. If she had been a woman who cursed, the evil words would have rolled off her tongue like money pouring out of a drunk's pocket. But she did not curse; she knew no woman who did.

Along the town's long wide main avenue were strung numerous businesses, but four saloons, the most lucrative and prominent, dominated the street. Their high false fronts, once lavishly painted, were dulled with weather and age. Only their names — The Blackjack Saloon, Zang's Spirits, Boot and Spur, The Cactus Saloon — reflected their zesty spirit. Batwing doors allowed casual entry to the spacious interiors — or a rough and hasty exit into the horse and cow dung spattered street if a cowboy became too rowdy. By eight o'clock each night considerable crowds filled the places and clouds of cigar and cigarette smoke floated in thick layers. Spirits flowed freely, served by tough bewhiskered barkeeps in stained aprons and rolled-up shirt sleeves held in place with thin black satin arm bands. The steady clink of poker chips and loud talk and laughter could be heard from noon till the following day's early morning hours. Lofty crystal chandeliers illuminated gaudy wallpaper designed to cheer the heart of a lonely man and encourage him to spend his hard earned cash at green felted gaming tables or at the bar as he leaned on its richly polished surface, his foot propped up on the shiny brass rail; or as he sat at a table listening to the ladies in their flashing, colorful and provocative dresses as they laughed with red lips at anything he might say — or cried with him if he needed that. The Blackjack Saloon and Zang's Spirits, the more elegant of the four public houses — were two-story buildings with rooms upstairs where a man

11

could purchase a bath and get a decent night's sleep. But the rooms weren't necessarily just to recover from a long day's travel.

It was with ill-concealed anger and impatience that Blanche now walked toward the Blackjack Saloon. Instead of wasting precious time to stop at such a horrendous place as a saloon she would have preferred to use that same time to take a moment to stop at the drugstore, a favorite place of hers to browse. Long and narrow, the store was pleasantly decorated inside with subdued wallpaper that lent credibility to its wares. Shelves aligning the walls were stocked with a host of patent medicines, most of them heavily laced with alcohol. Diet enrichers, cod liver oil, female remedies, medicated dressings, herbal nostrums, and pressed soaps abounded, along with bibles and books for pleasure or learning. There was jewelry and perfume in pilfer-proof glass showcases, and stacks of ready-to-frame art prints from far-off cities. Sweets in large green-tinted glass jars could be purchased for a penny. Albert Smith, its cadaverous-looking owner, was the town's only doctor even though he had only read a book or two on animal care. Even so, Blanche knew he could have given her *some*thing to ease her discomfort as he had occasionally done in the past. But she didn't dare take even a moment to stop.

As she passed by the drygoods store, her face a deep scowl, she remembered with contempt the discussion she had listened to while shopping there one day not long ago, that had gone on among the town's toothless old coots as they had rocked back on spindle-backed chairs surrounding the cold pot-bellied stove, chewin' and spittin' and stealing pickles and crackers from the oak barrels nearby: "Nosiree," old John Jacobs had said. "It ain't the hot weather 'nur Texas' possible readmission into th' Union, that's on my mind these days. But don't git me wrong, boys. They's pressin' issues an' importan' as hell to us ranchers and th'

12

politicians. But them things is takin' a helluva big back seat to that crazy Wyomin' Territory's latest move."

"An' them not even a state yet," Ansel Jason had added, nodding in agreement as if his and the rest of his cronies' very lives were threatened. "Them dadburned fools up there is thinkin' 'bout wimin's suffrage. Not only thinkin' 'bout it but seriously considerin' it. An' they's talkin' as early as eighteen an' seventy. Women votin' an' holdin' office! Next thing, the ladies'll wanna be wearin' pants an' ropin' steers! Godamighty!"

Blanche had read the article in April's *Samson's Town Monthly*, a newspaper delivered each month to Starcross by stage. Thomas Johnson, ancient as the hills and owner of Johnson's Drygoods and Honest Scales, had sold the seventy-five copies before high noon, something he'd never done before. And most of them sold to the ladies, once the word was out. Well, Starcross's women had concluded immediately, if Wyoming could do it, why not Texas? In fact, why not the entire nation? The article had struck fear in the hearts of Starcross's men. And it had made its women just a bit too uppity if you asked them. But, no woman bothered to trouble herself. Blanche was glad the men were nervous these days. It helped make her own discomfort a little more bearable right now.

Blanche's thoughts were interrupted by Sheriff Maynard leaving his office as she passed his jail. "Day, Ma'am," he said briefly, and with a generous smile politely tipped his hat.

"Good day, Sheriff," she replied.

The Sheriff's Office, set purposefully on the main street, was built of thick adobe, its two homely rooms within separated by more adobe, the larger room containing a small stove, desk and chair, and gun rack, the second room consisting of a cramped cell with thick iron bars and a single tiny window facing the alley. The cell was empty now and would probably stay that way. Sheriff Maynard was hard on

13

a man who removed his gun from his holster for any reason other than to protect himself. To a man, the cowboys and drovers carried their weapons hung low on lean hips, with hats pulled down over eyes darkly shaded by large brims. Clothing smelling strongly of cows and horses was rarely changed. Spurs jangled and boots clunked heavily on Starcross's sidewalks from early evening to early morning. But with Maynard keeping an eye on them, the fun-seeking men learned fast they'd damned well better be careful in his town. But he'd always been polite to Blanche and she deeply appreciated his kind smile now.

On a day like today the town had a look of abandonment about it although a few people had begun to stir now that the sun had reached its zenith and was headed for the western horizon.

Blanche continued toward the Blackjack, passing the millinery shop, Joan's Restaurant, and several saddlehorses with drooping heads tied to hitching posts, the mounts' swishing tails warding off biting flies. She knew Matthew had gone to the saloon this afternoon instead of coming back to school after lunch, the third time this week alone that he had skipped class. That she couldn't even keep her own brother in school made her already difficult job that much harder. He made her a laughingstock and she almost hated him for it, but not once had she let it show. Never once had anyone ever known how impotent he made her feel.

Her brother was soon to be eighteen, and Blanche knew he longed to be out on his own. For some odd reason, he wanted to run a saloon. How strange, she thought, that at his age he would select such an occupation. It seemed at times that their father encouraged Matthew's poor attendance at school, even knowing his son was spending the time at the Blackjack.

Blanche saw through her father's reasoning. Alexander Bartholomew worked at the bank — was founder and president in fact. Having himself a good business head, he had recognized early that Matthew did, too. Naturally he would have preferred that his son go to work with him in the bank, but if Matthew wouldn't and wanted to be a saloon keeper, he might as well be a good one and who better to learn the ropes from than Harry Lattimer, Starcross's most successful saloon and gambling hall owner?

Blanche knew that later tonight at the dinner table, as they all gathered together for their evening meal, Father would turn to Mother and say teasingly, "Matthew skipped school today, Julia, but he's your son." And she would retort, "He takes after you, Alexander, with nothing but business and making money on his mind," which would be much closer to the truth. Mable would then tease Blanche for being so boring a teacher that she couldn't keep the children in school. Everyone but Blanche would laugh. Deep in her heart she wanted to beat Matthew for the humiliation she endured in his behalf.

Blanche swatted at an annoying fly near her face and longed to be home right now. Each day, she waited impatiently until she could escape to her own pleasant bedroom and relax completely. The Bartholomew home was kept comfortably cool with big tall trees surrounding the two-story building lending abundant shade in the summer and a strong windbreak during the wild Texas storms. Blanche looked forward to the moment — almost upon her now — when she could finally go upstairs, lock her door and strip from her body all her hated garments. To do nothing, to lie with eyes closed, not moving, for an hour before her assistance was required in the kitchen. It was the highlight of her day to rest undisturbed, uninterrupted by children, heat, or Julia, who wisely realized that Blanche needed time to herself after her day at school.

A couple of years ago when Blanche had finally made the decision to spend an hour resting totally nude, she had put a lock on her door to assure her privacy. For a long time she had battled with her soul as to whether she was committing a sin against God, agonizing over the right and wrong of wanting to take off all her clothing just to cool off for a little while.

Rarely in her life had she ever been without clothing of some form on her body, the exception being once a week when she undressed for a hurried bath in the kitchen, the warmest room in the house. Of course, this forced everyone else to stay clear of the area until she was through so her bath was always quick. The thick oak tub, a heavy cumbersome vessel and only large enough for a body to sit in, was dragged in from the back door and set in the middle of the floor. This was not only an unsatisfying way to bathe but uncomfortable as well. So she, as did the rest of the household, hurried for the convenience of all; in moments she was back in clothes again.

What a delicious feeling then, at the end of each day, to peel off the hot sticky layers. The panties pulling at her crotch, the petticoats binding her thick legs, the dresses tight on top and cumbersome on the bottom, forever dragging in the dirt.

She had made her decision, bought a lock and installed it herself. Julia worried for weeks why one of her children would need a lock on her door from her very own mother; but Blanche would not explain, would not defend herself. She had just done it, she had given herself an hour alone in her room each day without a stitch on.

She reached the Blackjack Saloon and stopped in front of its batwing doors to peer inside. The interior looked dark and cool and inviting. The idea of entering reached her consious level before she could shake it off. A faint aroma of cigar smoke and beer drifted her way as her eyes adjusted to the dim light within. Looking past several tables, each already occupied with a cowboy or two, she could see Matthew

16

sitting on the railing in front of the long mahogany bar where a few men lounged. A spittoon was gripped tightly between his knees. With a rag, he was vigorously shining its smooth surface brighter than a new penny. She didn't know how to get his attention and had already buried the idea of walking inside. Her only choice was to wait until someone came out or was about to go in.

A voice filled with surprise came from behind her: "Blanche, what are you doing here?"

Blanche turned swiftly, guiltily, toward two women who, like her, carried parasols against the pounding sun and were dressed in a style of dress similar to her own. But their dresses were gaily colored pastels, one of blue and white, the other of green. These ladies didn't have to wear dark, depressing colors to look thinner.

"Good afternoon, Mary, Eleanor." Blanche nodded to each as she spoke, knowing that in seconds her face would show the splotches of red that appeared whenever she was extremely embarrassed.

"Looking for someone?" Mary asked. Always beautiful, always in control, Mary was tiny and petite, never failing to make Blanche feel as big as a pregnant mare.

Blanche looked down on the two women from her five foot, eleven inches and took a customary step backward to lessen the angle at which she saw them. "My brother is inside," she explained.

"Indeed?" spoke Eleanor, a short, sharp-tongued, pointed-faced woman. "Strange place for a schoolboy, isn't it?" She raised an accusing eyebrow.

"Yes, it certainly is." There wasn't much more Blanche could add. Matthew had skipped school. Mary and Eleanor knew it. Blanche wasn't going to make excuses for her brother's bad behavior. And she would try with all her might not to let the ladies' self-righteousness upset her.

Mary flicked an imaginary piece of lint from her sleeve.

17

"Well, I hope he doesn't stay long, Blanche. He's so young."

Blanche forced a sweet smile to conceal her discomfort. "I'm sure he'll be along soon."

"You shouldn't wait in front of the door, Blanche," Eleanor advised. "It's unbecoming."

"Yes, of course." Blanche stepped away from the door.

Mary asked, "Are you playing the organ on Sunday, Blanche?"

"Yes, certainly," Blanche answered. Yes, yes, YES! she wanted to scream. Every Sunday she played the church organ. It was expected of her and she did it. She enjoyed it, but if only once someone else would take over for her. . . . She had been deathly sick a couple of times, but still she had been there.

"That will be nice, dear," Eleanor said.

"Yes, Blanche." Mary reached out a slender hand and gave Blanche's arm a patronizing little pat. "You play so beautifully."

So did Mary, but Blanche knew that Mary would never play on a Sunday. It was beneath her.

Blanche smiled tightly and watched them walk away, their heads together like two conspiring schoolgirls. From a distance she could hear laughter as Mary glanced back at Blanche, giving her a light wave of a hand.

Blanche waved back, wanting to use her great size to pick them both up and bash their haughty little heads together. Had she been a man she could have easily done so. But then if she had been a man, tall as she was, weighing what she did, they wouldn't have found her unattractive at all. And her weight would not be fat, but muscle on bone from cowboying, a job she would have done as a man. But she wasn't a man. She was too weak, too tall, too fat — a lady schoolteacher waiting for a brother who probably knew she was waiting at this very moment but was deliberately avoiding her.

18

The harsh laughter of a woman's voice from inside the saloon drew her attention. Blanche stepped back to the batwing doors to peer inside. A woman stepped up behind a cowboy seated at a table and put her arms around his neck. The cowboy said something to her and she walked away with another laugh as a different woman joined him.

Blanche turned her attention to the sidewalks for someone who might help her, but there was no one in sight. She sat down to wait on a bench beside the saloon's doors and prayed that a man would come out of the Blackjack soon because she felt again what was surely a surge of blood. No one could sweat between her legs that much.

The batwing doors swung open. Blanche got up quickly to call to the exiting cowboy but paused when she saw the woman she had just observed within.

She'd never spoken to a harlot before. She knew the woman was a harlot; Matthew had told her about the two women working at the Blackjack. And her father had confirmed to her that all dancehall girls were harlots. That's what they were there for. That was how they made their living.

Ignoring Blanche, the woman walked over to one of the posts supporting an overhead roof and leaned carelessly against it, taking a puff from a small cheroot and shocking Blanche into speechlessness. She had never before seen a woman smoke. In fact, this was the closest she had ever come to one of those . . . women.

A cowboy came out of the Blackjack and walked over to the woman, the silver spurs strapped to his boots jingling musically. A wide-brimmed hat perched on the back of his head covered black curly hair reaching nearly to his shoulders, a red-and-black-checkered flannel shirt rolled up at the sleeves and opened at the throat showed strong and hairy arms and a hairy chest partially concealed by a red bandanna knotted at the throat. His black pants were tucked snuggly into high-heeled boots, and he wore his wide gunbelt and holster with its sinister looking revolver low on his hip and tied loosely with leather thongs to a muscular thigh. Tall and lean, he was as handsome a man as Blanche had ever seen, even with his day-old beard. She thought of her own fiancé, Steven Trusdale. If Steven looked like this man, life with him wouldn't be too bad. At least he'd be good-looking.

The cowboy rolled a cigarette and struck a match on the bottom of his worn boot. Possessively he draped an arm across the woman's slender shoulders. She stood submissively for a moment before shaking him off, saying, "Quit, Gene. It's too hot."

He chuckled and said, "I can show you what hot is," and kissed her ear.

A real man, Blanche thought. Romantic, aggressive. Not like Steven.

The woman put a slim arm around the cowboy's waist. "You'll have to wait, dearie," she said. "I'm taking a rest now."

The cowboy gave her a little squeeze and said, "I'll be back."

In a bored tone the woman answered, "I'm sure. You always are."

Blanche watched the cowboy walk over to his horse and mount up with graceful ease. He tipped his hat to the woman and then to Blanche, catching her off-guard. She blushed and turned away but not before she gave the cowboy a small involuntary smile.

And, she had forgotten to ask him for help. Angry with herself for letting a little unexpected attention distract her, she resigned herself to a second wait. Another cowboy should be along soon.

Blanche turned her attention back to the woman who still leaned against the post. About five feet tall or so, gracefully slender, she wore a bright red dress trimmed in

20

black. It was a beautiful dress by Blanche's standards. And shocking. Without sleeves or shoulders, the dress was cut low exposing much of the woman's back and bosom. The brightly colored garment came only halfway between knee and ankle showing a trim calf and high-heeled shoes. The woman wore her black wavy hair cut short, reaching only halfway down her neck, but curling around her ears in a carefree manner. She looked cool and at ease leaning against the post, smoking like a man.

For just the briefest amount of time Blanche wanted to destroy her for having the courage to dress in something so comfortable and lively, and for so boldly holding that cheroot. Blanche certainly didn't want to smoke, but she would have enjoyed a choice in the matter.

The woman must have felt Blanche's intense stare for she turned to look at the tall lady dressed in black. "Going to a funeral?" she asked sarcastically. She faced Blanche and leaned once more against the post, blowing smoke off to one side.

Blanche dropped her eyes and turned her head away, knowing she had been rudely staring. "I . . . I'm sorry," she stammered. She sat back down looking at the dusty sidewalk. If Matthew didn't come soon she'd just give up and go on home and talk to him later.

The woman walked over to Blanche and stood in front of her. As if sensing Blanche's discomfort she spoke more compassionately. "You look lost. You need something?"

Blanche glanced from side to side in confusion. If anyone saw her talking to this saloon girl, her reputation would be ruined. "I'm fine," she managed to get out. Sweat poured down the sides of her face and she pulled an already damp linen handkerchief from the sleeve of her dress and pressed it to her cheeks.

"Hey, honey. I didn't mean to embarrass you." The woman sounded sincere as she sat down beside Blanche.

21

"You do look lost, you know." Her perfume drifted Blanche's way, expensive and heady. "You waiting for someone?" she asked. The kindness in the woman's voice made Blanche overlook for a moment that she might be seen talking to a harlot as she wondered about the woman's strange accent, one she hadn't heard before. Her first thought was to ask what part of the country she came from – but that would have been completely insane. She shouldn't even be sitting here.

"Come on, tell me. I won't bite."

Blanche finally looked directly at her. Up close the woman's face was buried beneath paint, powder, and rouge, her eyes heavily made up with blue eyeshadow. Somehow she had pasted on fake eyelashes, giving her an air of false innocence. Her eyes were green with flecks of gold and Blanche could sense that beneath the powder the woman's face was probably very smooth because the flesh on her neck and shoulders showed her to be young; perhaps only twenty-three or four. The bone structure across her shoulders reminded Blanche of a living marble statue of curves and shadows and sensuous shapes. She wanted to reach out and run her hand across the woman's shoulders and down her arms to feel the textured velvet look of her skin. She was a beautiful thing to gaze upon.

And then an unexpected and freakish thing happened to Blanche. Her heart skittered in pleasant unexplainable beats. She swallowed stupidly and only the sound of the woman's voice broke the spell she had unknowingly cast upon Blanche.

"Well?"

Blanche blinked several times and then said, "My brother is working inside. I'm waiting for him to walk me home."

"Who, Matthew?" The woman had perfectly even white teeth.

More rapid blinks. "Yes."

22

The woman took a final puff of her cheroot and expertly flipped it into the dust of the street. "Damned kid. I told him he shouldn't be skipping school. I'll get him for you." She stood and walked over to the batwings."You're Blanche, aren't you?"

Blanche nodded, shocked again — this time by the woman's foul tongue. But working in a saloon, it probably mattered little if she cursed.

"Pretty name," the woman said. "Matthew has mentioned you a few times."

"Thank you," Blanche replied, acknowledging both the compliment and assistance.

"Mine's Teresa."

Teresa. Blanche silently repeated the name. Teresa. Like the sound of lovely chords Blanche played on the organ. Not just any chords, but the special ones that she sometimes made up when she practiced on Thursday nights. Teresa. She had never heard a name like Teresa before.

"What is it?" A harsh male voice broke into her thoughts like a herd of wild horses loose in an empty barn as Matthew barged through the batwings.

"It's time to come home," Blanche said.

Matthew's eyes narrowed to tiny slits as he stood straddle-legged before her. Not quite as tall nor nearly as heavy, his efforts as an imposing figure fell short as Blanche stood unmoving, looking down at him. He snapped viciously at her,"Says who?"

"Careful, sonny. You aren't boss yet." Teresa, with a fresh cheroot, had followed Matthew and now stood beside him. She blew a big puff of smoke directly into his face.

Angrily, he pawed the smoke aside. "Neither are you, Teresa, so don't go giving me orders. I work for Mr. Lattimer."

"And I own him. So get going Matthew, and don't come back before school's out. You get under foot." Teresa left them without a backward glance. Somehow her abrupt departure left Blanche feeling strangely let down.

By a harlot?

"Let's go Matthew," she commanded sternly. "Without delay."

CHAPTER TWO

"You could slow down and walk more like a lady," Matthew said. Clearly angry, he trotted in his effort to walk alongside her; but his five foot seven inches was no match for her desperate necessity to get to the privacy of her room without delay. She was sure to mess everything she was wearing if she didn't get there in the next few minutes. The heat and sweat made the insides of her legs chafe and her discomfort was almost more than she could bear.

"I wouldn't be here at all if you took a little more responsibility for your life, Matthew," she responded tightly.

The whole thing would be settled later at dinner unless, as she expected, Father laughed it off.

Finally home and unpleasantly breathless, Blanche barely muttered a quick hello to Julia and Mable at work in the kitchen before going straight upstairs to her room. Matthew had turned off toward the barn to feed the animals and wouldn't be in the house before it was time to eat. That was good. It would give her time to organize her thoughts and perhaps talk to her mother about him before dinner.

Stripped at last, Blanche put her blood-soaked rags in a cloth bag she would later take out back and wash in the wooden tub when no one was around. She poured water from a pitcher on her dresser into its matching bowl and with a washcloth began to sponge herself clean of the day's accumulation of blood and sweat. She could hardly stand the odor of her own body nor its shape. Forced to lift the folds of her stomach from her thighs in order to cleanse herself, unusually worn from the day's trials and tremendous heat, she nearly cried in frustration at how she looked and what she was. She couldn't imagine how other fat women dealt with their weight. Much better than she, apparently. She was the heaviest woman in Starcross.

Daily there was a battle at the table as Blanche tried to refuse food her mother pressed on her, her mother insisting that if Blanche didn't eat she would get sick.

She was already sick. She was sick of eating. Lately, as she walked to school with her packed lunch, she fed it to the dogs along the way until several had begun to follow her faithfully each morning. So far she'd managed to get away with her little trick but she knew eventually someone would catch on.

She discarded the rose-colored water into her chamberpot and poured a little fresh water into the bowl, rinsed it, and then poured another bowlful for another sponge bath. On the terribly hot days like today she sponged down completely before her "quiet time."

The water, although warm, felt good as it cooled the numerous folds and planes of her body. This was her special moment in the day, and she performed her task slowly and methodically, being sure she missed no part of herself. Finished, she tucked clean powdered rags begween her legs, brought them part way up her belly and back and then tied a light strip of cloth around her waist to hold the rags in place. Refreshed, she rested on her bed, closed her eyes and emptied her head of thought. It was the most peaceful time of her existence; her time to escape from herself and the day's daily demands.

Sometime later — not much because of the delay at the Blackjack — came the expected light knock on her door.

"Coming," she answered. Reluctantly, she rose to dress. She had hung her underwear over the back of a chair and her dress on a hanger from a hook on the back of the door. They had dried out nicely but just knowing that all that sweat was still in the cloth made her cringe.

Her body heat began to rise in the confining clothing, but with the day cooling off already, in another hour or so it wouldn't be so bad.

Downstairs, she made her way through the dining room toward the kitchen. Big and airy and comfortable, with the windows opened and the drapes pulled against the direct rays of the sun and dust, the house was pleasantly cool. The living room was filled with several comfortable chairs and a large sofa with a playing table off to one side for chess or checkers. In front of the sofa was a long table for tea. On the floor were two over-sized oval rag rugs of colorful cloth her mother had braided; another was in the dining room under a large rectangular shaped table surrounded by eight chairs and positioned beneath a fifty-candle chandelier. Off in one corner a triangular shaped knickknack hutch was crowded with ornaments that Julia had collected over the years.

27

Beside the adjoining door to both rooms hung a large family portrait of the Bartholomews painted when they had first lived in the house. Blanche had been thirteen. Each day as she came downstairs, her eyes rested on the painting. She had been thin. And pretty. Now she hated the girl in that painting who stared back at her.

In the kitchen, graceful, red-haired Mable sat at a large worktable polishing silver. She said, "I don't see why I have to do this. He's not my beau."

Instantly, Blanche felt her stomach tie into a knot.

"Be nice, dear," Julia said in a singsong voice. She wiped her hands on her apron and then brushed strands of fine hair away from her face with a slender hand. "You just keep polishing like a good girl." Julia turned to Blanche and in a voice with too much gaiety said, "Steven is coming for supper. He stopped by today to bring some fresh butter. Wasn't that nice?" Julia was talking too fast; she was trying too hard to sound happy.

Blanche leaned against the sink, her hands on its edge supporting her, her knuckles white with tension.

"I told you, Mother," Mable said, catching Blanche's reaction.

Blanche contained herself in silence; she rarely let her emotions show just because of remarks like that from Mable.

"You should be happy, Blanche, that you've got a beau. At your age, you can no longer afford to be choosy." Julia was still using her gay, singsong voice, as if being bright and cheery would make everything all right for Blanche; make her a princess and Steven a prince.

"You could have asked me first, Mother, if I was up to seeing anyone tonight."

"There was no time, Blanche. He was here way after lunch."

"Besides," Mable put in, "you two are engaged. You shouldn't be putting him off at all, if you ask me."

"No one's putting him off, Mable," Blanche said, turning

28

to her sister. "No one's asking you, either."

"I just become absolutely starry-eyed when Roger comes to call," Mable said. She stopped her polishing to extend a hand to touch the fabric of her mother's dress, the same design and pale blue color as her own. "He's going to ask Father for my hand this weekend. We've decided. It's time."

"Why Mable, that's wonderful," Julia said reaching eagerly for her. The news was not a surprise. At twenty, Mable was bound to be married soon. As Mother and daughter embraced each other, theirs was joy so obvious that Blanche wondered how she had missed that same joy when Steven had asked Father for her hand.

Blanche walked over to hug Mable. If this was what her sister wanted she wasn't going to begrudge what a woman was supposed to feel for a man. "I'm very happy for you, too, Mable. You'll make Roger a wonderful wife."

She meant it. Mable was born to spend the rest of her life happily being what Blanche supposed all women desired in life: to be a wife and mother. She knew she was the exception.

Once Mable had made her announcement she could talk of nothing else. Blanche began peeling potatoes, only half participating in the discussion until Mable asked, "Blanche, when are you and Steven going to set your wedding date so that Roger and I can set ours?"

A small shock of fear raced through her as she replied, "Oh, don't wait for us, Mable. We haven't quite decided yet."

Instantly Mable began to wail, "Mother, Roger and I can't get married before my older sister does. It wouldn't be proper. It's not proper." She stamped a tiny foot to emphasize her point.

"She's right, Blanche," Julia casually agreed. "Younger sisters do not normally marry first in proper families."

There it came again. The big push to get her out of the nest and into her own home. Suggestions and hints had been dropped for years by Julia, becoming more and more pointed: Blanche was nineteen, it was time to think seriously about getting married, most girls her age were long since married. Blanche was twenty-three, most girls her age were already mothers. Blanche was twenty-five, all the girls her age were mothers with children about to go to school. Now Blanche was twenty-eight and was teaching the children of many girls with whom she had gone to school.

And Mable was twenty and banging at the altar door, feeling that she should have been married three years ago.

Blanche could have crumbled under the pressure at that moment except for the one thing she was sure she had inherited from her mother − her inner strength. "I'll talk to Steven." She bent without further word to finish the potatoes.

Promptly at five forty-five, Alexander arrived home with Steven Trusdale at his side. "I found Steven by the gate," he said, turning to the sweating young man. Dutifully, Blanche walked to Steven's side giving him a slight smile. "He says he's joining us for dinner this evening."

"That's right, dear," Julia said, automatically hanging Alexander's coat, hat, and gun belt on a coat tree by the door. "Blanche, it's so hot. Why don't you take Steven's coat?"

"Oh, no, thank you, Mrs. Bartholomew," Steven protested. "It isn't necessary." Blanche knew it could be two hundred degrees and Steven would wear his suit coat. And wear it stylishly: middle button fastened, top and bottom ones left undone. Underneath and bulging the right side of his coat, strapped to his waist was his gun. An extremely proper man, he was never out of step for whatever any occasion called for. Steven, like Blanche, was fat; as fat as she at least − a thing that perhaps had drawn them together. That, and their both being well beyond the usual marrying age. They were realistic enough to know that for them this was it in Starcross, each other or nothing. And nothing was unacceptable in their social circle of friends and family.

30

Steven's face was round as a pie with little blue pig-like eyes. He wore long bushy sideburns and a moustache which seemed to add more weight to his face. He was not quite as tall as Blanche, a private unmentionable embarrassment to them both. She did her best not to stand too close to him in public.

To his credit, Steven had his own ranch several miles out of town and several hundred head of cattle. He had been prosperous and diligent and had made the land work for him. He could provide well for his future bride.

Blanche, for all her years, had not gathered fancy linens, made special clothing, or collected things such as silver and dishes to bring with her on her wedding day. Once or twice Alexander had mentioned a money dowry but she had never pressed for details and he had never elaborated. Even so, she knew she was expected to leave eventually, dowry or not, to make a home and raise a family of her own.

With Steven.

"Why don't you and Steven go sit down and relax, Alexander," Julia told the two men, "while we finish setting the table?"

Steven smiled weakly as they left, Alexander's big arm across Steven's shoulder.

"Mable, go and fetch Matthew," Julia said. Mable went to the barn as Blanche and Julia buried the dining room table under mounds of food: potatoes, salads, meats, and sweets. More than Blanche would want to consume in a month. But she knew that this table would be cleared of every morsel this evening. And only she and Steven would pay for it. She had to work at smiling and chatting as she and Julia completed the table and then waited for everyone to gather, take their places, and prepare for grace.

Finally they were seated, heads bowed while Alexander gave the usual brief thanks. As he prayed, so did Blanche: not for a bountiful table — that was all this house ever saw — but

31

for strength to get through the evening. She was determined to talk to her father about Matthew's frequent skipping. She preferred not to bring it up in front of Steven, but his presence might be to her advantage. He believed schooling was important. When he and Blanche had gone to school together years ago, he had been the class's top student. Of course, it hadn't gotten him anywhere to speak of but was an achievement nonetheless.

The talk flew across and around the table as silver clacked against plates and food was passed again and again. Blanche took only small portions but still was forced through politeness to take more than she wanted. It was easier than arguing with Julia. Finally Blanche thought enough casual conversation had gone on. She knew Matthew had just been waiting for her to say something; he had been silent and sullen throughout dinner. "Father," she began. "I'd like you to speak to Matthew about school."

Alexander looked up from his heaping plate to glance at his son. "What about it?" He immediately turned his attention back to his food.

"About not attending." Blanche waited for the family jokes to begin.

"Call it skipping, will you, for Christ's sake?" Matthew growled at her.

"Matthew!" Julia spoke sharply.

"Skipping? Did you skip today, Matthew?" Alexander hardly missed a beat with his fork.

"I was at the Blackjack."

"When do you think," Alexander asked, "that you'll be ready to start your own saloon?"

"Father!" Blanche wasn't prepared for this new twist in his sense of humor.

"Anytime," Matthew answered coolly, looking directly at Blanche.

"You have to be eighteen first," Alexander said. "It's the

32

law."

Blanche slammed her spoon down on her plate with a loud bang. The sound seemed to reverberate around the room. "He needs schooling first," she said sharply.

Everyone looked at her, surprised at this uncharacteristic outburst. But she felt strongly about Matthew's education. "He needs schooling," she insisted.

"And you need to keep away from harlots," Matthew countered.

"What do you mean, Matthew?" Julia asked quietly. Her eyes flew first to Blanche and then to her son.

"She was talking to one of the dancehall girls outside the saloon this afternoon," Matthew accused. "If anyone saw her, people will laugh me out of town."

Julia looked at Blanche and in a firm voice said, "Please explain yourself, Blanche."

"Explain myself? Explain myself?" she repeated. "This is ridiculous. I'm trying to discuss the importance of Matthew going to school and you, Father, are discussing how soon he can open up a saloon. And you, Mother, you're only worried that I was talking to a dancehall girl. What about Matthew? He skipped!"

"Which one was Blanche talking to, Matthew?" Alexander asked.

"The one they call Teresa," Matthew said with a sneer.

"Ask me, Father," she said angrily. "I'm the one who spoke to her."

"So, you admit it then, Blanche," Julia said. "Do you know what people say about people who associate with those kinds of women? Do you know what they'll say about you?"

Ignoring her mother, Blanche turned to Steven for support. "Steven, please explain to Matthew why he should finish school before starting any kind of business."

Steven only swallowed a couple of times as new sweat popped out on his face. Blanche looked at him for a couple of seconds and then gave an impatient sound of disgust. She should have known better. How he made that ranch work for him with his wishy-washy ways remained a mystery to her.

She turned to Alexander to explain about the dancehall girl. Strangely, Teresa's face almost materialized before Blanche, so clearly did she have her in her mind. She could have reached out and touched her. Blanche blinked a couple of times to drive the image away. "The woman was only trying to help me, Father."

"She's a tramp," Matthew growled cruelly.

"She's part of a business, Matthew," Alexander advised. "You have to look at her that way or you'll never work well with the ladies you employ."

"It's ridiculous to call them ladies," Julia said.

Alexander turned to Blanche. "I know her, Blanche. She comes into the bank now and then. Nice woman, but. . . ." His voice became unusually fatherly. "Matthew is right. She is all those things you hear about.

"Blanche." Lord, now it was Mable's turn. It was going to be so good to get to bed tonight. Just to be alone.

But Mable asked, "When do you and Steven plan on setting your wedding date?"

A blow!

Almost physical.

Steven looked first at Blanche and then at his plate. Thank goodness he wasn't much on talking. Most times Blanche found that a big help. Like now. She would handle the matter herself, as tactfully as she could, without letting everyone know how easy it would be to kill Mable right here and now. She said in a carefully controlled voice, "When we get time to sit down and talk about it Mable, we'll let you and everyone else know."

Ignoring Blanche's underlying warning to let things alone, Mable turned to Steven. "Steven," she said in a sickeningly sweet voice, "Roger is going to ask Father for my hand this

34

weekend."

Alexander's head came up from his plate. A big smile filled his dark, handsome face.

"It's supposed to be a surprise, Father," Mable said. "So please act it when Roger asks."

His pleasure at her news was obvious, making Blanche feel even further pressured. She and Steven had already been engaged a year and she had deliberately put off their wedding date, sidetracking Steven every time he brought up the subject.

"Better get going, Blanche," Matthew added, enjoying his older sister's noticeable discomfort.

Mable carelessly reached for the pitcher of water on the table, averting her eyes as she coyly spoke. "Steven, you wouldn't want to see Blanche's younger sister get married first, would you? It's not proper, you know."

He knew. His sweat glands told everyone at the table that he knew. But a forkful of food into his mouth was his answer.

"Well, Steven?" Mable pushed. She didn't give up easily. She was going for the jugular. Carefully she poured him a fresh glass of water.

Blanche spoke sharply in his defense. "Let Steven alone, Mable. He came to visit me. Not you. We'll let you know what we plan to do, without your help."

With dinner over, Alexander stood. He put his big hands on the edge of the table and announced, "Enough talk, everyone. Let's go into the living room."

Immediately, Matthew excused himself, claiming work in the barn. For once Mable volunteered to help Julia clean up. "Go walk with Steven, Blanche," she said generously.

That was all Blanche needed right now; a walk in the sun. And why did Mable enourage them? The answer screamed at her.

And somehow, Matthew had been exonerated from

skipping school while she had been scolded for talking to a harlot. Now she was expected to spend the evening with a man she had no more feeling for than old Thomas Johnson over at the drygoods store.

"Well," Alexander said. "It looks like I'm alone."

And how he loves it, too, Blanche thought. A chance to sit and prop up his feet, smoke a long black cigar, and read undisturbed. She'd give her right arm to be in his position. "Let's go, Steven," she barked at him. Meekly he got up and followed her to the front door.

"Do you want your parasol?" he offered.

"No," she snapped. "Let's just get out of here." Her impotence was more than she wanted to think about. A fast walk down by the Brazos River would do her good. If she were alone it would do wonders.

Blanche and Steven wandered back through town passing the stable and blacksmith's shop, run by a bull of a man who wielded a twenty-pound hammer as if it weighed nothing. Blanche listened to the ringing of his heavy sledge as he fashioned wheel rims, horse shoes, building nails, or any oddity one might request from the artist of iron even at this hour.

They passed the barber's shop before turning left onto Baker's Street, heading toward the river and through the more residential area, passing one- and two-story homes of white clapboards, a few with white picket fences. The good up-keep of the houses was in sharp contrast to the dilapidated shacks of wood or adobe inhabited by drunks or the lazy with scrawny squawking chickens and emaciated dogs running loose. Trees growing randomly over the flat plains broke the monotony of the landscape and offered shade to the homes. Later this spring, when this unusually hot weather let up, there would be flowers growing in folks' yards, and almost every dwelling, no matter what its status, would have its own garden of vegetables and herbs nearby.

It was a constant battle against the severe Texas weather that battered the buildings of Starcross. Untended exteriors were left silver-gray, cracked and splitting. Within two years fresh paint blistered and curled off clapboards exposed to the hot summer sun and was blown free by fierce winds. During dry seasons powdery grains of dust settled over everything, keeping storekeepers and housewives and young girls busy dusting surfaces and shaking out garments and rugs. But right now, with the sun low in the sky, the buildings took on a healing glow, hiding paint chips and dust and pleasing Blanche's eye for neatness and cleanliness.

The river flowed on the western side of town. Trees and bushes grew everywhere, cleverly decorating the limitless flatland of the prairie and along the river's banks on either side, housing the animals and birds. Although the shrubs weren't beautiful in appearance, they served to break the monotony of the hundreds of square miles of surrounding flatland.

The water level of the river was so low that Blanche and Steven walked on parts of what was usually water-covered banks. Blanche closely observed the land she would normally not have seen. There was nothing spectacular about the clay bank, but she studied it to preserve the memory against a time when the bank would no longer be visible.

She was deep into her thoughts, feeling better just for being here, when Steven spoke for the first time since leaving the house. "Uh, Blanche, about what Mable was saying."

"What about it?" She wanted to walk along the river and not think about anything.

"Have you considered a date?"

"For what?"

"Our, uh, marriage?"

"Oh, Steven, stop stammering." Couldn't he just once be manly about something and say whatever it was he wanted to say? "I told you before," she said, "that I'd think about it."

"But that, uh, was two months ago." He looked pathetically apologetic.

"You're not listening to me, Steven. I said I'd think about it and I will." As soon as she thought she could bear the feel of his whiskers against her skin on a daily basis. As soon as she could adjust mentally to the weight she would feel lying on top of her body any time he wanted to be there — as was her duty.

Tentatively, Steven stepped close to her and took her in his arms. The evening had cooled sufficiently to allow her body to stop its heavy perspiring and, she saw, Steven's own.

Cooler and more comfortable, she allowed him to hold her beneath the shelter of a mesquite tree. It wasn't too bad for a moment but, as always, Steven's breathing became more rapid and, irritating the very life out of her, his nose started to whistle as his breathing rate increased. Then, as he held her close to him she felt a bulge against her pelvis because of his apparently large male endowment. As he became more enamored he pressed against her a little more and then a little more until she couldn't stand him. She hated that part of his body. Hated it and didn't want it. As many times as she had tried to become excited by his maleness, she had never been able to. How many times she had lain awake nights thinking of him standing nude before her? He was her fiancé. She should be aroused by him. She tried desperately to be, once even went so far as to touch herself while thinking of him. All that had happened was that she had felt shame and had somehow let herself down.

"That's enough, Steven," she said pushing him away.

"Why?" he protested. "When we're married. . . ."

"Yes," she said holding him back. "When we're married. But we're not, yet, so don't."

Steven never argued, never quarreled. He backed off. Just once she wished he would say something, be more aggressive. Like that cowboy she'd seen today. Maybe it would have

38

made a difference.

For another hour or so they wandered along the river bank before turning back to the house. The sun had escaped the Texas sky for the day and cool gentle breezes had moved in. A soft darkness settled over the land obscuring the hard lines of the distant buildings, producing a soft edge to the harsh desert world.

Along with the soothing breezes, the thought that tomorrow was Friday put Blanche in an almost heady and benevolent mood toward Steven. As they walked toward the house she impulsively reached for his hand. Surprised, he smiled at her as he matched her steps back toward the house.

How bad could it be, she questioned silently, being married to this man who really was quite devoted to her? She began to total the amount of time he would actually touch her in a twenty-four hour period. There would be the lovemaking of course, the time she most dreaded, and the sleeping side by side. But she wouldn't necessarily have to sleep in his arms. There would be a considerable amount of touching and holding and kissing at first because, she assumed, marriages always started out like that. But then, after she and Steven had fit into a routine, the physical contact should lessen. She calculated the time she thought she would have to physically give him. It couldn't be more than two, perhaps three hours total, in a twenty-four hour day; and probably not even that much every day. Couldn't she handle three hours a day for a home of her own and a man who would certainly see to her needs? Wouldn't it be worth it to be independent of her mother's disappointed eyes and her father's patient tolerance of her?

As for teaching, that would be out entirely. Women didn't teach once they married. That would certainly solve her unhappiness with her futile efforts to keep Matthew in school. He would become someone else's problem.

Mable did have a right to marry secondly. Otherwise it

definitely would be an embarrassing situation to her. To the whole family actually; a family which always went by what etiquette and protocol and tradition dictated. Blanche would hardly be fair if she didn't marry Steven first. She knew she would marry him. Had to. This was the end of the line. She absolutely could not live with her parents for the rest of her life. She was the town joke now because she had waited this long.

Three hours of bodily contact? Of course she could handle it. She would have her own home and a life of her own with only one other person to deal with instead of an entire household.

In an expansive mood, Blanche paused beneath a mesquite tree and said to Steven, "Why don't we talk about setting a wedding date soon, Steven? We've waited long enough, don't you think? We'll discuss it this weekend. You are coming over, aren't you?" She spoke rapidly as if to pause for even a moment would cause her to lose the momentum of her words. She rushed to get them all out before she changed her mind.

Joyfully, Steven took her in his arms and kissed her passionately. She thought of the cowboy who had smiled at her today but Steven's mustache scratching her mouth drove him from her mind. Blanche returned Steven's kiss thinking that this kiss would only take a minute or so. That wasn't too much time in a twenty-four hour period for all the other benefits she would gain.

But at the moment she couldn't think of one.

CHAPTER THREE

As the last child left, Blanche returned to the empty school room to finish closing windows, straightening her desk, and gathering her things together. The day had been deliciously tolerable with the cooler weather and her monthly time nearly over now. If each day could be like this one, she knew she could live forever.

Walking toward town, Blanche knew it would be useless to stop by the Blackjack for Matthew. He had skipped school last Friday afternoon and had done so again today. She would be wasting her time if she stopped. No matter what she said about the importance of education, Matthew had just about had his fill of school. He'd be working steady in the saloon soon, learning how to be better at the business than Lattimer was. Her father openly approved. Her mother seemed unconcerned. It was time for Blanche to give up trying to educate her younger brother.

Blanche had no excuse whatsoever then, to walk farther down the sidewalk and past the Blackjack Saloon, the biggest and the rowdiest saloon in town reputed to have the best women and the best whiskey. She rarely ever went by way of the Blackjack, except when she had to make a stop at the bank or the drygoods store or the dress and millinery shop. When the cowboys drove their large herds through town on their way to Samson's Town, no woman in her right mind would walk unescorted by the saloon. Men poured through the doors, so eager were they to reach the whiskey and the women in the powerful Blackjack Saloon.

She rationalized that she *might* stop to shop; that it was a shorter distance going home this way than using the opposite side of the street, thereby saving a few steps. She had taken the same route on Tuesday and again on Wednesday. Each day as she approached the saloon, walked by its open doors, passed the building with eyes straight ahead, she found herself listening intently to the sounds of the piano player plunking out his melodies, the hoarse laughter of cowboys, the muted clink of poker chips on felt table tops, the sound of chairs scraping against the wood floor, not really sure what it was she expected to hear.

On Thursday, one week from the day she had waited miserably in front of the Blackjack for Matthew, there on the bench before the saloon sat the cowboy who had smiled at her last week. Lord, he was handsome. He made Steven look like an old potato. If she were marrying him. . . .

With him, looking as cool as a beautiful spring day, sat Teresa, her right arm resting across the back of the bench, and a cheroot held loosely in her left hand. As much as the cowboy was handsome, Teresa was beautiful. If Blanche were a man she'd be sitting where the cowboy was now.

That's what she didn't understand.

The thought was too radical for her. It left her feeling just slightly ill as she forced her mind to again accept the cowboy as the one she had been looking for all this time.

But it didn't work.

Recklessly, she let false desires for the cowboy go. She didn't want him. She admitted why she had been walking by the Blackjack every day. She had been hoping she'd see Teresa again; had been listening for her voice; had at some time last Thursday made that decision and hadn't known it until this moment.

The cowboy got up and went inside the saloon, leaving the saloon girl alone. A strange sense of relief filled Blanche.

As Blanche walked up to her, Teresa leaned comfortably back against the bench and took a deep drag of her cheroot, blowing smoke up and away. She wore another very low cut dress, strapless this time, orange with black lace trim around the top and at the hem. Blanche briefly wondered how the dress stayed up. She looked at the small woman's sculptured shoulders, at skin appearing so soft that again, as on last Thursday, she longed to reach out and feel the fineness of it. She imagined it would feel as smooth as the marble piece that covered the top of her dresser.

Teresa blew a perfect ring of pale blue smoke in Blanche's direction, dissipating it with a flick of a hand. "Hello, Blanche," she said.

Blanche paused before the dancehall girl. Another woman would have called her Miss Bartholomew. "Good afternoon, Teresa." She would have called another woman Miss Something-or-other, their having met only once, and not very formally at that. But formality seemed out of the question. And Blanche didn't know her last name.

"Have you given up on Matthew?" Teresa asked.

"Yes," Blanche said. "I assume he's here again."

Teresa nodded, shrugging. "I didn't help much last week." She took another puff of the cheroot. "I tried. I thought I might scare him out of here for good. It's no place for boys his age."

"Thank you for trying." As an uneasiness settled over her, Blanche began to move on. Suddenly, she feared being seen talking to Teresa and hated herself for her own weakness. She had deliberately walked this way daily, hoping Teresa would come out of the Blackjack so that she could talk to her. And now. . . .

"Here," Teresa said. She patted the bench beside her. "Sit down and rest for a minute."

"I . . . I. . . ." Blanche stammered, still moving down the walk. She liked Teresa without understanding why. Liked her very much. But a proper lady just did not associate with dancehall girls no matter what. She answered weakly saying, "Another time, perhaps."

Teresa smiled with knowing eyes. She stood stiffly and flipped the cheroot into the street saying, "I understand perfectly." Without another word she walked into the Blackjack.

Blanche stopped then, to watch Teresa's back disappear through the doors, their squeaking hinges protesting usage until they were still. She stood for a moment as if hypnotized. She was glad she was alone, for she felt red splotches of shame on her face and neck, and felt a small trickle of sweat snake its way down her throat to the cleavage between her large breasts, causing an unbearable tickle. She longed to reach up and claw the maddening sensation away. She deserved this punishment; she had snubbed someone without valid reason — except that proper ladies did not talk to dancehall girls. Impulsivly, she swallowed several times, a habit of hers whenever she was badly upset.

44

At home that evening she was cranky. A bitch, Matthew had called her. Yes, she was that all right, because of her shameful treatment of Teresa. What in the world could anyone say even if she did sit and talk to a dancehall girl? It wasn't as if Blanche were inside the Blackjack Saloon with her foot propped up on the brass railing, her elbow on the bar and a whiskey in her hand. But she knew if it were to happen again, if Teresa were to ask her to sit down, she would do the same: she would refuse. She didn't have much choice in Starcross.

And, she thought, neither did she have much courage.

Friday after school, as if she couldn't help herself, she again walked toward the Blackjack. She wanted to apologize to Teresa for her behavior yesterday. She would explain, if she could. It wouldn't be easy. Apologies never were. It amazed her that she intended to say anything at all about her rude behavior. Teresa was nothing to her. Just someone she had met briefly.

And liked.

She could feel the tension building as she came closer to the saloon and she actually began to hope Teresa wouldn't be there today. There was no reason to expect her; she'd shown only one day out of the whole week so far. But soon Blanche could see the small woman sitting on the bench. This time she wore pink. How many dresses did she have, Blanche wondered. She felt shabby and dumpy-looking in her own plain brown dress. As she stepped up onto the sidewalk and approached Teresa, Blanche had little idea of how to even begin her apology. She still didn't want to be seen in lengthy talk with a . . . dancehall girl.

But Teresa made it easy. In the strange accent that Blanche had wondered about last week, she said, "Hello, Blanche. I just thought I'd sit out here today and greet you as you walked by."

So Teresa knew that Blanche wouldn't sit and chat. And

45

why. And still she had been willing to wait outside just to say hello in spite of yesterday's snubbing. Blanche wondered what kind of stuff Teresa was made of. It was at least a plane above herself.

As Blanche stopped momentarily, Teresa added through the smoke of her ever present cheroot, "You can do that, can't you? Say hello, back?"

"Of course," Blanche answered, relieved now of the burden of apology and by Teresa's understanding of her plight. Her familiar perfume drifted up to Blanche's nostrils and again she wondered what it was. Intoxicating struck her as a good word.

As Blanche started the rest of her journey toward home, Teresa waved a hand, seemingly almost dismissing Blanche. The awkwardness of yesterday was gone but Blanche could still feel the shame. But, on the positive side, some sort of understanding had sprung up between them and she moved with a lighter step.

The weekend dragged by in spite of evening walks with Steven both Friday and Saturday, a walk alone by the river Saturday morning, and playing the organ Sunday at services. The worst was the constant chatter of Mable, nearly driving her mad, about their coming weddings. In six weeks, as Blanche and Steven had finally announced Friday evening and much to everyone's relief, she would be Mrs. Steven Trusdale. She did her best not to let her disquieting fears interfere with Mable's own enthusiasm.

With unusual and anxious anticipation she looked forward to Monday. And not just Monday, but Monday afternoon. She hoped to see Teresa out in front of the Blackjack, sitting on the bench as she had been on Friday.

The longed-for day finally arrived and crawled slowly by, filled with the sounds of studious children. At last the final child flew off the steps leaving Blanche's mind free to hope.

Teresa didn't let her down, brightening her day when

46

Blanche saw her sitting there. They spoke only briefly but it was enough. Her evening's work on her wedding dress, with its yards and yards of material, seemed more bearable. Bearable, too, if not almost pleasant, was an unexpected walk with Steven that evening.

On Tuesday, again Theresa was there. And on Wednesday — each new day wearing a colorful and cool dress, looking relaxed and sure of herself and in control, puffing freely on a cheroot. Blanche envied her easy living style. Some women were more bold than others. Blanche wished she could be like that.

On Thursday, Blanche closed the school as usual and began the five-minute walk to the Blackjack, striding rapidly toward her expected brief meeting with Teresa, a pattern she had quickly fallen into. But she could already see at a distance that Teresa was not there. She slowed her steps to allow time for Teresa to come out of the saloon. By the time Blanche had reached its doors, she had delayed to a conspicuous pace and knew that Teresa would not be out. No matter, she told herself. She had tomorrow to look forward to.

On Friday, Teresa wasn't sitting on the bench either and as hard as Blanche listened for her as she passed by the saloon she did not hear Teresa's voice among the rest. That left the weekend stretching long and empty before her. She could have asked Matthew about Teresa but didn't want to endure his righteous eyes.

Teresa was a trollop, a convenience for the cowboys — perhaps even the very personal friend of Lattimer himself, as she had indicated last week when she had told Matthew that she owned him. Yet somehow it was unimportant what Teresa was or what she did. What drew Blanche even closer to her was that Teresa hadn't at any time, especially during their first meeting, scrutinized her. Neither her size nor her weight nor the obvious hair on her face. The last, alone, was

47

enough to endear her to Blanche. For Blanche was well aware that how she looked was a point of private interest and great humor among the women she called friends.

Very early on Sunday morning, she went to the river. The place had lately become a refuge. With just enough light to see by, she was at the water's edge as the first bird sang its morning song. Her heart and soul filled with hopeless longing for the birds' peace and beauty. Depressingly, she began to compare herself to them.

The males were the most striking in color, to tempt the female. Even in her drab colors the female was beautiful, for she had sleek lines and boundless grace and was unabashedly attractive to her mate who fought others of his kind to win her.

Near a mesquite tree, Blanche sat down on a rock that was fast becoming her own, and gazed absently across the wide river. Who would ever fight for her and find her irresistibly attractive? She and Steven were marrying each other for all the wrong reasons. No one else would have either of them; socially they needed each other; life was becoming hopeless in her present situation and she needed an escape, and for her at least, pressures at home were almost unbearable.

Lost in morbid thoughts, she sat for a couple of hours. Shimmering in the red sky, the sun looked like a squashed ball this morning, its slightly flattened bottom red-orange, its round top yellow as a buttercup. The unusual distortion cleared itself up as the sun rose higher and higher, leaving in its wake a brilliant blue sky, and in the distance miles and miles away, billowing white clouds holding the elusive promise of rain.

The approach of a horse and light buggy brought her out of herself. She was more than a little irritated that someone would intrude upon her private place. No road ran by here. Other than small boys coming to fish, rarely did anyone ever walk or ride this close to the river. She had claimed this particular spot on the bank as her own.

Turning to identify her intruder, Blanche stood quickly and watched with great delight as Teresa drove up in a small open two-seated buggy, handling it like an expert. She didn't look the type to ride in a buggy by herself. The top, with animated fringes dangling, should have been in place to protect her from the sun. There should have been some big handsome cowboy handling the reins with Teresa beside him looking like she owned the world.

Blanche's next observation was that Teresa looked almost alien in a plain, sober dress. Teresa should be much more like the colorful male bird with her flashy clothes and aggressive ways.

Teresa brought the prancing chestnut gelding to a halt beside her. "Get in," she said.

When Blanche paused, Teresa extended a hand toward her. "Come on. There's no one around."

Blanche threw caring what anyone else thought to the wind and climbed up, sitting on Teresa's right. Teresa cracked the reins against the horse's powerful flanks and said, "Getup, Stormy."

They drove along the river for several minutes without speaking. Blanche enjoyed the ride immensely, the sensation of escaping. Finally Teresa asked, "Where would you like to go and how much time do you have?"

Blanche looked down at a small gold watch pinned with a metal bow of gold to her bosom. The tiny gold hands on a white face read nine-thirty in delicate Roman numerals. "I have an hour and if you continue along this path, you'll come to a fork in the road." She gestured toward the west. "The road cuts back to the river. Several mesquite trees in a group offer a lovely shaded area. We can go there if you like. It's about a fifteen minute drive."

Teresa followed Blanche's directions and soon pulled

Stormy to a halt under the trees, wrapping the reins around the front bar of the buggy. She sat back, looking straight ahead, and sighed, folding her hands in her lap like one of Blanche's well behaved children. "I've never been here before," she said contentedly.

"No?"

"No. I've always driven north along the bank."

Blanche gave a light laugh. "I never go north, only south."

"So between us we know about five miles of the Brazos."

"At least."

Another minute or so passed before Blanche spoke. Shyly she said, "I walked by the Blackjack to say hello Thursday and Friday. I'm sorry I missed you."

"It couldn't be helped," Teresa said. "I would have been there if I could."

Blanche wanted to ask why she wanted to be there. It would have done her heart good to hear Teresa say, *Because I like to say hello to you.* But the dancehall girl remained silent.

Blanche settled into the corner of the buggy seat and draped her arm carelessly across its back and a little behind Teresa. The repose of the moment was almost intoxicating. She would never, ever sit like this with Steven. When driving with him, she remained always in a rigid, formal position, he in charge, the reins held stiffly in front of him, the left rein in his left hand, the right rein in his right; she, sitting upright, hands in her lap. With Teresa driving, she had dared slump a little and mold her body to the padded leather seat. It was downright comfortable.

"I'll try to be out front tomorrow but if not tomorrow then Tuesday for sure," Teresa said gazing to her left.

There was something odd in the way Teresa was avoiding looking at her. She sat staring out over the land, deliberately averting her eyes. Confused, Blanche said, "Teresa?" wonder-

50

ing if Teresa were having second thoughts about coming here with her. "If you'd like to go back. . . ."

"No, I don't want to go back," Teresa said in a strained voice. She shifted slightly.

With her arm behind Teresa and her body only inches away, Blanche felt protective toward her new friend. But, not believing for a minute that it wasn't herself who was causing Teresa's discomfort Blanche said, "I have to assume you haven't looked directly at me because of something I've done to displease you. I'm sorry if I have." She began her uncontrollable swallowing, the heat splotches rising on her skin. The thought also crossed her mind that up close, Teresa found her repulsive. All that facial hair would turn anybody away.

"It's not you at all, Blanche," Teresa said, only halfassuring her. "It's something I didn't want you to see. I really shouldn't have stopped this morning. I don't know. Maybe I was just looking for a little sympathy."

"Sympathy?" What wouldn't she want Blanche to see?

She looked down on Teresa's rich, glossy, dark hair casting thread-thin rays of sunlight off each individual strand. She admired the conservative, pale-blue dress Teresa wore, fitting much like Blanche's, tight at the top and covering her neck, shoulders, and arms, and flaring at the bottom. It reached to her plain, high-buttoned black leather shoes. Her face, scrubbed clean of its makeup, was smooth and creamy. Away from the Blackjack Saloon, Teresa could have been any one of the ladies who lived in town and strolled its streets and sidewalks on pleasant days.

"I needed to get out," Teresa said. "To get away from the Blackjack for a while." Teresa looked again to her left avoiding Blanche's eyes. "I watched you sitting by the river for quite some time yesterday morning. I decided then that I would have a carriage rented for this morning and drive out this way if you went again."

51

Blanche said, "You could recognize me from the saloon?" How nice to think that someone would care enough to see if she were there.

"From my window upstairs," Teresa answered. "I can see up and down the river for quite a distance."

Teresa had deliberately watched for her. Blanche forced the smile from her lips. It would be childish to appear so pleased. Softly she asked, "Why shouldn't you have come here this morning, Teresa?"

As Teresa turned to fully face her, Blanche gasped at what she saw. A large yellowish bruise, days old and almost gone, marred the smooth complexion on the left side of Teresa's face. The mark began above Teresa's temple and stopped halfway down her cheekbone, part of it covering her eye both above and below. Blanche was astonished and sickened at the size of it.

"Did you fall?" Blanche whispered.

"Lord, no, honey." Teresa laughed. "Dancehall girls don't end up looking like this from a fall."

The anger Blanche felt welling up within her forced her beyond tact or discretion. "You were struck, weren't you?"

"That's putting it mildly," Teresa said.

Without thinking, Blanche reached up and put a cool hand on Teresa's face. Gently her fingers touched the ugly mark. "Why . . . how . . . ?" She'd never known a woman who was struck before. "Is that why you weren't out front, Thursday? Were you hit on Thursday?" She clasped her hands together in her lap to hide their angry shaking.

"Wednesday evening," Teresa answered. "Late. It's nothing, really. I've made too much of this. I'm sorry."

Blanche refused to begin her swallowing. She would be rational and calm. "Would you tell me about it?" she asked. "I'd like to know."

Teresa gave her a dubious look.

"Please, I mean it, Teresa. I'd like to know." She wanted

to know this more than she had ever wanted to know anything in her life.

Teresa sighed, staring off into space. "My period started Wednesday. I always have a bitch of a time on the first and second days."

Blanche flinched at Teresa's profanity and then said, "Period?"

"You know. The monthly curse," Teresa explained.

"Oh," Blanche said stupidly. She had never heard a woman's monthly time called either of those names before. It did seem like a curse to her. A great huge joke God had played on women.

"I guess it was a big disappointment to Lattimer coming when it did," Teresa said. "He's usually more reasonable."

It took Blanche a couple of seconds. Then disgust and revulsion overwhelmed her as the explanation sunk in. "Are you saying," she stammered, "that because he couldn't . . . couldn't. . . ."

"Screw me?" Teresa laughed. "Believe me, Blanche, men can be very demanding."

"So it seems," Blanche barely managed to utter before turning away. She was never going to let Steven get like that — using her like a . . . a thing. No man had those kinds of rights. A wife had a duty to fulfill, but she wasn't an object, like a chair or a fork; or a dancehall girl to be used at a man's whim.

"Let's forget it," Teresa said. "I insist." She reached over and patted Blanche's hands. "We still have time left. Let's get out and walk awhile."

"Of course." Blanche stepped out and joined Teresa who had already jumped down on the other side of the buggy. If Teresa was going to forget what had happened, Blanche knew that she must, too.

They strolled along the bank of the river talking about their different lives. The contrast was so great that their comparisons caused them tears of laughter. The feeling of friendship Blanche experienced was like a found treasure.

Reluctantly Blanche checked her tiny watch. Services began promptly at eleven. She'd have to leave now to make it on time. "I must return, Teresa."

"So soon?"

"I play the organ at church," Blanche explained.

They turned back to the buggy with forced steps. "This has really been good for me, Blanche. You're a good woman. It was kind of you to ride with me today."

Blanche stopped. "Teresa, you know I wouldn't even be talking to you like this if you were sitting in front of the Blackjack right now."

"I know that."

"Then, I'm hardly worthy of being called a good woman."

"Of course you are, Blanche," Teresa insisted.

"No, I'm a hypocrite and we both know it."

Teresa gave a little laugh. "I disagree."

"How can you?" Blanche argued, stepping up into the buggy.

Teresa joined her and picked up the reins saying, "Gitup, Stormy," cracking them against his rump, and heading back to Starcross. "You're no hypocrite. You just do what you have to do. I do what I have to do. There's nothing hypocritical in that."

"I think you're being very generous, Teresa. Very generous."

Teresa dismissed Blanche's comment with a smile.

A short time later Teresa returned Blanche to the river bank. "Do you come out here often?" she asked. "I never noticed you before yesterday. But then I really wasn't looking."

"Yes," Blanche said, climbing down. "But rarely this

early. I've just been very restless lately. I've needed to be alone."

"I hope I didn't spoil your solitude."

"Not at all. And what about you?" Blanche asked. "How did you come to be up early? You work long hours." She didn't want to say *late night* hours. Blanche knew exactly what Teresa did at night. If she had allowed herself to envision Teresa's livelihood, she could almost have become physically ill. She pushed aside fleeting thoughts of her parents and that night long ago.

"I haven't been working," Teresa said. "Lattimer doesn't want anyone to see my face and know what a bastard he really is. He's been telling everyone I have a bad cold, he's been sending my meals up to my room. I had to get out of there this morning before I went crazy."

"Does he know where you are?" Blanche hardly flinched this time when Teresa swore. "Will he be angry?" *Will he hit you again,* Blanche wanted to ask. But she didn't dare.

"I have my own room," Teresa said. "Lattimer's still asleep, I imagine. He usually doesn't stir before noon. Another man opens up for him and he won't tell I went out. In fact, he rented the buggy for me yesterday."

Teresa started to speak again only to stop. She said good-bye briefly and quickly to Blanche before driving off. Blanche waved to her and watched her for a minute or so before turning back to the house.

Her father met her at the front door. He spoke softly, quietly, as the smoke from the cigar held between his teeth rose in a thin straight line. "Morning, Blanche," he said. "Been out walking?"

"Good morning, Father," Blanche said. "Yes, I was." Why did she feel so guilty?

"Down by the river?" Alexander asked casually.

"Yes," she replied. "I was restless." She didn't hear

anything in her father's voice other than interest but somehow he made her terribly uneasy. "Excuse me, please. It's time I got ready for services now." She thought she caught a look of — what? Curiosity? Concern? Not anger. It was something else altogether.

"Take your time," he called after her as she went upstairs. She turned back to give him a brief smile. He had followed her to the foot of the stairs and stood with one hand on the railing gazing up at her. The look she couldn't identify still on his face.

A while later, with all of them in a four-seated buggy, Alexander driving, and Matthew with his feet hanging off the rear, it was as if her earlier conversation with her father had never taken place. Amid the normal Sunday bustle his strange look was gone. Blanche impatiently brushed the incident aside as part of her overactive imagination.

Blanche thought again about Teresa's words. Teresa was wrong about her. She indeed was a hypocrite. She'd just proven it again. Otherwise, why hadn't she admitted what she'd done this morning — taken a buggy ride with a dancehall girl?

But she couldn't admit it. She already had too many faults as it was; too much hair, too much weight, too much height, lack of grace. She couldn't openly display one more: that of thinking a dancehall girl could be a friend. That would have caused the Bartholomew household no end of uproar.

She argued with herself and fought off waves of shame.

CHAPTER FOUR

"Are you practicing tonight, Blanche?" Julia asked. She, Mable, and Blanche stacked the last of the supper dishes, filling the kitchen with familiar sounds.

"At seven," Blanche answered.

"Which way are you going?" Mable hung up her towel and sat down on a stool next to the sink.

"To school?" Blanche asked. A warning sounded in her mind.

"Yes," Mable said. "To school. Which way are you going to school?"

"By way of Mexico, Mable," Blanche answered defensively. There was only one way to get there. Through town. "Do you want to go?"

"No," Mable said flippantly. "I wouldn't want to be seen standing in front of the Blackjack Saloon, talking with a common trollop."

So, the family knew. Since she and Teresa had gone driving last Sunday morning, she had stopped by the Blackjack daily on her way home purposely to see Teresa. "I take it Matthew has been watching me," she said.

"Not only Matthew," Julia replied. "Others have seen you."

"I don't see any problem, Mother," Blanche said. "We only speak for a minute."

"It was quite a bit longer than a minute yesterday, Blanche," Julia said. "It is not a proper thing for you to be doing."

Blanche stood defiantly with her hands jammed on her hips. "And what, may I ask, makes it all right for Matthew to skip school and spend his time in the Blackjack when he isn't even old enough to be there, and not all right for me to be outside the place talking to Teresa? What, exactly, is wrong with her?" She was nearly choking with anger.

Mable began to speak but Blanche cut her off with a slashing hand. "Mother, *you* tell me. I want *you* to answer. Do you know that she is very nice to me? She doesn't make me feel like an overgrown brood cow like everyone else I know. She is a pleasant person." Blanche defended her as she would anyone who had done nothing more than not fit in with Starcross's sense of what was right and what was wrong. "Who decided anyway, whom I should see and whom I should not? Matthew? Mable?" She was about to say, *You?* but stopped in time.

"She's a saloon girl, Blanche," Julia said angrily. "A dancehall girl. She . . . she. . . ."

Blanche lost her head. "Screws indiscriminately?" She spoke heatedly using Teresa's language. The word was out before she knew it.

"Blanche!" Julia gasped. A trembling hand flew to her throat.

"Mother," Mable wailed. "Blanche is even starting to talk like a trollop."

Blanche turned on her sister. "How would you know, Mable? Do you know what screw means?"

"No, but I do and so does your mother." Alexander had come in from the living room drawn by the loud voices of his women. "Please don't use that kind of language, Blanche." He turned to his wife and youngest daughter. "Blanche is over twenty-one. Leave her alone on this. She'll work it out."

Stunned by her father's unexpected support, Blanche could only stare at him as her built-up anger drained away.

"Alexander, you do realize that people will talk," Julia stated levelly. "Do you know what they'll say about her? About us?"

"We'll survive it, Julia," Alexander replied.

Mable protested vehemently, "Blanche has real girl friends she could visit if she'd only get out once in a while instead of sitting alone in her room so much or watching the stupid water go by in the river all the time."

"The issue is closed," Alexander answered flatly. He turned abruptly and left the kitchen.

Blanche glanced toward her mother and sister who stood staring openmouthed after him, then she followed him into the living room taking a chair nearby as he sat down. Casually, he picked up a book from a small end table and began to read as if she weren't there.

"I don't understand, Father." Blanche waited for a delayed and severe tongue-lashing.

Alexander rested the book in his lap. He rubbed a

thoughtful hand across his mouth and then spoke with quiet authority. "Three things, Blanche," he began. "First, I don't ever want to hear that kind of talk from you again. You've hurt your mother and your sister and owe them an apology immediately."

She had no doubt of that. What had ever possessed her?

"Secondly," he continued. "You'll work it out. And, lastly, the issue is closed."

She stood and walked back to the kitchen. His words made little sense to her. If he wasn't going to scold her then she wasn't going to wait around and give him the opportunity to change his mind.

She entered a quiet kitchen, "I'm sorry, Mother. I'm sorry, Mable. I shouldn't have spoken that way. It was crude and uncalled for."

Mable said nothing, leaving the room almost before Blanche could complete her apology.

Julia asked, "Are you going to continue to stop at the Blackjack?"

"Yes."

"Then why apologize?"

"I'm apologizing for my rude tongue, Mother. Nothing else."

"I see," she said. She looked away and absently brushed an imaginary crumb from the worktable with a flat opened palm. "What did your father say to you?"

"He repeated what you heard in here."

Pain showed in Julia's eyes but Blanche would not allow it to influence her. She would not be dictated to. She had to have something that was hers only. Teresa's friendship was going to be that something.

"She'll ruin you, Blanche," Julia said.

"No, she won't, Mother," Blanche said tiredly. "She's just someone I can talk to. What harm can there be in that?"

Resolutely, Julia said, "She's not to be invited here. I'll

60

not have that kind of woman in my home."

It was a decree. And final. She left Blanche standing alone in the kitchen. A moment later Blanche heard her pleading voice in the living room and then a firm retort.

The discussion was truly over, then. As Father said it was. Whatever happened from here on in was up to Blanche.

Later that night, long after the rest of the house was still, Blanche lay awake thinking over her father's words: *You'll work it out.* She decided he had meant she would work out whether or not she would continue to see Teresa — whether or not she would embarrass and hurt her family further. As far as she was concerned, the issue had been settled long before her father had ever walked into the kitchen. Ten minutes after Teresa had dropped her off last Sunday morning, she had decided. She was going to continue to walk to the Blackjack each day; she was going to talk to Teresa; she was not going to change a thing. Until this evening's argument, the only question she had had was what she would do when her parents found out.

You'll work it out.

Friday afternoon, when she again stopped to chat with Teresa who had faithfully been out front each day, Blanche boldly asked her if she would care to meet by the river the next morning. Without hesitation Teresa said, "Yes."

That evening Steven came for supper and was more talkative and open at the table, speaking easily with everyone, even joining in some of the bantering that normally went on at supper. He was different tonight. Assertive. Not at all like his usual self. Blanche had never seen him this way.

After supper it was he who suggested first that he and Blanche take a walk together. He took her by the hand and did not release her. They strolled through town, Steven possessively walking to her left, and casually window shopped, he making suggestions as to what he would like to see in their home once they were married. Then he steered

61

her toward the river.

They stopped under a tree, Blanche still marveling at his behavior. She liked it. Liked the way he took the lead and kept it. Suddenly though, he turned her roughly toward him. "I have something to say to you, Blanche. I expect you to listen." He spoke with unusual conviction. She felt like a trapped animal as he held her close to his face, his grip tightening. He said, "Did you notice we never went near the Blackjack this evening?"

"No, I didn't notice," she answered tartly. "Should I have?"

"Mable was out to see me today, Blanche. She tells me you're speaking daily with one of the women from there."

She looked into his small eyes and saw his determination to dominate her. "Oh, let loose of me, Steven." She broke from his grip and rubbed the circulation back into her arms. "Mable talks too much. She has nothing else to do."

"Your mother sent her," he said.

"I don't care if my entire family sent her," Blanche shot at him. "They're meddling and they know it."

In an instant he had grabbed her again and yanked her to his chest. "I don't want my wife associating with that kind of person."

"Your wife?" she snapped. "Let go!" Again she broke his grip and quickly stepped out of his reach. Her eyes blazed as she said, "I'm not your wife yet, Steven."

"When you are . . ." he warned with a pointing finger, "you will not be allowed to talk to that creature called Teresa."

He had cheapened her name just speaking it. Blanche turned away contemptuously. "Goodnight, Steven."

"Blanche, I'm telling you for your own good. I have a reputation to maintain, too, and you'd do well to protect your own a little better. Very soon it won't be only yours you'll have to worry about, but ours. I intend to have a respectable home and family and wife."

"Oh, go home, Steven, before your sacred reputation is damaged." Blanche stalked back toward the house. She had had enough of his manly ways.

Steven caught up with her, again grabbing her by the arm. "You will be my wife, Blanche. You know it and I know it. So you just get your little problem straightened out quick."

Lord help her, she'd marry him. Even with all her bravado, she knew she'd marry him.

"I'm warning you, Blanche," Steven went on. "After we're married. . . ."

"That's after we're married, Steven," she said yielding to the inevitable. "So let go! This is the last time I'll tell you."

Wisely, he didn't try to force himself on her again nor follow her. If he had she didn't know what she would have done. All that ridiculous grabbing. She could not tolerate it.

It struck her that even if she wanted to continue seeing Teresa after her marriage, it would be impossible. Steven's ranch was fifteen miles from town. She'd still be coming in each Sunday to play the organ and for occasional shopping trips but Steven would insist, she was sure, that he come with her just to keep her away from Teresa. Tears stung her eyes as she realized how little time she had left with Teresa. She was glad now that she had asked her to meet by the river tomorrow.

The following morning, Blanche sat thoughtfully on her rock. Steven had certainly surprised her last evening. He'd shown her a side of him she didn't know existed. Even with her height advantage over him, he stood his ground. He was much stronger than she had ever thought.

The approach of Teresa's buggy interrupted her meditation. Blanche checked her watch. It was just a little after six. "You're early," she said with a big smile. "I didn't expect you much before eight."

"We had so little time last week," Teresa answered. "Would you like to ride or walk or sit?"

"All three," Blanche said. "But not here."

"To the mesquite grove, then?"

"That would be fine."

In twenty minutes they were sitting on a blanket Teresa had brought with her in the buggy. The early morning air was chilly.

Teresa lit a cheroot. "Would you like one?" she offered.

Blanche smiled slightly. "No, I don't think so, thanks."

"Nasty habit." Teresa took a deep, satisfying drag. "Are you glad school's almost out?"

"In a way, I am," Blanche said. "But, it's the last I'll be allowed to teach anymore so I'm sad about that."

"Allowed?" Teresa said. "Why is that?"

"I'm getting married in four weeks. If you're married, you can no longer teach."

Blanche thought Teresa would ooh and ah. Women always did at the announcement of a wedding. Teresa didn't. Instead, her voice sounded small and far away as she asked, "Are you excited?"

"Scared, really," Blanche answered honestly.

"Why?"

"It's so permanent. And I'm not sure it'll be much different than living at home with my parents."

"There isn't much freedom in either situation, is there? Even if you're not married or living at home, it's like that, Blanche, believe me. If you're involved with a man. . . ."

Blanche knew the ending to the trailed off sentence. She said, "Well, I'm hoping I'll be happy for the most part. My younger sister will marry three weeks after I do and she can hardly wait."

"It's good for some," Teresa said absently.

Blanche looked over at Teresa who was once again scrubbed shining clean of makeup and dressed conservatively in a plain white, long-sleeved blouse, tucked into a black skirt with a small belt to dress off her outfit. Next to her, Blanche felt like a giant bag of flour.

"Have you ever met Steven Trusdale?" Blanche asked. "He's who I'm marrying."

"Maybe," Teresa answered, crushing her cheroot into the ground. "I don't remember off-hand. I don't know if I would tell you if I did. You might not like it."

It was Teresa's first reference to her job — if it could be called that. If Steven had bedded Teresa, it wouldn't have made a bit of difference to Blanche. What she wouldn't have liked was having Teresa bed with him.

Or anyone.

She stopped, thunderstruck at this realization. Something had gone wrong with her thinking.

With difficulty she said, "Steven is built like me. Only just a little shorter." With these words she finally privately admitted that she was just as ashamed of how Steven looked as she was of herself.

For the first time in their short relationship, Teresa deliberately, slowly, and meticulously looked at Blanche. "He's built like you, you say?"

Blanche nodded and swallowed.

Blanche wondered what was going through Teresa's mind and then began to dread her reaction as the small woman studied her closely, eyes starting at the top of Blanche and traveling the length of her body and then back up again.

Finally Teresa spoke. She screwed up her forehead and pursed her lips and said, "Well. Hmmm. Well then, your children will be able to beat the living shit out of you, won't they?"

Blanche sat frozen, unblinking, staring at Teresa for several seconds trying to decide whether or not she had been ultimately insulted. Teresa stared back at her giving her look for look. Then Blanche threw back her head and roared. She laughed until the tears ran down her cheeks and Teresa laughed with her. Gasping, Blanche said, "Can't you see them now? Little butterballs strong enough to throw their parents clear across the room. I think I'll have ten and turn them loose on Steven." She howled anew, fresh tears streaming down her face and the two women gripped sides that ached with laughter as Stormy nickered softly at their sounds.

They finally caught their breath, their laughter slowing to chuckles and then to smiles and then to restful sighs. Then they reached for each other and held one another tightly as if to let go would be to drown.

They stayed that way for several seconds. It felt so good and so natural to Blanche to cradle Teresa's head in her large hand and hold her close and protectively against her. Teresa lay her head against Blanche's breasts, her arms wrapped awkwardly around her thick waist.

The moment passed and they pulled shyly away from each other.

"I bet I haven't laughed like that in a year," Teresa said. "I hurt." She rubbed her sides.

"The last time I laughed like that was at school a few weeks ago," Blanche said, "when Tommy got a grasshopper down his pants and it kept biting him. Can that boy move!"

"Do grasshoppers bite?"

"Tommy says they do."

Smiling, Teresa sighed and leaned back on her elbows to let the rising sun warm her face. She closed her eyes against its direct rays. "If I never went back to work, it would be too soon," she said.

"Why do you stay there?" Blanche asked.

"Where else would I go? If I moved somewhere else, my past would become known. I've met a lot of cowboys, Blanche, and cowboys get around."

"You're not from around here, are you?" Blanche said stating an obvious fact. "Your accent is different. Not

66

southern nor Texan."

"New England. I'm from Connecticut."

"You're a long way from home. How did you happen to end up here?"

"It was as far as I could go on the money I had," Teresa said. "I had to leave."

"Why?"

"A child. And no father."

"So you left?"

"I ran," Teresa answered. She sat up and wrapped her arms around her knees. "My father would have killed me if I'd stayed." She paused thoughtfully and studied something far off in front of her. "I was very young. My father put my baby in an orphanage right after she was born. He hated her and hated me. I got tired of his whipping me, stole all the money I could find in the house, took the first train I could, and finished the trip in a covered wagon to Samson's Town. From there I took the stage to here. Then my money gave out. You can travel pretty far on not too much when you have to. Lattimer took me in right away. I was lucky."

Lucky? Blanche wasn't so sure. What would happen to Teresa when she was thirty? When she was fifty? What happened to old dancehall girls?

Teresa broke into her thoughts. "Tell me about your wedding dress. Is it pretty?"

"It's white. That's the most important part to me."

A pained look crossed Teresa's face. "Well, we can't all be virgins, I suppose," she said angrily. She began to rise.

"Teresa!" Blanche grabbed her arm. "You don't understand at all," Blanche said, and sat her back down. It was easy to do, she was so little. "I know what you're thinking. But you're so wrong about what I mean — you can't even imagine."

"What is it you mean?" Teresa's voice was hostile, her

67

eyes wary.

"Have you ever looked at what I wear?" Blanche asked. "You wear fancy, colorful clothing all the time. Every day. But me, I always, always wear either brown or black. That's all. Never another color. Haven't you ever noticed? It's common. Drab. Good heavens, I wouldn't care if the gown were pink and orange just so long as it was different!" Blanche still held Teresa by the arm. She released her by saying, "Now do you understand?"

"I guess I never really paid too much attention to what you wear, Blanche," Teresa said. "All I saw was someone who didn't work in a saloon who was willing to talk to me about something other than cows, bulls, whiskey, and bed." A thoughtful furrow creased her forehead. "Why do you wear only black or brown?"

"It makes me look smaller, slimmer," Blanche answered.

A shrug and a slight *humph* told Blanche how unimportant this was to Teresa. She could have kissed the hem of Teresa's skirt in appreciation.

"You're very different from the other women I know, Teresa," Blanche said.

"So are you," Teresa answered quietly.

They sat for a time without speaking, watching big white clouds drift by in the vast sky. It was enough just to enjoy the peace and solitude here, without having to guard themselves against the day.

A while later Teresa said, "Let's walk." They wandered down by the riverside until the brush along its banks thickened enough so that they could no longer follow its course, and they talked about nothing and everything and learned little things about one another.

Finally Teresa sighed and said regretfully, "I should turn back now." She hugged herself and then flung her arms wide. "Ohhh, I could walk on forever."

"To where?" Blanche asked.

68

"To green hills — gentle, rolling, green hills. To grass. To real trees and shade. Like where I come from." Teresa stopped and looked out over the open spaces of Texas. "It's so empty here."

"How can you say that, Teresa? There are at least two hundred people in Starcross and there must be that many in Samson's Town."

"Four hundred people," Teresa remarked. "That many used to come to my church every Sunday, back in Connecticut."

"Four hundred people in one building?" Blanche couldn't believe it. She'd heard and read about New York City and Boston and other great northern cities. She hadn't ever talked to someone from one of them. "It's hard to envision that many people in one town let alone in one building."

"I didn't live in the city itself. I only attended the church. That's where I met my daughter's father," she said offhandedly.

"Was he nice?" Blanche asked.

"He was gentle, dashing. I was naive."

"Do you know where your daughter is now?"

"No," Teresa said. "I know she was adopted and she's in a better place than I could ever offer. I'm satisfied. I couldn't have given her anything. I have no regrets. Would you like to take the reins?" She handed them to Blanche.

Driving back, Blanche again felt protective toward Teresa. She had felt that way several different times lately without being able to describe how exactly.

All the way back to Starcross, they pointed out scenes of interest and chattered like two magpies. As she pulled Stormy to a halt, Blanche asked, "Would you care to go again tomorrow?"

"I'd love to but I can't," Teresa answered. "Once in a while I can get away but Lattimer just about killed me last

week when he'd learned I'd gone. He doesn't want me looking tired at night and insists I sleep late in the mornings. It's
not hard to do." After a moment she added, "What made
him so mad last week was that I still had a black eye. He was
afraid someone might have seen it. I sneaked in the back way
but he was up already."

Blanche handed the reins to Teresa and stepped down
from the buggy. "How did you get out this morning, then?"

"I just went. He was sleeping."

"He'll be angry."

"Very."

"Will he hit you?"

"Probably not. It cost him too much money last time."

Blanche's brows knitted in confusion.

"He gets a cut of my take. Of course, I get a cut of the
drinks I hustle, so it works out even."

Blanche just shook her head. She could hardly stand hear-
ing how Teresa was used. She was nothing more than a piece
of furniture to Lattimer.

She's so much more to me, Blanche thought.

"I'll meet you next week," Teresa said, "and talk to you
after school on Monday."

"All right, but only if you'll let me rent the buggy this
time. You pick it up."

"Done," Teresa agreed. "See you then."

Blanche waved and watched Teresa until she was nearly
into town. On her way back to the house Blanche told herself countless times that Teresa was living the life she wanted
or she wouldn't be doing it. She would do something else.
Anything. But if she did work at something different, she
would have to move further than Samson's Town to escape
her past and that would take her a much greater distance
from Blanche.

She entered the house by a rear door leading directly into
the kitchen. Breakfast had been finished for some time but

on the worktable, carefully covered, were fried eggs and toast, left for her return. She began to clean the food away without eating. She did not need it.

She was nearly finished putting things away when Julia came in with a dozen eggs in a cloth-covered basket. "Where've you been?" she asked lightly. "The last time I remember you missing breakfast was during the Christmas play when you were so nervous. Are you all right?"

"I'm fine," Blanche said. "I went driving with Teresa this morning. Down by the river." There was no sense in evading the issue. She saw her mother's lips tighten. Blanche felt she should tell her the rest. "I'll be going next Saturday, too, Mother. Early. Don't wait breakfast for me."

"What do you find to talk about to someone like that, Blanche?" Julia bustled about the kitchen, busying herself, putting the fresh eggs in a shallow bowl and then up on a shelf out of harm's way.

Blanche said carefully, judiciously, "We talked about my wedding gown and Steven, and things we saw along the river. Nothing much."

"She's not from around here," Julia said. It was an accusation. "What's her last name?"

"I don't know. I never thought to ask."

"You talk with her every day and spent this morning with her and you don't even know her name? Isn't that a little odd?" Julia was staring at Blanche.

"It hasn't seemed important. Her name is Teresa. That's all I can tell you. And, no, she isn't from around here at all. She comes from the east."

"She's welcome to go back," Julia said. "We don't need her kind around here."

Blanche took a deep breath. "All right, Mother," she said as calmly as possible. "It's obvious that we can't come to any terms about Teresa. Father said the issue was closed. I refuse to discuss Teresa any further in this house. This is

71

your home. Yours and Father's. Soon I'll have my own. There, I will do as I please. Until then don't ask me where I've been if I'm gone any length of time because undoubtedly I will be with Teresa. I will not accept your accusing eyes nor your fretting over my whereabouts."

Blanche got up from the stool and walked to the dining room door. Turning to Julia she said, "I want you to know that I love you very much. I apologize to you for not being able to do what you want, for not being all you had hoped I would be. It's never been possible — and I've disappointed you and Father because of it. I'm glad you have Mable and Matthew to make up for me. I'm different — I don't know why, but I am. If you can, Mother, love me for the way I am. Not the way you need me to be."

Blanche left then, going directly to her room, leaving Julia alone in the kitchen. As she reached for her door handle, she could hear quiet sobs from below.

Mable came out of her own room. "That was quite a speech, Blanche. Wait'll Father hears what you said. I can't believe you would say those things to her."

"I know you can't, Mable, but the words needed to be said."

"Aren't you even sorry?" she asked tearfully.

"More than you'll ever know. My greatest fault lies in being myself. You should try being me sometime."

"You're not making any sense, Blanche." Mable wiped tears away.

"I know," she answered. "But the words feel right to me." Quietly she closed the door behind her, shutting herself off from the rest of the world.

72

CHAPTER FIVE

"It was a wonderful play, Miss Bartholomew. The children all knew their parts so well."

"It gets better every year, Miss Bartholomew. It will be a shame to lose you."

"Would you consider helping the children next year, Miss Bartholomew, for the holidays and special events?"

"Great, Miss Bartholomew. Just great!"

Blanche stood just outside the door of the school accepting congratulations for a job well done with this Friday's final graduation exercises and entertainment. The parents of every child had come tonight, knowing this was Blanche's last time to be here as their child's teacher. It was a wonderful show of support from her community for her efforts over the years. Even Matthew had managed to be pleasant and perform his part well in the play. Caroline and James would be getting married soon and that announcement, too, had added excitement to this evening's events.

Steven came out of the school with Alexander to stand at Blanche's side. He leaned toward her and whispered, "I'll walk you home afterward. I'll tell you then, how well you did tonight." She smiled at him and let him put a possessive hand on her elbow.

"A very nice job, Miss Bartholomew," a lady said to her as Blanche was speaking to another parent. She turned to nod a quick thanks to the mother. But, this was no mother. It was Teresa. She had somehow gotten herself out of the Blackjack and had remained unrecognized throughout the two-hour long presentation. She had dyed her hair blonde, combing it back and up in soft waves. Her face was very carefully made up to be attractive without being brazen. Her dress was a lovely shade of blue, trimmed at the neck and cuffs with white lace, appropriately conservative without being prudish. She wore a small hat of blue with a few tiny white flowers on it, and carried on her wrist a small white handbag.

Teresa offered a congratulatory hand to Blanche as she spoke. Blanche tried desperately to hide her shock and quell the beating of her heart as she took Teresa's warm fingertips. She could only mutter some incoherent answer in response, quickly releasing her. Teresa left immediately, fading into the night.

"Who was that?" Steven asked.

"I don't know," Blanche lied.

Alexander rocked back on his heels, his admiring glance following the lady in blue and said, "She's certainly lovely, isn't she?"

"Yes, quite," Blanche agreed. She turned away from her father; once again she had seen a look she couldn't identify cross his face. A look that made her uneasy.

Soon afterward all the parents and children were gone. Blanche said to Steven, "I'm tired. It's been a long day. I'd really like to go straight home." She was a little more than tired. She was still trying to recover from seeing Teresa. All she wanted was to sit down and put her head in her hands and rest. If Steven had recognized Teresa, what would he have said? Or done?

All week when Steven had come in from his ranch to see her, he had demanded to know if she had seen Teresa that afternoon and Blanche had refused to answer. But she could see the anger in his eyes and knew he knew the truth.

She was almost ready to give in to his wishes, it was so much easier than fighting him. Easier, too, than seeing the hurt and pain in her mother's eyes and listening to Mable's nagging. Matthew didn't even speak to her these days unless he had to. Only her father continued to treat her as he always had.

Soon none of it would matter because she wouldn't see Teresa any longer. Just four more times by actual count. Three, after tomorrow. And no more at all on a daily basis now that school had finally finished for the summer.

"Come on, Blanche. What's the trouble? You're lagging." Steven spoke sharply, a tone he had taken more and more frequently lately. He had insisted that they go down to the river, a place that Blanche felt was more like home than home, these days. And in the dark night, it was very pleasant.

Steven pulled her to him and kissed her. As always his nose began to whistle but Blanche forced its unpleasant sound from her ears and concentrated on what she was supposed to feel for him. He began to rub his hands up and down her back. Trying to perceive what he was experiencing she let him have his way without argument, letting him

75

fondle her breasts through her dress and wondering what his attraction was to them. She had never let him become so familiar before, but with their marriage so close she was desperate to grasp whatever it was that women felt toward men. Her mother certainly felt it. She knew Mable was just waiting for that first night. James and Caroline stared moony-eyed at each other constantly. What in God's name was wrong with her?

Steven pressed against her and she could feel him rock-hard against her body. He began to push slowly but rhythmically, then faster and faster until he was gasping and burying his face in the hollow of her shoulder whispering hoarsely, "Hold me. Hold me."

Blanche could have been the trunk of a mesquite tree. She held him until his breathing steadied. She thought she knew what had happened to him. But with all his clothes on? Impossible.

He started moving against her again but she had had enough and whispered as if she could hardly resist him, "I think we'd better go now, Steven."

He held her closely, still pressing against her. She waited with concealed impatience until he stepped back. "I guess you're right." His voice was still breathless as he said, "You're a fireball, you know that? A real fireball. On our wedding night, the whole sky will light up."

She had never felt so used.

They walked slowly back to the house. Steven with his arm around her waist all the way there.

After Steven left, she walked into the living room to say goodnight to her parents, but only Alexander was there. "I want to talk to you," he said.

A stab of fear went through her as she took a chair opposite him. She had had about all she could possibly stand tonight. "It's not that serious, Blanche. Relax. Take a seat."

Was her tension that obvious?

76

"The lovely lady you denied knowing tonight," he began, "was Teresa. Why did you lie to Steven? You knew who she was."

Shock hit her for the second time tonight. She never expected this. Until now her father had left her alone about Teresa. Had he changed his mind?

"You know, Blanche...." He interrupted himself to light a cigar. A cloud of smoke billowed around his face. Added tension built in her. Blowing out the match and tossing it into a tray beside him, he said, "I have many friends. But there are even those I call friend I would never ask to my house."

"I would never ask Teresa here, Father," she said.

"That's not my point, Blanche. You know that all my friends do not fit into this part of my life. At the bank they do, at the Blackjack where we have a drink together now and then, they do, and out on occasional hunting trips. But not here. Not in this house."

"I don't understand your point, Father," Blanche said.

"My point, Blanche, is that even if they don't fit neatly and precisely into my way of life it has never been a reason to deny that I know them and like them. And, I would add, they probably wouldn't want to join in everything I do. It would bore some and cause mental anguish to others because your mother would make them feel very unwelcome. But in my heart, they'll always be special to me — and I'll not deny them."

"Steven is making it so difficult," she said.

"Then fight him!" Alexander said strongly. "He doesn't own you."

"And Mother?"

"She'll adjust. She has for me."

"It's a great deal to ask of her, Father. I'm hurting her terribly."

"Why not just forget Teresa, then?"

77

"I can't."

"Why?"

"I almost think I need her."

"Almost?"

"I need her," she whispered.

"Why do you need a trollop's friendship more than you need to yield to your family's wishes that you give up this little tramp?"

"She's not a tramp!" Blanche said vehemently.

"Yes, she is, Blanche."

No! her mind screamed. But in the end she had to agree. "Yes . . . she is," she said very softly. The truth was the truth.

But, it was so unimportant.

She said, "I'm well aware that she makes her living hustling drinks and sleeping with cowboys. But it doesn't matter to me, Father. What does matter is that she makes me feel like a real person. Can you imagine how it feels to be able to talk to someone who doesn't laugh at me the minute they think I'm out of earshot? I know what the ladies around town say about me. I know!"

Alexander rose and walked over to Blanche. "Come here." He reached for his daughter and took her in his arms. For the first time in months she felt safe and secure and honestly loved.

"Blanche," he began. "Someday you're going to love so hard that you'll fight and die if you have to just to keep that person. You'll see happiness in everything around you and everyone will look like they're smiling and you'll be sure they're smiling just for you."

"I'm marrying soon, Father. Steven."

"Yes, I know." She could feel his chest expand as he took a deep breath. He said, "You'll love hard and only once, I think, Blanche. You're that kind of a person. And nothing on earth will make you change your mind." He let go of her then.

She didn't understand at all how she could ever fall in love in the manner he described but somehow his confusing words left her with a sense of release from the week's endless tensions.

Later, she lay awake thinking that she had better fall in love with Steven soon or she was in a great deal of emotional trouble. She was sure she didn't love him right now. Not like Mable loved Roger. Things just didn't feel right. To her, love only looked like an endless trap.

She stopped these useless thoughts and rolled over to think about Teresa's unexpected appearance tonight. Talk about joy! She had thought her heart would explode. If she could experience that feeling with Steven in the form of love — which was greater than friendship — then she would easily be the happiest woman in Starcross. She fell asleep trying to think of ways to transfer the happiness she felt toward Teresa to Steven.

The following Saturday morning it was cloudy with rain threatening but there wasn't a storm brewing that would have kept Blanche away from her drive with Teresa. She wanted to ask her a thousand questions about last night. And maybe even a few about Steven; about what she was supposed to feel toward a man. If anyone could help, she was sure Teresa could.

Teresa pulled up early and said, "Get in." She smiled but seemed withdrawn, and Blanche sensed a strain between them.

To loosen things up, Blanche said, "I see you got Stormy again. He's becoming an old friend, isn't he?"

Teresa merely nodded, and without asking Blanche her perference this morning, drove to where they usually spent their time together, passed it, and continued on for another fifteen minutes before stopping. They were dangerously far from town.

"Teresa, give me the reins." Blanche took them from her hands. She turned the buggy around and drove back toward the mesquite grove. They rode silently until she pulled Stormy to a halt under the trees.

Like the first time Blanche had sat beside Teresa, she again put her arm on the back of the seat. "Look at me," she said.

Teresa stubbornly stared straight ahead.

Blanche took Teresa's chin in her hand. "Look at me," she insisted. She turned Teresa's face toward her own and Blanche could hardly meet her dark eyes.

Towering over her, Blanche felt like a fortress shielding Teresa from all her pain.

Someone she would fight and die for? Her father's words bounced around in her head.

"Tell me what's wrong."

Teresa didn't move. Made no effort to pull away. She looked steadily into Blanche's eyes.

Blanche would not swallow. Would NOT! Would not turn splotchy red. She'd croak first. She took a deep breath and let it out slowly to allow time enough to regain her composure. She chided herself for her unexplainable boiling heart but with a steady voice said, "Teresa, I'm a friend of yours. Please tell me what's bothering you."

Teresa threw off Blanche's question with a wave of her hand, a self-deprecating laugh. "Oh, you know how I get, Blanche."

No, Blanche didn't know. A couple of weeks ago Teresa had quickly brushed off her black eye after going through a mood. What was she brushing off now, Blanche wondered.

Teresa's disposition brightened as they walked to the boulder they had closely studied some days ago, and climbed over some smaller rocks that rested against it and onto its

80

top. In spite of the cloudy day, it was still pleasant to be here.

Blanche struggled with how she could ask Teresa about Steven — and soon, while she still had an ounce of courage left in her cowardly body.

"Teresa," she began shyly. "I have some things I'd like to ask you. Things I don't dare ask my mother. I . . . need to know them before I get married."

Teresa looked at her. "Yes?" she asked, and sniggered.

"About . . . about marriage."

"Ha!" Teresa burst out loudly. "What do I know about marriage?"

Blanche said, "Well, not about marriage, exactly."

"Do you mean sex?"

Involuntarily, Blanche swallowed. "Yes."

"What about it?"

"I don't know much about it."

"It'll come to you. Don't worry."

"I'm not so sure, Teresa. You see, I don't. . . ." How could she possibly tell Teresa that she felt nothing for Steven?

"Do you want me to tell you what to do?" Teresa asked. "Is that it?"

Red-faced, Blanche said, "No, I know what to do. I just don't know why I don't feel anything for Steven yet." There! It was out. Let her laugh.

Graciously, Teresa didn't. "Oh, don't worry, Blanche. You will. I guarantee it. When you're lying there with all your clothes off and he lays down beside you and you feel his skin next to yours, you'll feel something then."

"Do you feel something?" Blanche asked.

"No."

No? Teresa felt nothing for the men she slept with? It wasn't possible. But it was good news. Lord, what was wrong with her mind? She couldn't own Teresa any more than

Steven could own herself. "I don't understand," she said. "Not at all. How can you not feel something?"

"You just said, Blanche, that you don't feel anything for Steven. Why can't I not feel anything for the men in my life?"

"I guess because I've never actually had . . . had . . . intercourse with a man and think I'll feel something only after I do. And you . . . you have and therefore should feel something."

"I don't. I did with my daughter's father. He was a little exciting. Not much though," she added as an afterthought.

Blanche absently drummed her fingers on her knees. She looked far off into the distance. "Would you have fought and died for him, Teresa?"

"I guess not," she said after a moment's thought. "I'm here. He's in Connecticut."

"Do you think you'd ever fight and die for someone, if you had to?"

Teresa gave her a strange look. "Fight and die for someone? Yes, I would," she said looking away. "I'd fight and die, and burn down towns if I had to. That is, if I knew that that person would do the same for me. That's a strange question, isn't it, coming from a woman about to be married? You'll fight and die for your husband, Blanche, if you're ever forced into such a situation."

Blanche shrugged. She was supposed to feel like that. She was supposed to be willing to give her all for her man. Father had said so.

As they strolled along the river, Teresa withdrew again. She seemed to be fighting with herself over something she wanted to say. Several times, with a word or a sigh, she began, only to stop and start over again. Blanche felt something close to irritation at the way Teresa unconsciously teased her with her secret. But Blanche had never been pushy. She despised that trait in a person. She lived with people like that;

was about to marry one. Her rationalization steadied her and she was able to let Teresa carry on her struggle without interfering.

Finally, with the morning gone, it was time to return.

On her way back to the house Blanche counted the days and itemized all that she would be doing until she could see Teresa again. She would go to church twice. She would see Steven at least six times, go to sleep seven times, eat so many meals, see so many people, do certain things. And then she would see Teresa again.

Later that night in bed, she dreamed. She saw herself walking through a large two-story house full of empty rooms. Each room had a bed and a window with a thin white curtain which billowed softly from a pleasant cool breeze. The rooms were bright and sunny.

From somewhere upstairs someone was calling her name. She thought she should be terrified because she was alone. She waited for terror to grip her. When it didn't, she ascended the stairs, following the voice, her steps echoing loudly throughout the building. She became confused. Now there were two voices. She looked in the direction of the voices. Both were coming from different rooms to her right. She walked down the hall opening each door looking to see who called. When she reached the next to last door she found Steven alone in the room. He lay on the bed waiting for her. He beckoned with his hand for her to come to him.

His nude body was hairy and grotesque. That he was terribly unpleasant to look at was not supposed to matter to Blanche because he was her husband now and knowing this she dutifully walked toward him. He swung his legs over the side of the bed and sat on its edge as she stood before him. Slowly and reluctantly she took off her clothes, dropping them at her feet piece by piece.

Steven began to breathe deeply. Blanche looked down on him and saw that he was ready. She stepped to him and put a hand on his shoulder. She bent to let him kiss her heavy breasts, gritting her teeth to keep from screaming. Then another voice began to call her name. She had forgotten there had been a second one when she had walked toward her husband.

Steven followed her out the door. His engorged penis kept poking her unpleasantly in the backside as he walked closely behind her. "I want you," he kept saying.

Blanche opened the last door in the hallway and there on the bed lay Teresa covered with a large white lace blanket that allowed Blanche only a faint glimpse of her small slim body, but Blanche knew she was nude. She walked over to Teresa, longing to lie down beside her. Without turning, Blanche said, "Go, Steven. I'll be right in. I promise." She turned to look at him but saw instead Julia who was saying, "She'll ruin you, Blanche."

"No, she won't, Mother," Blanche answered. "Go on. I'll be right there," and Julia faded into Steven. Without knowing how, she knew he now waited in the next room for her.

Guilt weighing heavily upon her, she slipped in beside Teresa and lay on her side looking down on her. Teresa looked up and tenderly and shyly Blanche leaned over her, and as if by accident, brushed her lips with her own while on her way to her ear to whisper that they would meet on Saturday. The delicate touch was enough to make Blanche want Teresa in ways she had never wanted Steven. Her heart pounded violently in her ears and her hands clenched into tight fists as she fought to keep from touching Teresa's enticing body. When she could no longer bear being next to her for another second, Blanche started to get up.

Teresa said, "You haven't gotten one message I've sent you so far," stopping Blanche, freezing her with her words.

Blanche tried to understand what Teresa was saying. The words must have been terribly important. Otherwise Teresa

84

wouldn't have said them.

Unable to stay there any longer, Blanche moved with Herculean effort from Teresa's side. She tidied the lace blanket to make sure no one could detect that she had lain there.

As she walked out the door, Teresa said, "You shouldn't go, Blanche."

But she couldn't stay. She was married. And her husband waited for her.

She returned to Steven's room and stood outside the door until he called her. With an enormous crushing sense of loss she turned once to look back at Teresa who now stood in the hallway with the lace draped seductively around her body. Blanche tore her eyes away and walked over to Steven. She lay down beside him, aching with defeat. He took her in his arms and lay on top of her, his massive weight crushing her, driving her deep into the mattress. Unable to move, she felt him force her thighs apart with his legs as she listened to him whistle through his nose. Her terror of him mounted as she wondered frantically if he would hurt her. She wasn't ready. She had never been ready. Not for him. Just as she felt him begin to penetrate her, she awoke.

She sat bolt upright in bed, her nightgown drenched and her breathing labored as she fought for air. Her dream was still with her. Her loathing and fear for Steven's touch, her passion for Teresa. Then suddenly the meaning of the entire dream came crashing down on her: what she had done, how she had felt, lingering emotions still so strong that a single thought of Teresa set her heart beating wildly out of control as she drew her knees up against her chest and fought renewed visions of nearly kissing Teresa and barely being able to keep her hands off her.

As heat rose within her she felt a sudden moistness between her legs. Was this passion? Was this finally it? Was this how she was supposed to feel about Steven?

85

It was grand. Grand!

The new sensations overwhelmed her, and an uncontrollable urge drove her to explore. She lifted her gown and worked her hand between the warm fat of her thighs to reach herself to know what was happening.

She discovered she was hot and swollen. Once she had touched herself she could not remove the finger she had placed there. She was slick, wet, nearly dripping. She pressed an exploring finger against a slight mound of soft, firm flesh. Only a team of horses could have pulled her hand away.

She hardly dared make a move or even breathe for fear of committing some sort of sin. She was only curious about her body. That was all. She was just learning about herself. For marriage.

Her hand involuntarily began to move. The other hand strayed with volition to a breast. She slid her fingers up to a swollen nipple and began to squeeze it and to run her palm over it, caressing it softly. The motion forced her onto her back where her hips started moving almost by themselves and her thighs fell apart.

Hardly aware that she was doing so, she easily convinced herself that it was all right because soon she and Steven would be doing it together and she needed to know how, now. She kept her mind on him as she continued to caress her breast and nipple. She moved her hand rhythmically with a slow, steady movement until her speed increased effortlessly. Almost at a peak now, she turned on her side to bury her face in the pillow to drown out sounds she couldn't control.

At the height of her ecstasy, she cried into the deep folds of her pillow, "Teresa, Teresa, Teresa. . . ."

CHAPTER SIX

Blanche played the organ this morning as she had never played before. Normally there would have been one or two sharps or flats she shouldn't have hit. Today she made no errors. She concentrated solely on the keys before her and the pedals at her feet. It was her way to forget the sporadic cramps rumbling in her stomach.

And other things.

She would have given anything to wash last night's dream and its results right out of her mind.

She had fallen asleep instantly afterward, she had been so

87

relaxed. But upon waking she had remembered. Every detail. And tried to forget and then remembered again more clearly than before. Her thoughts simply would not go away. Memories of her lips brushing Teresa's during the dream had caused her to experience again this morning that hot sensation between her legs and it frightened her. She could think of Steven lying nude on the bed and nothing happened. Nothing. But when she thought of Teresa in the same circumstance under a piece of lace she could hardly keep her hands away from her own body, her desire was so strong.

But it was wrong. All wrong! Those feelings were supposed to be for Steven. Not some slip of a woman. But for her husband-to-be in two more weeks.

On the family's return trip home, her calves ached from pumping the pedals so hard. She had received many compliments afterward on her fine playing at service and several ladies had tittered that it must be love because Steven, having ridden in late, had taken a conspicuous front row seat and had stood by Blanche's side gazing proudly at her as these praises were lavished upon her. Blanche found comfort in his nearness, clinging to him and keeping her hand firmly on his arm.

As Julia and Mable prepared dinner, Blanche and Steven wandered outside to the shadier side of the house until they were called for the midday meal. Blanche spoke of their future, of the changes she would like to see made in Steven's house if he would let her and the comfort she wanted to provide for them and the types of special foods she would create for him. He was enraptured with her, and for all appearances, she with him.

Later, after supper, they returned to the riverside and when near darkness had settled over Starcross, Steven half-made love to her. She didn't try to slow him down. He put his hand on places under her dress and over her undergarments that had never been touched before.

88

But not like last night, by herself.

Having set a precedent in her behavior, she allowed him to carry on this way for the rest of the week so that by the following Friday night, she was convinced that last Saturday's nightmare, as she now called it, was cleansed from her mind and Steven was the only one who was going to arouse her. Not dreams. Not fantasies. Not Teresa. Just Steven. Arousal hadn't come yet, but it would in time.

Secure in her mind, at peace with herself, she didn't feel the same compelling need to see Teresa the next Saturday morning as she had in the past, but she went early to the river to wait.

It wasn't long before Teresa pulled Stormy to a halt. "Ready to ride?" Teresa asked cheerfully. And then on a more somber note, added, "And talk?" She began the drive south along the Brazos.

Teresa remained silent until they were settled on a blanket beneath the mesquite grove. Blanche waited patiently while Teresa made sure there were no small sticks or stones underneath to pester them, Blanche knowing that Teresa was stalling for time. Whatever she had on her mind was not going to come easy in the telling.

"What did you want to talk about?" Blanche finally asked.

"I'm leaving Starcross."

"Leaving?"

In an instant Teresa's brief words shattered all Blanche's past week's carefully built up shields of indifference.

"Leaving?" she repeated almost inaudibly. "When?"

"In two weeks. I've saved enough money to get myself back to New England. I've had enough of saloon life."

Teresa couldn't be serious. Leave Starcross? She couldn't leave Starcross. What would Blanche do without her? Her earlier resolutions and strength vanished like sugar in boiling hot coffee.

Blanche blinked rapidly. She put her hand to her breast as if to lessen the severe pain that had settled there and lay like a heavy chunk of lead in the middle of her bosom. "This is quite a surprise, Teresa," she barely managed to utter.

"I've got it all planned," Teresa said, apparently unaware of the devastating effect of her words on Blanche. "I'll take the Saturday express to Samson's Town and then catch a second stage the next morning to Preston. From there I can travel east by train. Maybe I'll just stay in Chicago, for a while."

Blanche remained mute. There was nothing to be said. Nothing. She listened politely, feeling splotches of heat pop out on her body as Teresa continued to explain, laying before Blanche all her well-thought-out plans. She would travel very light, taking only the barest of essentials in one suitcase and in her handbag. Nothing more. She didn't want to be slowed down by cumbersome possessions. She wanted to get out. Fast!

"The stage reaches Samson's Town by nightfall," Teresa said. "There are six ten-minute stops along the way while they change horses and then you're there. You arrive at night, very tired and hungry, but in a day's time I can be a hundred miles north of here. Lattimer wouldn't bother coming after me at that distance."

"You mean he doesn't know?" Blanche asked. "He won't like it."

"Oh, he'll be killing mad at first," Teresa said indifferently. "But in the end he'll just steal a girl from one of the other saloons. They'll be glad to work for him. He pays good on drinks and the cowboys aren't too rough."

Blanche pulled her knees to her chest as she had last Saturday night in bed, causing her old dream to leap into her head. Quickly she straightened her legs and rested her hands on thick thighs.

90

"Blanche," Teresa said softly. "I want you to go with me."

The unexpected request struck like a bolt of lightning, transfixing Blanche. When she could finally speak, she said, "Surely you're joking, Teresa."

"No, I'm not. I'm about to change my entire life. I'm inviting you to change yours, too."

"And what would we do, Teresa? Where would we go? You don't even know where you'll end up or even that you'll be welcomed."

Teresa asked, "What is there for me here? A life with Lattimer? A future as a dancehall girl? I hate what I'm doing. I don't want to do it any longer. I know damned well I'll never set foot in your home. Now or in the future."

Teresa's words stung but Blanche could not deny this truth.

"And I don't want to travel alone," Teresa continued. "That's why I'm asking you to come, too."

"It's out of the question," Blanche declared. "I have a home here. A family. I'm about to be married. How can you ask me to give up the security of a town I've grown up in and the security of a loving husband to move hundreds of miles away to a place I don't know? How would I live? What would I do? I'm fit only to teach. And look at me, Teresa. I'm so big that my weight wouldn't even allow me to make such an extremely lengthy trip even if I were willing, which I'm not. And after I got there, as a fat —" And then to emphasize her point she repeated, "— fat woman, it's doubtful anyone would hire me for any type of job at all based on my looks alone."

"Are you convinced about all this?" Teresa asked.

"Well, you really haven't given me much time to think about it have you?" Blanche said with more than a touch of anger. "You come rolling up in your buggy and say, I'm

91

leaving, come with me, and expect me to pack my bag and be gone."

Teresa said, "You aren't required to give me an answer this morning. Anyway, I wouldn't accept anything you said immediately, whether it was yes or no."

Blanche put up a hand to stop Teresa's words, but Teresa interrupted with a raised hand of her own. "Talk to me next Saturday, Blanche. In the three years I've been here, you're the only woman who isn't a prostitute who has ever spoken decently to me. You've given me a glimpse of what I'm supposed to be. Not some worthless tramp but a clean-living woman. I'm going back to New England to be just that. You're responsible for my change in life, Blanche."

"Don't say that, Teresa. I'm not responsible for anyone's behavior except my own."

Teresa spoke sharply. "I'm trying to thank you. Without ever realizing it, you've given me the strength to take this step. I'm scared, believe me. I'm really scared. But that isn't going to stop me."

Seeing Teresa brush at tears she was trying to conceal, Blanche reluctantly agreed. "All right, Teresa. I'll meet you one more time."

Teresa looked at Blanche and said with unwavering eyes, "I'll be waiting for either a yes or a no. If you go, you should travel the same way I do. Light. And bring any money you may have. If you have none, I have enough to at least get us there. We'll leave in exactly two weeks. At six in the morning."

The day of Blanche's wedding.

Blanche said, "I already told you, Teresa, my weight alone would slow us down."

Teresa exploded furiously. "What the hell is wrong with your weight, I want to know? Jesus! Listen, Blanche," she said. "That is no excuse. Nothing about your weight would interfere with traveling. Men twice your weight ride around

92

on horses all day long day after day and live to tell about it. So what's the problem?"

The problem was the fear that Teresa was right and that Blanche would actually consider the idea.

"We've discussed this all I care to, Blanche," Teresa stated firmly. "How about you?"

"Definitely," Blanche agreed. She never wanted to discuss it again.

Not long after, the conversation began to lag. Blanche checked her watch saying it was time to return to Starcross even though they had spent only a short time together. Teresa did not argue.

Blanche didn't even wait to watch Teresa drive any distance to town before she began her own troubled return trip to the house. For Teresa to go back East alone was one thing. To join Teresa in her foolhardiness was the most ridiculous idea Blanche had ever heard. For two women — even worse, a woman alone — to travel unescorted would bring all kinds of perilous situations. Wild Indians and crazy white men who would love to prey on single women were just some of the worst threats she could think of immediately. She herself would have little problem with men but Teresa would have boundless trouble — she was beautiful. Then, there was the incredible distance. That alone was mind-staggering.

And who would manage all the arrangements? Blanche knew nothing of traveling. Short of trips to the stores and to the bank, she knew nothing of handling money either. What if she and Teresa ran out of money before they reached their destination? What would happen then? Father wouldn't be there to help. And Mother — as trying as she could be at times — wouldn't be there to say, "There, there, dear, it'll be all right." She would be completely on her own for the first time in her life, save Teresa. Completely.

And just how helpful would Teresa be? How much did

she know about traveling great distances? Just because she had traveled west once didn't mean that she could travel east with the same apparent good luck she'd had coming to Starcross. And as for that apparent good luck, Teresa had never told Blanche any details of her trip other than it had been cheap and a chance to get as far away from her father as she could on the money she had. And look where she had ended up. In the Blackjack Saloon as a trollop. How could that be called good luck?

And, too, how could she herself possibly travel with just a single suitcase? Her dresses were so big, one alone would nearly fill it. She would need to take other things — dusting powder, lots of it, to keep her thighs from chafing which they did without letup all through the very warm spring and the fast approaching hot summer. She'd need soap and towels and stockings, underwear, and an extra pair of shoes. She could never fit everything into one suitcase.

Undoubtedly there would come a time, too, when she would be unable under any circumstances to avoid undressing in front of Teresa. The very thought of it. . . . To have that tiny slip of a woman see her many layers of fat folding over each other and see the way she had to swing her legs around her own weighty thighs in order to walk. And all that hair on her belly running in a line from her navel to her crotch and more on her arms and legs than ten women ought to have. . . . She would never, ever be able to face that situation. Never!

Even as difficult as things had been lately, could she possibly leave her mother and father and Matthew and Mable? And that problem would automatically clear itself up in two weeks. In two weeks, Teresa would be gone.

Forever.

CHAPTER SEVEN

If it were possible for a week to drag more slowly than this one, Blanche could never remember the time. Yet, she filled every waking moment with activity. Nightly walks with Steven, final touches on her wedding dress, visits with people she cared nothing about — any device to keep her busy. How she longed to get her final dreaded meeting with Teresa over. But the interminable week gave Blanche time to try to frame her words of refusal to Teresa. A hundred times a day, and a hundred times a night as she lay in bed, she searched for words. And at the end of each of her mental conversations, she was defeated.

She wanted Teresa to stay in Starcross. She was the only woman who meant anything to her. The separation hadn't yet occurred and she could already feel the loss, the pain building in her chest. The feeling stayed with her, following her around like a shadow no matter how she tried to bury her traitorous thoughts.

She took time one afternoon to go to the bank to withdraw her savings. She would give it all to Teresa as a going away gift. She could not imagine any circumstance where she would need it nearly as badly as Teresa would.

Large plate glass windows on either side of a door painted with ornate gold and black lettering denoted the bank's name and hours of business. The letters stared back at her as she took a deep breath before entering. The bank, with its large walk-in vault and eight-inch-thick door with a two-handled combination lock, was a safe establishment in which to deposit money. A few foolish souls had tried to rob the place; those that Starcross didn't bury rode empty-handed out of town on the run and were not heard from again.

Teresa would not be heard from again either, ever again. . . .

Alexander waited on her personally, saying as he handed her the money, "Steven will be pleased. He'll be able to put in his new well much sooner now."

Defiantly, Blanche said, "It's not for Steven, Father. Teresa's decided to leave Starcross and go to Chicago. I'm sure she'll need it far more than Steven needs his well."

She expected Alexander to fly into a rage, to shout down the building that this was the last straw, this was her entire working career's savings, how could she so easily give it to a near-stranger? But in quiet sorrowful agreement he said, "That's very commendable, Blanche. Very commendable," and completed the transaction without further discussion.

Confused and amazed, Blanche wordlessly tucked the

96

money into her purse and left hurriedly, unable to face Alexander's penetrating eyes.

At last the dreaded day arrived. She dressed carefully, wanting to look her best for Teresa this final time. She asked herself, "Why bother?" and went ahead and dressed carefully anyway, knowing why.

As she left the house she knew she was covered with red splotches. She swallowed continuously but walked with her head held high and her step firm.

She wasn't at her rock five minutes before Teresa drew the buggy to a halt.

Teresa got down and faced Blanche. "I can guess what your answer is, Blanche." She looked the tall woman straight in the eye as she spoke.

Blanche nearly wilted under Teresa's steadfast gaze. "I have no choice, Teresa. You know that."

"Everyone has choices," the smaller woman told her.

"I don't."

Teresa reached up and placed a soft hand against Blanche's cheek. Her eyes seemed to search the depths of Blanche's soul.

Blanche stood unmoving, fearing she would grasp this tiny creature to her breast and crush her to death with love.

With a little smile Teresa said, "You never did get over your red splotches, did you?" and dropped her hand from Blanche's burning cheek.

"I was hoping you would never notice," Blanche said. Heat of embarrassment rose up her neck, reddening her further.

"I see much more than people realize," Teresa said. "They think I'm a toy, a plaything. I'm not." And then she added, "And I'm going east."

Even though Teresa knew already, Blanche had to say it: "I will be staying, Teresa. I have to." She fought back tears.

97

"I won't try to change your mind, Blanche. You must come freely or not at all."

Teresa's statement disappointed her. Teresa could have at least tried to change her mind; she could have shown that she cared that much.

"I . . . I have something for you," Blanche said, removing from a deep pocket in the skirt of her dress the money she had withdrawn. She pressed it into Teresa's small hand. "I want you to take it."

Teresa began to protest.

"No," Blanche insisted. "You'll need it. Take it, please."

Teresa looked at the roll of bills bound with a narrow yellow ribbon. "It's a lovely gesture, Blanche. Lovely." She brushed aside an involuntary tear. "But, I can't." She handed back the money.

"If you don't take it, Teresa," Blanche threatened, her voice choking, "I'm going to throw it into the Brazos." How else could she lessen the guilt she felt letting Teresa go like this?

As if sensing Blanche's determination, Teresa thanked her softly. "It will be a big help." Again she brushed away a tear.

Her heart aching, Blanche said, "Come to my wedding before you go." She wanted to plead, to beg Teresa to be there.

"No," Teresa replied. "The stage leaves at six. I'll be on it. I've made all my plans, such as they are, and I might weaken if I have to wait even one extra week for the next express. And then where will I be? Back in the clutches of Lattimer. I couldn't stand that again." An involuntary shudder took her.

"You're right," Blanche reluctantly agreed. "I have no right to detain you."

Softly, Teresa said, "Thank you for understanding, Blanche."

Heaven help her, Blanche didn't understand anything right now. And she didn't need Teresa's kind words. She had come here to make a final break with her and a final break it would be. Right now. Speaking quietly, Blanche said, "All right, Teresa. Go back, then. I don't see any point in our staying here any longer."

Teresa turned to walk back to the buggy. Unable to help herself, Blanche reached out a restraining hand. She couldn't just let Teresa go like this. The two women gazed at each other for a long time and then for one last time, held one another so closely that it nearly took their breaths away.

Oh, Lord, how Teresa felt in Blanche's arms, pressed against her large breasts; how comfortably Teresa's head tucked beneath her chin; how protective she felt toward the smaller woman. If she were only a man, she would take Teresa for her own. She would fight and willingly die for her. A thousand different times if she had to.

Appalled at such unnatural thoughts, Blanche was brought up short and stepped back, putting space between herself and this woman who was forever unsettling her.

No matter. This was it. This was the final time. It was over, goddamn it, over!

Teresa drove off, Blanche watching her one last time. She was almost out of sight now, partially blocked from view by the buildings. Blanche took a big, strong, brave, determined deep breath and then crumpled in a sobbing heap against her rock wishing she were dead, miles away, already married for ten years.

When she got back to the house everyone was just sitting down to breakfast. She avoided the kitchen, going straight to her room. She collapsed on her bed wanting only to lie there unmoving forever. Over and over she saw Teresa's receding back as she drove away, heard Teresa's final pronouncement: "I'm going east."

Blanche lay there trying to get up but was held to the

bed by the weight of her own depression.

Giving up on the day, she eventually undressed and put on her nightgown and crawled into bed. In five minutes she was asleep.

She was awakened by a soft knock on her door, Alexander calling her name. He walked over to her bedside. Softly, he said, "Blanche."

"Father. Is something wrong?" she asked heavily.

"I was going to ask you the same thing," he replied sitting down beside her.

She asked, "Father, did you ever love someone that you shouldn't?"

Alexander contemplated his daughter, a pensive look on his face. "Women have their little secrets. Men should be allowed theirs, too." He bent over and kissed her. "Go back to sleep now. No one will bother you."

The following Friday, the Bartholomews gathered to toast Blanche and to be together for the last time as the original family before adding a new member. It was a happy affair, all the family telling stories from their pasts that left them laughing hysterically. Blanche thanked goodness for wine. It helped her forget tomorrow and enjoy only tonight.

When she went upstairs to bed, Blanche took with her her wedding gown which had hung in her parents' room until now. Julia would come up in the morning and help her dress. Mable would fix her veil at the church. Matthew would hold the ring. Father would give her away. Julia and Steven's mother would thank God and cry.

Alone in her room, sitting on her bed, her gown still in her arms in great fluffy heaps of white billowing out in front of her and onto the floor, she asked aloud to the surrounding emptiness and golden glow of the three chimney lanterns, "And whatever will you do, Blanche Irene Bartholomew?"

A sudden loud knock interrupted her, startling her nearly

out of her wits. Alexander peeked in. "I wanted to see you alone before I went to bed." He smiled and entered. He took the gown from her hands and gave it a little shake and hung it in the closet for her. "Beautiful," he said sincerely.

"A lot of work for one day," she said.

Alexander wandered over to the window and looked at his reflection staring back at him through lace curtains. "It's hard to believe you'll no longer be here," he said.

He's sad, thought Blanche. Somehow this surprised her. She didn't think her father would be sad. Just happy that she was finally out of here.

"You know, Blanche, if you had never married, I wouldn't have minded. It was your mother who was the worried one."

"It's time that I did, Father. You and I both know it."

Alexander came over and sat on the bed beside her. His breath was sweet with wine. "I haven't mentioned a dowry before." Alexander put an arm around her. "I've been putting something away for you and Mable over the years so that when you married, you'd go as proper brides. I'll give yours to Steven after the wedding tomorrow."

"We are a proper family, aren't we, Father?" Blanche said. "Leading citizens in Starcross."

"We are," he agreed.

"That's rather a heavy burden to carry at times, do you know that?" she asked.

He kissed her and left her alone. She got up and walked around the room touching things and running her hand over old and familiar objects on her dresser. Walking over to her gown, she fingered the fabric she had so carefully fashioned into her first light colored dress in years. It was a beautiful dress, she had to admit, even if she had made it. What a waste, she thought, to wear something this costly and lovely only once.

She sat on the edge of the bed and stared at the crates

101

and suitcases sitting off to one side out of the way, waiting to be taken to Steven's tomorrow afternoon.

As the late night hours passed into early morning, certain she was in control of herself, she allowed herself to think of Teresa. She remembered their first meeting, their rides together, their talks. Their time had been so short. To have had more time, to have spent carefree and endless hours with her. . . .

Too late Blanche realized her mistake. The gate was opened, old heartbreaking feelings returned to devastate her. She lay down on the bed, burying her face in her pillow, crying pent-up tears into the silence.

I'm leaving.

The finality of the terrible words echoed off the walls of her room, striking her from every side, touching every quaking nerve in her body.

I'm leaving.

All she'd have to do is take a suitcase. The small one. The one there on the end. It was ready for such a trip. And Teresa already had Blanche's money — plus her own. All she had to do was just grab the suitcase and run.

No! her mind screamed. She ran out of her room and downstairs, trying to make it to the backhouse. Halfway there she vomited up stale, sour, stinking wine.

It was awful. She threw up so hard she had to kneel and and to put her hands on the ground in front of her to keep from falling forward. It went on and on and on. Finally, the spasms passed and she was able to sit back on her haunches and rest.

My God, she entreated, why did this woman trouble her so?

Back in her room, she washed her face and brushed her teeth. She put on a fresh dress, not her gown, and sat again on the edge of her bed. Exhausted, she wanted the morning

102

light to come as soon as possible. It would be here in another hour. In two, Teresa would leave.

And, God help her, in two, Blanche would leave with her.

PART TWO

THE CONNECTICUT YANKEE

CHAPTER EIGHT

"Quick, get up!"

From a deep sleep, Teresa felt her shoulder being roughly shaken. She moaned and moved away. "Get lost, Lattimer," she snarled.

"Teresa, it's Blanche. The stage leaves in —" There was a brief pause and then a near hysterical voice: "— three minutes. You've got to get up."

Teresa sat up quickly and just as quickly grabbed her head. "God, what day is it?" Remembering she was nude, she pulled a sheet up over her breasts. "Give me my dress, will you?"

Gaudy garments hung everywhere: from the door, on hangers against the wall, and in the closet. A large dresser with an even larger mirror was buried beneath jars and canisters of facial powders and paints. The wallpaper, a brilliant red print, glared unpleasantly in the early morning light.

Teresa swung her legs over the side of the rumpled bed and grabbed her undergarments. Rapidly she began to pull them on. "I thought you weren't going. Not that one," she said to Blanche who had picked up a bright orange dress. "That one."

"I thought you weren't staying," Blanche retorted. She handed Teresa the dress she had worn the day they had first gone driving together. Not too neatly, Teresa yanked it over her head.

"My hat," Teresa said pointing to a chair nearby, frantically tugging her clothing into place. Blanche grabbed the hat and Teresa jammed it on her head groaning loudly from the pain. Even her hair felt like it hurt. "To hell with it," she growled, flinging the hat to the floor. "I couldn't leave without you," she said to Blanche, straightening the last of her buttons. She picked up her shoes and stockings. "I'll put these on in the stage. How much time do we have?"

"One minute. What do you mean?"

"Get my suitcase. I was all ready to leave and then backed out at two this morning."

The two women hastened out the door and down the stairs. "Let me out, Sam," Teresa called to the man who cleaned the Blackjack each morning.

He came from around the bar looking at the suitcases in Blanche's hand. "Lattimer know?"

"Hell no, he doesn't know," Teresa replied impatiently. "And don't you tell him either."

"I'll miss you, Teresa," Sam said. He gave her a brief

kiss on the cheek.

"I'll miss you too, Sam," she said. "But it's time to move on. What time is it, Blanche?" she asked over her shoulder. They were out of the building and running.

"Six," Blanche replied.

They reached the stagecoach in time to hear the driver yell, "Gitup!"

Teresa ran out in front of the coach waving her shoes and stockings at the six-horse team, unmindful of the great size of the beasts and their beginning forward motion. She screamed at the top of her lungs, "Hold it, Charlie, you old bastard! You owe me! You stop this goddamn stagecoach right now or you're never gonna be able to go home again."

Cursing loudly, the grizzly bearded man hauled back on the reins trying to quiet the startled horses, and spat tobacco juice at her. From beneath a dirty sweat-stained hat, piercing black eyes glared at her. "Hell, I don't wait five seconds fer nobody. Not even fer President Grant!"

"I'm warning you, Charlie," she yelled, threatening him with a shoe. "I'll tell your wife all about you and I'll do it right now!"

He glowered fiercely at her and then grunted, "Pay at the first stop."

Blanche, standing by with both suitcases, breathed a sigh of relief and slung their bags unceremoniously into the coach. She and Teresa climbed in, slamming the doors shut. Teresa noted with relief that they were the only passengers this morning. She couldn't have endured chit-chat from anyone today.

As they collapsed against the seats they heard Charlie yell, "Gitup!"

Moving the baggage out of the way, Blanche asked, "Are you sick?"

"No, just a damned hangover. Acquired it through lack of faith." Teresa put a shaking hand over her eyes to shield them momentarily from the bright morning sunrise. She had a splitting headache. At two this morning she'd gone downstairs, gotten a bottle of Lattimer's best rum, and returned with it to her room. Slowly and methodically she'd drunk every damned drop, gone outside and thrown up, and then staggered upstairs to sleep it off and face one more day.

But who the hell ever knew what the turn of a card would show? Here she was this morning, with Blanche by her side. And wondering how it had all come about. If Lattimer didn't come gunning for her she'd be perfectly happy. Happiness wouldn't be hard to accomplish after the last three years of her life.

She looked over at Blanche who stared wide-eyed out the window as the horses warmed to their task and the stage began to pick up speed. Teresa could see she was scared. Probably more scared than she'd ever been in her life. She didn't blame her. What Blanche was going through today was what she herself had gone through three years ago in Connecticut.

Worse yet, this was Blanche's wedding day. The lady had guts. "Don't worry, Blanche." Teresa smiled. "It'll all work out. For one thing I won't be getting drunk anymore." Brave words from someone who didn't have an idea in the world what the next week would bring.

"I'm not your mother, Teresa, and I'm not worried." Then Blanche corrected herself. "Well, maybe I am a little."

"Maybe you are a lot," Teresa amended. "When did you decide to come?"

"I don't really know," she said. "Probably right after you asked me. My suitcases have been all packed for my wedding trip to Steven's for a number of days but I must have been planning to leave Starcross permanently because of the way I packed."

"Why?" Teresa grunted, hauling on her stockings and shoes. "What's in your suitcase?"

"The barest of essentials," Blanche replied.

Teresa became thoughtful and then said, "There's no turning back before Samson's Town. But there is a return stage tomorrow morning."

"I won't be turning back," Blanche answered firmly.

The bouncing stagecoach rolled rapidly over the open plains of Texas. Caring nothing for the comfort of more room by using the second empty seat, Teresa and Blanche sat close together seeking solace from one another as they began their perilous journey. They unrolled the windows' heavy canvas curtains in a futile attempt to fight the dust thrown by the thundering hooves and rolling wheels. Eventually, the sun forced them to raise the canvas and they stared with gritty eyes at the landscape as Charlie skillfully guided the horses over bumpy roads, across wooden bridges spanning dry gulches, and around large boulders and groves of trees. They listened to him yell "Gee!" and "Haw!" at sharp bends as the coach leaned frighteningly away from the curves. The tense passengers were roughly jostled in the rapidly moving coach, coughing frequently and wiping grit from their faces and wondering if they could last to Samson's Town.

During the brief rest stops, they got out and stretched their legs and tried to calm their queasy stomachs, while a fresh team was speedily exchanged for the worn panting horses, great breaths of hot air blowing from their nostrils, heads hanging low, sides heaving, froth dripping from their massive chests and hindquarters and dark splotches of sweat soaking their thick necks and sides.

Nervously, the women tightly held each other's hands as they rode. By clinging to one another, there still remained some contact with the world they had known until just a short time ago — a certainty unlike the future ahead of them.

The driver stopped the stage for the final time at nightfall. They staggered off the coach, hauling their suitcases with

them, and stepped up onto the wood sidewalk shaking dust
from their clothes.

"I told you the trip would be endless," Teresa said.

"Is there a hotel?" Blanche asked exhaustedly.

"Down this way," Teresa replied. "Come on."

They walked through the settling darkness, bumping into
cowboys filling the sidewalks and exiting the endless saloons
lining the bustling street. Horses filled hitching rails, heads
hanging low as they patiently waited long hours for their
riders. Mixed music from tinny pianos drifted on the night
air and loud singing could be heard from several quarters.
Stores and shops, tucked in between the public houses, were
closed and dark, yielding to Samson's Town's night life.
Townsladies and gentlemen were noticeably absent.

"Hey, a real lady," a passing cowboy said, grabbing
Teresa as she walked by. His breath was potent with drink.

"Hiya, cowboy," Teresa answered in a friendly tone.
"You go have a good time, you hear?" she said smiling. "I
just got off the stage and wouldn't be good for a thing
tonight."

Disarmed by Teresa's good-natured teasing, the cowboy
let her go and bellowed laughter as he staggered down the
sidewalk.

Teresa hissed, "Damned drunken fool," and brushed at
her arm where he had grabbed her. "Come on, Blanche."

Gunshots exploded from somewhere down the street and
two windows shattered just to Blanche's left. Instinctively,
she ducked and clutched Teresa's arm. Several cowboys on
horseback galloped by, yelling and challenging each other to
shooting contests.

Nonchalantly, Teresa said, "Nothing much has changed
in three years."

"The place is so wild," Blanche said nervously.

"Only at night," Teresa answered. "The men are harmless. There must be a cattledrive going through. Come on.

112

Let's try for a room. I'm dead."

They entered a large two-story hotel. Several chandeliers brightly lighting the interior gave its orange wallpaper a warm glow. There was heavy horsehair furniture in the spacious office. A tired looking clerk sat behind the counter intently reading a newspaper. From the hotel's dining room, odors of cooking food drifted to the famished women.

"I stayed here three years ago," Teresa said. "It's not bad."

"Good," Blanche said strongly. "Once I get settled, I don't want to go out into this madness again."

Teresa chuckled to herself. Blanche didn't know what madness was. "Any rooms?" she asked the bored-looking clerk.

"Three left, ma'am."

"We'll take one," Teresa said with authority. "Two beds."

"Ain't got but doubles, ma'am. One in each room." He wrote in the guest book as he talked. "Two rooms. Sign here." He pushed the book toward Teresa.

Knowing they must watch every expense, Teresa stated, "I said one room, please. It will be sufficient, I'm sure. For a week."

"Yes ma'am," the clerk said and changed his entry. Teresa paid for the week and he handed her the key. As they walked away they could hear him mutter, "Damned uppity Yankees."

Blanche turned to say something, but Teresa grabbed her arm. "Never mind, Blanche. It isn't worth it."

"But we're not Yankees."

"I am. And pretty soon you will be, so forget it."

In the dim light filtering into their small room from the hallway, Blanche dropped her suitcase at her feet. She sat down heavily in a worn leather chair. "I'm so tired I could die," she said.

113

"So am I," Teresa groaned. "But I've got to eat first so I'll have the strength to." She made her way to a single small dresser and lit the room's only lantern then lay down, unmindful of the quilted bed cover as she crossed her feet.

A single large window was covered with a thin lace curtain. The shade was up and a gentle breeze stirred the curtain slightly. Small oval rugs were placed on each side of the bed on the wide plank floor. The room's walls were papered a pleasant shade of blue creating a restful atmosphere throughout. "Come on," Teresa said before the room overwhelmed her and she fell asleep forever. "Let's go eat."

In the large dining room they sat near a window, its lower half covered with a white curtain hung from a brass rod, the top by a valence. Red-and-white-checkered tablecloths on every table added cheer to the room already brightened by overhead chandeliers and by opal glass hurricane lamps spaced frequently along the walls. At this late hour there were only two other patrons, tired-looking cowboys who sat alone and who probably had just ridden into town and were preparing their stomachs for the volumes of whiskey they would drink tonight.

Teresa and Blanche ate tough thick beefsteaks almost impossible to cut with a knife, and boiled potatoes buried in butter and salt and pepper. They declined a generous helping of fried beans hot enough to start a prairie fire. Within the hour they were back in their room again.

The hotel provided only chamberpots for its guests. It did supply one for each side of the bed, however, and for that both women were grateful. Sensing Blanche's discomfort over their situation, Teresa said, "I'm going downstairs for a newspaper. I'll be back in five minutes."

When Teresa returned, Blanche was in a flannel nightgown up to her neck, tied in a neat bow. She had taken her hair down and it lay like a long, glossy fan behind her head. She had drawn the covers up to her chest and lay rigidly,

114

eyes staring straight ahead. "Relax, Blanche. Nobody's going to bother you." She smiled reassuringly and began to undress, not afflicted with the same inhibitions as Blanche.

She used her chamberpot as discreetly as the room allowed and crawled into bed nude, saying, "I never sleep in clothes in the summer. It's too damned hot for me."

She reached over and turned out the lantern on the small bedside table. In the darkness she asked, "Any regrets, Blanche?"

"None," came the confident answer.

Sun streaming in through the window woke Teresa early, but she lay in bed another two hours before stirring. Frequently, she would look over at the big woman who still slept by her side. Teresa's heart beat with excitement with the thought of the days and days ahead they would spend together. She would have to see about getting themselves East and she'd have to start today. It wouldn't be easy, but as long as Blanche was there with her. . . .

As much as she possibly could, she would try to make up to Blanche what she'd given up – a home, a husband, the family she had left, and the family she would have had with Steven. Maybe Blanche would get married when they reached wherever it was they were going. Maybe not, too. Teresa wouldn't mind rooming with Blanche the rest of her life. At least Blanche wouldn't be pawing at her every night. She wouldn't mind being held by Blanche, though, a strange thought Teresa didn't understand but didn't try to ignore.

Blanche, she had to admit, meant more to her than any man in her life ever had. Just knowing she'd see Blanche those Saturday mornings had made the weeks fly by, made things better. Even made her heart beat faster. She smiled remembering the excitement of the drive to the river. They were good memories. But now she was where she wanted to be. And with the person she wanted to be with. Now if Lattimer just left her alone. . . .

Stretching, she swung her legs over the side of the bed. She washed quickly, using water from the big flowered porcelain pitcher and matching bowl on the dresser, then dressed hurriedly, anxious to get downstairs to breakfast. Blanche didn't look like she'd be stirring for at least another hour.

Over coffee, Teresa asked the waiter about the next stage to Preston. Filling her cup, he said, "Ain't no stagecoach, ma'am. Everybody gits their own ride from here to Preston. Wells Fargo quit the run a year ago. No return passengers."

Teresa exclaimed in dismay, "But that's two hundred miles away!"

"Can't help it, ma'am," the waiter replied. "Nobody ever leaves here 'cept drovers. Bunch of 'em pullin' out tomorrow. Might be you could get a ride on one of their wagons."

"But there are so many people here," she said. "Where did they all come from?"

"East," he answered. "East. Everybody's comin' from the East. Nobody's goin' thataway. This here's a turnoff point fer west and south Texas. Can't recall the last time somebody went East. 'Cept for the drovers, that is. Them Yanks likes our beef." He suggested to her, "Go over to the blacksmith shop. Maybe the smithy knows somethin'. He talks to all the drovers. He's usually open on Sundays."

"Yes, thank you," Teresa answered, too stunned to say more.

No way out of Samson's Town? It wasn't possible. All roads ran north and south and east and west. Roads didn't just stop!

"Not all roads, ma'am," the big bull-like blacksmith informed her. "Seems like once people get here, they either stay in Samson's Town or head south or west. Once in a while a family will go back east but they usually go by wagon."

116

"Covered wagon?" Teresa said. Her heart beat with renewed hope.

"Yep." The big mustachioed man pumped air into a large bellows making the coals glow in a huge brick pit. "Doesn't happen much though."

With this information, Teresa hastened back to the hotel to find Blanche up and dressing.

Together, they made their way to the dining room. The tables were nearly all occupied now, ladies eating light breakfasts with their husbands before the beginning of the day's work. The two cowboys Teresa and Blanche had seen last night sat with elbows propped on the table holding their heads as steaming cups of coffee sat untouched before them. Two gentlemen completely dressed in black, hoslters worn low on their hips, leaned against the back wall facing the doorway. Teresa recognized their type immediately. Gamblers. Men who made a profitable living off the whiskey-saturated trailhands.

She drew long looks from the pasteboard professionals but ignored them as she and Blanche took a table near the entrance.

"Ladies?" the waiter said.

"Two coffees. One breakfast," Teresa said ordering for them both. "You'll find the breakfast much better than supper was," Teresa whispered as the waiter left.

"You're so sure of yourself, Teresa," Blanche remarked. "I wish I were more like that."

"You will be by the time we reach the East."

"Just where in the East did you have in mind?"

All right, Teresa honey, the smaller woman said to herself. Go ahead. Tell her just where in the East you have in mind. "Blanche, I honestly can't tell you. I don't know."

"But I thought you had this all planned out." Deep concern was visible in Blanche's eyes.

"Not exactly."

Thankfully, the arrival of the coffee momentarily interrupted Teresa from further explanation. She took a tentative sip and then said, "We've got another problem right now, anyway. One we have to solve soon while we still have good weather for a couple of months."

"Good weather? What do you mean?"

Somberly, Teresa related to Blanche what she had learned this morning. "And," she added, "we can't spend any time here. There are people who want to know where we are and we can't hang around to let them find out. I took the room for a week but I thought we'd be gone at least by tomorrow. Who would kill a horse to get here in one day?"

"Lattimer and Steven, not to mention my father," Blanche suggested drily.

"Are you still willing to go on?" Teresa asked. "Or would you rather return to Starcross?" She waited for Blanche to back out. Things were already becoming difficult.

"How would be the best way to get out of here?"

Teresa let out a sigh of relief, raising a small chuckle from Blanche. "The drovers would be terrible. I know all about them. Horseback would kill me within the first two days."

"Then it's the covered wagon," Blanche said.

Teresa nodded thoughtfully.

"Alone."

"That's right. Can you drive a wagon?"

"Two-team, not four-team."

"Would we need four?"

"I suppose not," Blanche answered. "Not if we didn't take everything in the world with us. We'll sell the wagon in Preston anyway, won't we?"

"Lock, stock, and barrel. Let's see," Teresa pondered, chin in her hands. "We'd need grain for the horses. At least a three weeks' supply of food. I don't know exactly how long the trip would take."

"Surely not three weeks," Blanche said.

"I think so. Ten miles a day. Two hundred miles. With an extra week for whatever delays we might face."

"Just us."

"Right."

"We'll need guns, then," Blanche said firmly. "Rifles. And pistols. I'm not going unarmed."

Teresa agreed. "And water."

"Where are we going to get all this?" Blanche asked.

"The blacksmith shop, I think, for the wagon. If we told him what we want, he should be able to find a wagon for us."

"For how much?"

"Eat first," Teresa told her. "Then we'll go hear the bad news."

A half hour later they heard the bad news. "Got a Conestoga behind the barn," said the smithy.

"Too big," Teresa said upon first glancing at the wagon. Still, they walked around the large Conestoga painted a bright blue beneath, bright red above, with canvas on hoops sheltering its long, boat-shaped body.

"It's all I got, ma'am," the smithy said indifferently. "Three hundred dollars outfitted, includin' horses and water. 'Cept for your grub and whatever else you want to take with you. Take it or leave it."

"Can two horses draw it?" Blanche asked.

"Big horses," the smithy said. "If you grained and rested 'em proper."

With no acceptable alternative, Teresa asked, "When would it be ready?"

"Give me a week," came the reply.

"Sooner," Blanche said.

"No, ma'am. It needs work on the wheels and axles. Money in advance."

Teresa reached into her purse. "In a week, then."

"It'll be ready."

Teresa gave Blanche a confident smile and they left, with

119

the blacksmith scratching his chin.

Back at the hotel, Teresa admitted, "That leaves us with just the money you gave me."

"It'll have to be enough," Blanche answered, and ran a worried hand across her brow. "I suppose we should start buying things tomorrow, don't you think?"

But they bought nothing, instead spending a busy day in careful planning. Not daring to be caught short, they would order enough grain and supplies to last four weeks; otherwise they would take only what they absolutely needed.

At the gun shop they chose two Winchester .44 carbines and two Colt Navy .36's from walls lined with weapons on display. They bought plenty of ammunition for their powerful and accurate hardware.

"You gettin' ready for a war, ma'am?" the gunsmith jested.

"In a matter of speaking," Teresa answered. "We'll pick these up in a week."

At the drygoods store they made prudent selections from its jam-packed interior. Hundreds of items filled every nook and cranny — tobacco goods, tinned goods, bags of coffee beans, dried beans, corn, sugar and salt, tubs and pots and pans. Pungent slabs of smoked pork and beef hung from a high ceiling on thick iron hooks. Along two narrow aisles were men's and women's shoes, pins, needles, scissors, mens' hats still in their original boxes, bamboo fans from the Orient, knives, guns, shells, holsters, bib overalls, pens, paper, lap slates, bolts of dyed cloth emitting a strong musty-sweet odor. The smell of leather, fresh-ground coffee, plug tobacco, spices, vinegar and nameless other fragrances mingled to tantalize the women's noses luring them to linger longer than necessary on this busy day. One tiny corner was set aside for the United States Post Office. In the middle of the crowded store sat a large pot-bellied stove, chairs surrounding it winter or summer. Blanche and Teresa slowly

120

made their way up and down the aisles pondering each selection. Finished at last, they would pick these items up just before they left.

Later that evening over dinner, Blanche said, "I feel like I'm dreaming."

"Some dream," Teresa scoffed.

Just as they were about to leave, a tall shadow fell across their table. Teresa looked up to see Matthew staring down at Blanche. A wide-brimmed hat, drawn low over his eyes, did not hide his anger and sadness. Underneath a light coat hung a gun and holster, the first Teresa had ever seen him wear. "Hello, Blanche," he said, completely ignoring Teresa.

"Matthew!" She did not conceal her surprise nor pleasure.

He remained standing, stern-faced, his eyes piercing. "You're to come home with me, Blanche," he ordered.

Tensely, wonderingly, Teresa watched the confrontation between brother and sister.

"That's no longer possible, Matthew," Blanche answered calmly. She reached up to put a hand on his arm. "I chose to leave with full knowledge that I wouldn't be going back."

"You broke Mother's heart."

"Mother has Father. She'll be all right."

Matthew glanced at Teresa. "Leave us alone, Teresa."

"She stays, Matthew," Blanche told him sharply.

Matthew glanced first at his sister and then at Teresa. He said nothing for a long moment and then asked, "Why'd you do it, Blanche? Why'd you run off?"

"I don't really know, yet, Matthew," she answered. "I'm closer now to the answer, whatever it is. When I find out, I'll let you know. I promise."

"Steven is mad enough to kill you," Matthew told her. "Mother was crying when I left and Mable won't come out of her room."

"And Father?"

121

"I would've handled things a whole lot different than he did, you can be sure. Damned different." He paused, his anger again visible in his eyes. "Where're you going?" he demanded.

"We're not sure. East," Blanche said.

"You're going with Teresa." A flat statement. An accusation.

"Yes."

"Why?"

"It's what I choose to do. You just have to accept that."

He snorted with disgust and reached into his coat pocket. He pulled out a large brown envelope folded in half. He handed it to his sister with a trembling hand. "Father said to give this to you."

"What is it?"

"He didn't tell me. A letter telling you to get home, I hope," he said angrily.

"Matthew."

Teresa knew that tone, the tenderness in Blanche's voice.

Blanche said in the soft, tender voice, "You are such a trustworthy brother. I'll miss you so."

"You don't have to." He pulled a chair alongside her and sat on its front edge. "Come home with me. We'll leave early in the morning. I'll take you home, good and safe." He put his hand possessively on the handle of his gun.

"No, Matthew," she said. "Please don't waste your time asking. Do you want to stay here tonight? I'm sure there's room. Several drovers left today."

"I'll get a room down the street. If I'm going to break from you, I'd rather it be right now."

"So brave," she said smiling. "I'll write," she promised.

He nodded, smiled weakly, and rose to leave. She stood with him and quickly they hugged each other. "Please give my love to Mother and Father and Mable. And please tell

Steven I'm sorry. It's a big thing to ask of a little brother."

"Not so little anymore," he said. "I'll tell them." He gave his gun belt a manly hitch. Then Matthew was gone.

CHAPTER NINE

Back in their room, Teresa said, "Matthew will miss you, whether he admits it or not."

"He's admitted it already," Blanche replied, and tucked the envelope, unopened, into her suitcase. "I'll write to Father soon, telling him I've received it. . . ." Her voice trailed off.

"Don't you want to read it?" Teresa said, watching Blanche place some clothing over the letter.

"Later. I'm sure it's just notes from everyone telling me what a mistake I've made. My separation from my family is complete now. There's only the future to look forward to."

Then, Blanche burst into tears.

Teresa crossed the room and led her weeping friend to the side of the bed. "It's been a long day, Blanche," she said softly. "Why don't you get ready for bed?"

Teresa laid out her gown for her, then went to the window to pull the shade, and peeked out along its edge to watch the boisterous nightlife below while Blanche changed. Soon Teresa heard her say timidly, "All right." Teresa turned to look at the frightened woman who had less idea than she of what the future held in store.

A few minutes later, Teresa climbed into bed beside Blanche. Nude as usual, tonight she somehow felt shy, and she rose to don a gown of lighter weight than the heavy cotton Blanche wore. In bed again, Teresa turned the unprotesting Blanche toward her and held her all through the night, while her own heart raced wildly in her breast and her own breathing was a strain to control.

It was unbearably exciting to hold Blanche. As big as many of the men Teresa had slept with, Blanche still felt so . . . different. Not at all like holding a man with a body as hard as saddle leather — and just as unyielding. Blanche felt so . . . wonderful, so . . . soft. No, she was not like a man at all. Her body, as big as it was next to Teresa's tiny frame, seemed to mold naturally and easily against her, filling the spaces between them, merging with Teresa as if they both had been carefully designed to fit together like two intricate pieces of a well-constructed clock.

And unlike the heavy sweating odor of the cowboy or the too-rich aftershave of the businessman, Blanche smelled good, a woman's smell, emitting a faint musky odor from the long day. A pleasant, almost intoxicating odor. Teresa could feel the bigger woman's large bosom pressing gently against her own, rising and falling in steady rhythm while she slept, Teresa knew, from tremendous emotional exhaustion. Teresa

125

vowed again to make up to the woman in her arms the loss of family and friends and home.

Toward morning Teresa managed to fall asleep with Blanche's head still resting comfortably in the crook of her arm, the other arm lying across her waist.

Throughout the rest of the week, Teresa kept a constant watch on the people around her, worried that Lattimer or Alexander Bartholomew or Steven Trusdale would show up and try to drag one of them back to Starcross. But by Sunday, the day before they were to leave, she was convinced that none of them were coming to Samson's Town. Thank God, Lattimer had apparently chosen to forget her, just as she half hoped he might, and Matthew must have convinced Blanche's menfolk that she wasn't ready to come back voluntarily, at least not yet. It struck both women as strange that except for Matthew's brief visit, neither had been pursued. Teresa reflected that maybe the contents of the envelope Matthew had given Blanche explained things — but so far it still lay undisturbed in the bottom of her suitcase, and she chose not to press Blanche on the subject.

To be sure they would be able to leave Samson's Town by Monday, she and Blanche had gone daily to the blacksmith's shop to check on their wagon. To make certain the big burly man understood that they would not tolerate delays, they stood around his shop by the hour, watching him work and pestered him when he stopped to shoe a horse or fill other orders. "There are other people who need me, too!" he finally bellowed at them but that didn't prevent them from coming back; they knew the wagon would be ready on time, if only for the blacksmith to get them out of his hair and out of his shop.

All the supplies they needed were packaged and waiting at the drygoods store and gunsmith shop. They would only have to drive up, pack the goods into the wagon, and leave this place forever. With each day, as they came closer to leaving, their excitement built. They hardly dared talk about it for fear of bringing themselves bad luck.

But more exciting than the events of the days were those of the nights. So exciting that not a word had been mentioned at all.

Each night since last Monday evening, as soon as they climbed into bed, she and Blanche had held each other. Every single night. They smiled shyly at each other, turned out the lamp, and moved into one another's arms. Mostly, Blanche would hold Teresa. Sometimes Teresa would hold Blanche, which made them giggle like children. Teresa didn't understand what was going on between them. She knew only that it was good.

Lying next to Blanche was startlingly different from lying next to a man. A time to sleep with someone and actually enjoy it. Teresa couldn't ever remember it happening before. Sleeping with her daughter's father had only been pleasant. This was exciting!

On the night before they were to leave Samson's Town, they celebrated in the privacy of their room with a bottle of wine and sipped the intoxicating drink until they were both heady. As the music from below drifted up to them, they moved unspeaking toward each other and danced together as their hearts beat beyond anything they had ever known before.

When the bottle was empty and the music had played its last note, Teresa didn't need to turn her back while Blanche put on her nightclothes. The wine allowed Blanche to change in front of Teresa and as Teresa did the same, she watched warm shadows from the dimmed chimney lantern cast a gentle glow on Blanche's large body.

"You're as big as a man, Blanche."

"I know. If the light were brighter you'd probably turn away from me."

Frowning, Teresa asked, "Why would I do that?"

127

"I'm more like a man than you realize, Teresa."

"I doubt it."

"I am," Blanche said.

"How?" Teresa asked. "Sit down. I'll brush your hair for you."

Blanche took a chair and began to pull the hairpins from her hair. It fell in a wavy cascade down her back. Teresa fluffed it and began to brush it in long, even strokes. "How?" she asked again.

"How, what?"

Teresa laughed. "Good wine, wasn't it? How are you more like a man than I realize? You certainly don't feel like a man. You have beautiful hair, do you know that?" It was thick and heavy in her hands.

"I'd like to cut it off."

"It's too pretty."

"Not that pretty."

Teresa persisted, "Are you going to answer my question?"

"Only because of the wine can I tell you this, Teresa. If you make fun of me, I'll kill myself."

"It can't be that bad," Teresa encouraged.

"It is to me."

"Tell me. I want to know."

"I . . . I. . . ." Blanche couldn't go on.

Teresa leaned against Blanche's back and rested her face in the rich thickness of her hair. "I want to know all about you, Blanche." Their physical nearness made the blood pound in Teresa's head. Slowly she slid her arms around Blanche's neck.

Blanche reached up and put her hands on Teresa's arms drawing her tighter to her. "I'm hairy."

"Hairy?"

"I have too much body hair. More than any normal woman should have. On my legs. On my arms. On my stomach. On my face. . . ." Her voice trailed off.

"What about it?" Teresa asked in a muffled voice.

"It's not normal."

"Who said?"

"Me. I say."

"I find it attractive."

"Attractive? You haven't really seen it."

"I like it. I find it very attractive."

Blanche stood to face Teresa, her near six feet towering over the tiny woman. They both stood trembling with emotion. She put her hands on Teresa's shoulders. "What's happening to us, Teresa?"

"I don't know, Blanche. I don't know." Teresa could barely get the words out.

"I . . . I feel things for you I don't understand. I. . . ."

Teresa put her arms around Blanche's waist. "Hold me," she whispered fiercely. She pulled Blanche tight against her body. Teresa knew what passion was, and what she was feeling right now was passion. Of a kind and intensity she had never experienced before. Nearly uncontrollable passion. Why it was happening with Blanche . . . with a woman. Her head whirled with desire. Her lips burned with longing for Blanche's own.

She tried to bring her world to a standstill as it spun around her. Her knees were weak from wanting. "I've got to lie down, Blanche. I haven't the strength to stand here anymore."

As Teresa let go, Blanche scooped her up in her arms as if she weighed nothing and stood holding her, looking down on her, their lips only the space of a breath away as if the wine they smelled from each other intoxicated them further. Blanche bent her face very close to Teresa's, paused momentarily, and then kissed her fiercely on the mouth.

Their breathing became very heavy and labored as the kiss became longer. One kiss became two and then three and finally Blanche carried Teresa to the bed where she laid her

129

down. She turned out the lamp and then leaned over Teresa and brushed the hair from her forehead. Teresa pulled Blanche to her and again they kissed. Their mouths opened and their tongues began to explore. Wildly, Blanche kissed Teresa's face and throat and when Teresa could no longer stand it, she gasped Blanche's name and pulled her on top of her.

Using her knees and elbows, Blanche adjusted her body, straddling Teresa's waist, and prevented her heaviness from crushing Teresa.

With her legs, Teresa forced Blanche's legs together so that she could wrap hers around Blanche. Her sensations were wild and like nothing she knew existed. "Touch me, Blanche," she begged. "Touch me." She pushed Blanche off her and forced a willing hand down to her thighs. She pressed Blanche's hand against her wetness. "Go inside, please." She pulled Blanche down on her once again.

Blanche put a thigh across Teresa's, and as their naked flesh came together she moaned, "Oh, God help me," and stopped moving.

Alarmed, Teresa whispered, "Blanche?"

Blanche sat up pulling Teresa with her. With maddening slowness, she pulled Teresa's small nightgown from her body and threw it to the floor. She began to remove her own but Teresa stopped her. "Wait," she whispered, and took it off Blanche.

Teresa got up on her knees and bent to Blanche's breasts. She held each one and sucked on the hardened nipples as Blanche buried her fingers and face in Teresa's hair. Blanche drew Teresa's face to her own and began to kiss her over and over until Teresa fell back onto the bed. Blanche followed her and moved her lips to Teresa's tiny breasts. She kissed them and licked them for a long time as Teresa moaned into the dark night.

Blanche began to kiss Teresa's belly and then her thighs.

130

Teresa guided her head toward her hips and let her legs fall apart as Blanche's mouth moved slowly toward her. She thought she would scream as Blanche's tongue touched her. She clutched at Blanche's hair as slowly and methodically Blanche licked her, as Blanche explored all of Teresa's folds and bumps and wet places.

Suddenly Teresa shuddered as she came in Blanche's mouth, her spasms repeating rapidly until she tore Blanche's mouth away. She pulled Blanche to her and violently kissed her wet face chewing on her lips and ears and biting her skin with gentle abandonment. Hoarsely she said, "Let me touch you. I need to touch you." Her hand found Blanche dripping with readiness. Teresa squeezed her and then spread her lips as an exploring finger slid inside her soft, yielding body. "You're so beautiful," she whispered to the woman who lay still now, with eyes closed.

Then, through clenched teeth, Blanche hissed, "Teresa, I want you. I want you."

Teresa was small enough to lay in Blanche's arms and suck on her new lover's breast while she caressed her with a free hand. She did it skillfully and with great love. She brought Blanche to near climaxes and then moved her hand away to squeeze her nipples and to caress her thighs and stomach. She sat up and climbed on top of Blanche fitting herself between Blanche's thighs to thrust her body against Blanche until she felt Blanche reaching a peak again. Lastly, she did as Blanche had done and lowered her face to Blanche's thighs and pushed her tongue into Blanche. She heard her gasp and she thrust her tongue into her several more times and then began that same slow, torturous licking Blanche had used, almost killing her with desire. In seconds Blanche was gasping with her spasms, clutching Teresa's face. Teresa crawled up to put her arms around Blanche and to hold her, burying her face in her hair.

They kissed, wanting to merge their bodies into one piece

131

of flesh, whispering words of tenderness and love. As their heartbeats slowed down and the night became real again, their world became complete.

"I love you, Teresa," Blanche said fiercely. "I don't understand why, but I love you."

"There will never be anyone for me but you, Blanche. I swear to you."

"That day at the Brazos, when you asked me to leave," Blanche asked, "did you know then?"

"I didn't know anything. I just wanted to be with you. Needed to be. It was worth the chance asking you to go."

"Are we in love, Teresa?" Blanche asked innocently. "Is that what we are? In love?"

"I don't know. I think so," she said.

"I saw my mother and father making love one night," Blanche told her.

"I'll bet it was beautiful," Teresa said.

"I wouldn't go that far," Blanche answered. "Before now, I couldn't see why my mother allowed him to touch her that way. Or she, him."

"Why? What were they doing?"

"What we did."

"With their mouths?"

"Yes."

Teresa laughed. "I thought we just invented it."

"You never. . . ."

"No!" Teresa said strongly. "There are some things I never would have been able to think of let alone do." She spoke pensively. "Why I allowed any of it to happen was. . . ." She fell silent for a moment and then said, "If I'd known you, Blanche . . . if I'd known we would fall in love, and I'm sure we are, I never ever would have slept with a man."

"But if you hadn't come to Starcross, you wouldn't have known anyway, so it doesn't matter," Blanche assured her.

"You're not hurt by what I did?"

"How can I be?" Blanche asked reasonably. "You were never mine. I didn't even know you existed until a few weeks ago. I promise you, Teresa, your past is just that. Past. Don't worry about it."

Teresa turned to Blanche and kissed her for her understanding and the night became magic all over again as they began to make love for the final time that night.

In the days they had been there, Teresa and Blanche had ordered a hot tub to be brought to their room each evening. They usually took a bath before supper, each conveniently staying out of the other's way, sitting in the hotel lobby, reading the newspaper until it was her turn. For this morning, however, they had ordered the bath for seven because by nine they wanted to be on their way out of Samson's Town.

Wild with love for each other, they were deliriously happy to be leaving, to be alone together to share whatever the future was going to bring them. Tenderly, they washed each other of last night's loving, fell onto the bed, loved again, and bathed again, laughing hysterically with joy.

Too excited to eat, they checked out, and nearly ran to the blacksmith shop with their suitcases.

"Everything's ready, ma'am," the blacksmith said to Teresa.

"Are the horses hitched?" Blanche asked.

"You're all set. Water barrels are full. But your husbands ain't here yet," he said in a disapproving voice.

Teresa and Blanche looked at each other and burst out laughing. After thanking him, they walked around to the rear of the shop to the wagon. Everything seemed in order. They climbed up onto the high seat. Blanche took the reins in her hand, released the brake and said, "Getup, horses."

First they went to the drygoods store and had the grain loaded. They planned to use the full sacks as a mattress, pulling blankets over themselves at night. Next, they loaded their remaining packages, placing them where they would be handy to reach in order of need. Finally, they picked up their weapons making sure they were obvious to anyone who might be watching two lone women leaving unescorted in one wagon.

"That's it," Blanche announced.

"There's one more thing I want to get," Teresa said. "I'll be right back." She disappeared around the corner while Blanche waited with the wagon. In twenty minutes she flung a final package into the back and declared, "I'm ready."

"What'd you get?" Blanche asked.

"I couldn't resist buying one more set of clothes," Teresa answered without any apology for using their precious money.

Gathering their dresses around them, they climbed onto the wagon seat once more. Blanche again took the reins, slapped them against the horses' flanks and said, "Getup, horses."

The big Conestoga began its journey.

Wide iron-rimmed wheels crunched over small stones and gravel and rocked gently over the rutted road while the big-hooved horses pulled the wagon with ease. Once away from the populated area, Teresa leaned comfortably against Blanche, knowing that this was where she was supposed to be. No matter if it was in Starcross, Samson's Town, or back East. As long as she was with Blanche, she was home.

"We've got to give the horses names, Blanche," Teresa told her.

"Before the day is out," Blanche promised.

Blanche held the thick leather reins easily in her big hands, sending an expert crack down the length of the straps to the left or to the right if either horse did not pull his load equally. The sounds of the creaking wagon, the squeaking of the harnesses, an occasional snort from a horse blowing dust from his nose, and the singing of the birds put Teresa in a near-hypnotic state as Samson's Town grew smaller in the distance.

As the town disappeared behind a rise of land, for the first time in their lives the women were completely on their own. Blanche pulled the horses to a halt on the empty prairie and rested the reins across the front of the wagon.

"Is something wrong?"Teresa asked in alarm. "What are you doing?"

"Something I've wanted to do since we left this morning. Sit on this wagon seat and kiss the daylights out of you."

Teresa looked into Blanche's eyes and read the love there. She had never seen love pouring out of anyone's eyes before and it took her breath away. "I love you, Blanche Irene Bartholomew. Desperately."

Blanche leaned toward her and softly kissed her on the forehead and then on each eyelid and finally on the mouth. Teresa could have fainted from the ecstasy of Blanche's gentle touch. Blanche took her into her arms and kissed her long and deep, leaving Teresa in a shambles.

"Blanche," she finally managed to say. But she could say no more because Blanche had again engulfed her in love. Blanche's hands roamed down the front of her dress and over her shoulders, down her back and across her thighs. Teresa lifted her dress out of the way so that Blanche could fondle her. And in the heat of the early morning sun with hardly a bird or a cloud in the sky to watch them, Blanche entered that private place of women that only they can understand and brought Teresa to levels of rapture not known to her even last night. Teresa fell against her lover in a weakened state repeating her name over and over again.

With her hand still there, Blanche said, "Let me again," and once more brought Teresa to new plateaus of love.

135

"Enough," Teresa gasped as a final spasm gripped her.

"I can feel it," Blanche whispered into her hair. "I can feel your love as it happens. It's beautiful."

"Let me touch you," Teresa said. She reached under Blanche's dress and found her wet and ready. She squeezed her mound and then slid a finger between the soft lips. "Oh, Blanche, I never thought love was anything. You have made it everything. Everything!" Gently she massaged the swollen flesh.

Blanche leaned back against the seat spreading her thighs wider. The movement caused her to climax sooner. Clenching her teeth she held Teresa tightly against her and gasped. She kissed her lover passionately, sucking on her tongue, exploring Teresa's mouth with her own.

They stayed that way for some time, Teresa's hand still in Blanche, Blanche's mouth on Teresa's. A roadrunner darting across the road in front of the horses caused the big animals to jerk, and their harnesses to jingle, bringing the women out of their frozen pose.

Carefully, Teresa removed her hand. Blanche jumped once, then relaxed. "The feeling is still there," she said. "I can hardly stand it."

They smoothed their dresses and again Blanche got the horses moving.

"We only have three weeks to reach Preston, darling," Teresa whispered to her lover, and shaded her eyes against the late morning sun. "We'll never make it."

Blanche laughed, and pulled Teresa to her side. "We'll make it, my love," she said. "I don't know how, but we'll make it."

Blanche sounded so sure, so confident, that Teresa felt completely safe from any peril their journey might offer. She was with a mighty woman, Teresa was sure of it. She was sure she had found a wonderful, what . . . mate? . . . to spend the rest of her life with. She sighed contentedly.

They seldom wore their sunbonnets as they traveled and the wagon's canvas cover remained rolled back continuously through the day. As they had hoped, they averaged almost ten miles a day. By the end of the first, with poetic flair they had named the horses Stormy and Night for all their precious memories. In two days they had mastered the art of cooking over buffalo chips. Their daily fare was almost always beans and hardtack, but the plain food wouldn't be necessary forever and they ate without complaining. Carefully, they conserved their water, carried in two large oak barrels attached to either side of the wagon, limiting themselves to drinking and cooking and watering the horses, and every third morning, dipping a quarter-pailful each to sponge themselves clean.

Life became perfect, extraordinary, something that could no longer beat them down or make them feel inadequate. They were full of tremendous confidence built by many small accomplishments: cooking with chips; taking turns off and on through the night at guard duty, recovering with cat naps through the day so that each could still handle her chores; driving the team and taking care of them; being wise enough to know when to rest and when to rise. For the first time in their lives they felt useful — to themselves and to each other.

The land began to change from its monotonous flat expanse to rolling terrain. There were more trees and shrubbery, and grass was more plentiful. More birds were seen and numerous small animals skittered in front of them, scurrying to get away from the huge object rumbling over their homes. Occasionally, the two women saw buffalo, the herds tragically thinned now from hunters who had worked for the transcontinental railroad that had finally finished cutting its way across the entire nation only last month.

By the sixth day of their journey, Teresa and Blanche had settled into a routine, taking turns gathering chips, cooking, cleaning, graining the horses, repacking after every meal — tedious tasks not at all tedious because they were performed for each other. It was another way to say: I love you, I want to do this menial thing for you. And because I do it for you, and by doing it, it is no longer menial, but terribly important. And I will do my best out of love for you.

Since they alternated the early morning guard duty it wasn't possible to awaken together. But whoever slept rose with the sun, a lifetime habit of Blanche's, one Teresa was still getting used to after years of sleeping late.

This morning, Teresa had early guard duty and sat on a rock near the wagon, a rifle across her lap, listening to the horses contentedly munching grass. She waited for the sun to rise to its daily morning splendor to splash mammoth streaks of red and orange and purple across the eastern sky until the sun peeked over the horizon, dissipating the multicolors to fill the space with blue. She listened for the first bird to chirp and then sing to wake a second bird with a different call until the air would be filled with the music of their mixed songs.

She looked expectantly to the east, waiting for that first streak of color as it began to splash across the horizon, but the grayness still lay like a sheet of lead over the sky.

She drew an impatient breath as just the whisper of a breeze from the west caressed her face and died away and the air became still again. Almost oppressive. Not a leaf rustled. In fact, she noticed for the first time, not a bird stirred. Neither were there the usual sounds of tiny animals scurrying beneath the shrubbery or along the ground. No early morning eagles or hawks or vultures soared a million miles above them with graceful abandonment.

Teresa checked her watch. She became uneasy. Blanche still slept. For the first time since they had been on the trail Teresa needed to wake her. She walked over to the rear of the wagon. "It's time, Blanche," she said to the sleeping

138

woman who lay wrapped in a blanket, gently snoring on the sacks of grain.

Blanche stirred and sat up. She brushed long hair away from her face, a motion that never failed to send a stab of heat along the insides of Teresa's thighs. That is, until this morning. There was something different about this morning. "What time is it?" Blanche asked heavily. "It's dark."

"A little before five."

Blanche crawled to the end of the wagon and looked out. Her brows knitted as she glanced at the western sky. Slipping her dress over her petticoats and quickly pulling on stockings and shoes, she stepped down from the wagon on three portable steps that could be conveniently attached to the rear. "I'll be right back," she said briefly.

Teresa sensed something had disturbed Blanche. Returning from a few moments behind a bush, Blanche again examined the sky, intently looking to the east and then to the west. "We'd better skip breakfast."

At the big woman's ominous tone the hairs prickled on the back of Teresa's neck. "What is it?"

"We're being chased by a storm." Blanche stood unmoving, studying the western sky.

"A bad one?" To compare the security of a building against being in a covered wagon on the vast prairie was impossible. There *was* no comparison. Teresa wasn't scared but she was definitely worried. If only Blanche would stop staring at the sky like that. No storm could be that bad. Blanche was making her nervous. "Is it bad?" she repeated.

Blanche ignored Teresa's question. "Make sure everything is lashed down. Tighten the canvas, cover things inside with that big tarp. Be sure everything's fast." Without another word, Blanche walked over to the horses who were tied to an improvised hitching rail: a rope suspended between two stout trees.

139

Blanche's voice galvanized Teresa into action.

In less than ten minutes, they were ready. Quickly, they climbed onto the high seat.

"We'd better try to find some type of shelter right away."

Even as Blanche spoke, Teresa was scanning the land for adequate refuge. How they had bragged to one another about sleeping underneath the open sky, gazing up at the stars and contemplating the wonder of it all like two silly schoolgirls. They'd know better after this.

Willingly, Teresa handed Blanche the reins, who cracked them smartly against the horses' rumps saying loudly, "Getup!"

Blanche was rapidly building the horses' speed. More rapidly than normal. Not properly warmed up, the team was already at a slight trot. A stinging pelt of rain on the side of Teresa's face and a strong gust of wind from the rear squelched her concern for the horses.

In another minute the rain poured from the blackened sky, drenching the women almost instantly. In no time at all dips and ruts in the trail had filled to overflowing, the wind built from heavy gusts to a single dull roar.

Teresa looked back to see huge streaks of lightning strike the earth. Suddenly, the horses screamed and reared, shying as a bolt hit a tree several yards to their left, cleanly splitting its trunk in half. Through the dense rain Teresa watched the divided sections topple to the earth in two different directions.

Blanche raised her arms high and brought the reins down hard on the horses' rumps bringing them back into line. "Haaaaa!" she yelled into the roaring wind, and forced them into a dead run. Teresa looked back inside the wagon, making sure nothing was jarred loose as the big prairie schooner began to careen dangerously from side to side, hitting unseen rocks and ruts. The billowing canvas cracked in the wind.

140

"Haaaaa!" Blanche yelled again, as lightning struck repeatedly nearby. "We've got to get to shelter right away, Teresa!" The words were ripped from her mouth as she spoke them.

"There!" Teresa shouted. She pointed in the distance to a huge pile of rocks and trees. "Get to the other side."

Blanche turned the horses slightly to the east and raced for the retreat. Without warning the team balked in a long skid, fighting their harnessess and the wagon that threatened to ram them from behind and nearly throwing the unsuspecting women over the front of the Conestoga.

"Whoaaa. . . ." Blanche hauled back on the reins bringing the horses to a dead halt.

"Goddamn it!" Teresa cried in frustration. "A gulch." In the driving rain, traveling at that speed, they had not seen the gap in the earth.

"We've got to chance it, Teresa," Blanche shouted over the howling storm. "We've left the regular trail. I don't know how far down or up the crossing may be. It could be miles in either direction."

Teresa said her first prayer in years as Blanche guided the horses carefully over the edge of the steep gully and down several rocky and slippery feet to its bottom, already five inches deep in water. The wagon rocked and tipped frighteningly as they looked frantically for a place to climb up the opposite side.

Nearly blinded by the rain constantly filling her squinting eyes, Teresa unsuccessfully wiped her face as she stared through the gray downpour. It was as dangerous to be in a gulch as out in the open. She expected at any moment to be engulfed by a wall of water cascading down through the gully in a flash flood. So far, the opposite side was too steep to drive up.

They crept along slowly, sometimes passing between jagged walls just barely wide enough for the horses and

141

wagon, scraping the water barrels until Teresa thought their oak slats would shatter into a thousand tiny splinters. Overhead, thunder reverberated and lightning split the sky.

"Up there!" Teresa suddenly cried out, pounding on Blanche's thigh with her fist. She pointed to a place fifteen feet ahead where they could probably work their way up the opposite bank.

A loud whoosh from the rear demanded their attention. They strained to look back around the canvas blocking their immediate view. But without needing to see it they knew it was water, water traveling toward them at a killing rate.

"Drive!" Teresa screamed, and slapped Blanche hard on the shoulder.

Even before Teresa's blow, Blanche was already beating the backs of the terror-ridden horses. They strained against their harnesses harder and harder as they rushed to escape the oncoming water. The wagon bounced sickeningly over rocks that threatened to break axles and wheels.

From alongside the seat Teresa grabbed the long horsewhip which had never before been touched by either woman. She lashed the team's rears unmercifully and repeatedly, shrieking their names. She peered around the Conestoga's canvas and saw the water gaining on them with frightening speed.

They had reached the path to higher ground and Blanche steered the horses up it. The panicked animals strained against leather, pulling the wagon inch by slippery inch up over the clay bank and gravel, fighting for footing as Blanche cracked their hides and Teresa cursed their existence, again and again bringing the whip down on them in stinging blows.

A violent jolt struck the Conestoga. With sickening sluggishness the wagon swung slowly to the side, its wheels scraping roughly over the gully floor. "Blanche!" Teresa shrieked.

"Hang on," came the desperate reply. Blanche stood up in the Conestoga. Her eyes bulged with the effort of working

142

the team. Teresa grabbed Blanche around the waist to steady her as the wall of water pushed powerfully — violently — against the wagon, threatening to tip it over.

The unnatural pull of the prairie schooner nearly yanked the team off its feet. In a frenzy, screaming in fear, the horses pulled blindly in an attempt to flee the weight threatening to pull them into the water gushing at their hind legs. In a final mighty burst of strength they hauled themselves and the wagon up over the side of the flooded gulch and onto higher ground.

Without mercy, Blanche continued to drive the panic-stricken animals toward shelter. After another minute of running they reached it. The women jumped down from the wagon and ran to the horses, grabbing their halters, the terrified, rearing animals nearly jerking the women's arms out of their sockets. Twice, Teresa was lifted off the ground by Night but she held on for dear life. She and Blanche put soothing hands on the horses' faces and talked to them as the exhausted beasts' sides heaved and their eyes rolled until only the whites showed.

The wind continued to scream and the rain came at them in stinging horizontal waves, slashing at their eyes and skin and tearing at their dresses. Still holding the horses and talking to them, speaking meaningless words, the terrified women watched lightning flow in wide streaks from sky to earth and from earth to sky. Twice, lightning balls could be seen at a distance bouncing playfully and dangerously along the ground.

Blanche and Teresa huddled together, standing close to the horses, feeling their breaths mingling with their own as the storm raged around them. Half an hour later, as suddenly as it had come, the storm passed over them. The western sky was peaceful, as if the storm had never been. The earth looked washed and clean. To the east, the tempest still raged, covering the land with its wrath and the sound of distant

143

thunder.

Teresa leaned against the side of Night's neck, weak-kneed and exhausted. Blanche reached for her and held her close, her face bent to Teresa's soaking hair. Her own long hair, never put up in this morning's haste, hung limp and dripping wet, covering both their faces.

"I never dreamed of anything like this," Teresa said.

Wordlessly, they began to unhitch the horses. They would have to dry everything out, give the horses plenty of time to rest and recover. And they needed to rest themselves, as well. At noon, as the sun began to warm the earth and dry the trail, the women rehitched the team. They had lost half a day, but they could make it up if they added just one mile for the next five days. Blanche took first turn at the reins while Teresa slept in the rear and then they switched. By five o'clock, they were more than ready to stop again.

That evening, they pulled up beneath a peaceful grove of trees.

They were nearing the end of their second week of travel, feeling trail-wise and confident. Now and then they had contact with someone coming from Preston. Once, the United States Cavalry had appeared off in the distance, and just yesterday, a thousand head of cattle and several cowboys went lumbering by a half-mile away causing the earth to tremble beneath them even at that distance as the herd headed first to Preston and then onward to Kansas.

It was time to stop for noon break to rest the horses, and also themselves from the bouncing ride. Teresa drew the team to a halt and wrapped the reins around the brakestick. Blanche, down first, reached for her. Teresa slid easily into her arms. They kissed hungrily. A little breathless, Teresa said, "I'll get us some lunch."

144

Reluctantly, they released each other. Blanche unhitched the team, leaving on most of their tack but removing the halters, hobbling the horses so that they could nibble freely and wander about without going too far. She walked out onto the prairie to gather buffalo chips.

From the back of the wagon, Teresa hauled out the ingredients she would need to prepare their meal. As she watched Blanche disappear a short distance away behind a large pile of rocks, it suddenly occurred to Teresa that her lady looked thinner.

The second day on the trail Blanche had announced she would like to start walking beside the wagon. That day she had lasted only ten minutes before climbing back onto the seat. Now, almost two weeks later, she could walk miles before tiring. And, almost three weeks after leaving Starcross, Blanche's dress fit noticeably looser at the top and through the waist. Funny, Teresa thought, that she hadn't noticed before.

She briefly considered mentioning it to Blanche, then dismissed the idea. She hadn't ever found Blanche's heaviness distasteful. She enjoyed feeling her lover's weight driving against her when Blanche lay on top of her. As if Blanche owned her. She didn't mind being owned by Blanche. Not that way. No, she'd never say a word to Blanche about her weight. She was exciting, however she was.

Lost in thought admiring the big woman, she was startled by an unexpected sound from behind her. She dropped the pan she had just pulled from a sack as an evil voice hissed into her ear, "Howdy, Teresa."

A calloused hand clamped roughly over her mouth. Foul breath reached her nostrils.

How was it possible that she hadn't seen her assailant? She tried to twist free to see him but a strong arm bound her against his body in an unbreakable grip. From behind her another voice asked, "Where's the other one?"

145

"By that heap 'a rocks over there, I think," came a gruff reply.

"I'll go get 'er. I like 'em big and fat," said the second man.

To speak so crudely of Blanche made Teresa nearly blind with rage. But her struggles were futile against the powerful man.

The raspy voice hissed again. "Lattimer sent me."

Overwhelming shock and fear paralyzed Teresa's mind.

"He sent you a message." Roughly, she was spun around, the hand still clamped over her mouth. "My, oh, my, oh, my. Ain't you a good lookin' one."

Teresa stared into eyes filled with lust. She had seen such a look on many a drunken cowboy, but terror seized her as she stared into these demented eyes. She tried to pull away from the dirty bearded drifter. She could feel him fumbling with his gun belt and then heard it drop to the ground. She knew she was going to be ravaged, and probably murdered — and so was Blanche. Where was Blanche, she wondered desperately.

The man dropped his pants and forced Teresa's hand to hold him. She fought to let go but he held her hand in a painful grip. So repulsive was his body odor that she began to faint. He let go of her mouth and slapped her back into full consciousness.

Her eyes rolled in mortal fear as he threw her to the ground and yanked her dress above her knees. Panting, he ripped away her underwear. She heard Blanche screaming off to her left.

Grappling with the horrified Blanche, the second man dragged the fighting, screaming woman toward his partner who lay on top of Teresa. Harshly he yelled, "Wait for me, you horny old bastard!"

But Teresa's tormenter was beyond waiting as he frantically tried to thrust himself into her. She fought

146

violently, kicking and scratching. A savage bite on his arm sent him into a rage.

Cursing, he whipped her to her feet and slapped her so viciously across the head that her neck snapped painfully back. Throwing her to the ground again, he collapsed on top of her.

As he made unsuccessful drunken attempts to enter her, Teresa rolled her head to the side. As she saw Blanche being equally violated, Teresa's shrill outcries shattered the silence.

In an unearthly voice unlike anything Teresa had ever heard before, Blanche began to scream. "The Lord is my Shepherd. I shall not want. He maketh me to lie down in green pastures. He leadeth me beside the still waters."

The man pinning her to the ground raised himself in confusion. Another prayerful shriek from Blanche caused even Teresa's attacker to pause. "Ah, she's just crazy," he said. "Slap the shit outa' her and get on with it." He began to force his way into Teresa again. "Goddamn it, bitch," he screeched, grabbing himself, trying to guide himself into the fighting woman. "Yer too goddamn small, you little whore." He slapped her again nearly knocking her unconscious.

She saw Blanche twist her head away from the bearded monster attacking her, heard her scream one more time and with strength possessed of the devil, free one of her arms. She swung at the man weighing her down and knocked him aside. He scrambled to regain his advantage but Blanche, now half-standing, struck him a second time with superhuman fury.

Badly dazed, Teresa cried weakly for help as the man on top of her began his painful penetration.

Blanche viciously kicked her assailant in the face, smashing cartilage and bone. Stunned, blood spurting through his hands, he grabbed for his nose. She yanked the gun from his holster.

The man on Teresa had barely begun his thrust when

147

Blanche grabbed him from behind.

"What the hell —" he growled.

Blanche lifted him with one strong arm and jammed the gun barrel callously against the bridge of his nose.

Teresa struggled to one elbow. As if in some dreadful nightmare, she watched the man's eyes widen in terrified apprehension. "Hey, hey, honey. Hold on. Hold on, now," he said in a horrified voice. He put his hands high in the air. "Lattimer sent me. I got a message for Teresa."

From somewhere deep inside Blanche came an unrecognizable animal sound as she bared her teeth and wrathfully shook him. His shorter stature was no match for her larger and taller size — and her savage anger. She pushed the barrel harder against his flesh.

He began to cry as he begged, "Please . . . don't."

Those were the last words he spoke as Blanche growled once more and then blew his brains out scattering bone and gray matter everywhere. She let him drop and strode over to the second man who scrambled to his knees. He looked with unbelieving eyes at his dead companion and then up at the wild-eyed woman who was pointing his own gun at him.

"What's Lattimer's message?" The voice was deadly calm.

"He . . . he said. . . ."

Blanche drew back the hammer of the gun. The click was loud and ominous.

The man stammered, stalling for time. "He'd . . . he'd forgive her if she came back."

He had spoken his final words. Again the gun roared and the top part of his head disappeared across the prairie. Two more shots thudded into his chest before Blanche returned to the first dead man and shot him again. With each bullet the weapon jumped in her hand and the body jerked from the impact. Then, there was only the click of the hammer on an empty chamber rhythmically snapping over and over.

"Blanche," Teresa screamed, trying to reach her. "Help

me. Help me, please." She sobbed loudly as Blanche still stood shooting at the dead man.

Blanche finally stopped pulling the trigger. She blinked rapidly several times and then, still dazed, let the gun slide from her hand and fall to the ground.

Teresa tried to stand. But she had been so battered that her strength was nearly gone. Blanche knelt by her side and tenderly pulled down her dress. "Are you all right?" she asked so softly that Teresa had to strain to hear.

"He almost got me, Blanche," she sobbed. "He almost had me. I thought I was done with that for good."

"You are, darling. I promise." Blanche's eyes still had a half-glazed look in them.

Effortlessly, Blanche picked up her lady and carried her to the shade of the wagon. She sat her against a wheel and then spread a blanket upon the ground. She helped Teresa remove her dress and then gently laid her down, spreading a light cover over her. Bathing her tenderly, unmindful of the amount of water she used, Blanche kissed each darkening mark. Methodically and meticulously, she applied a soothing salve on the scrapes covering Teresa's face and body. Carefully, she wiped the insides of her legs where Teresa had been badly bruised. The man had been big. Another second and he would have torn her wide open.

"God . . . God!" Blanche cried out. Tears streamed down her face. Teresa reached for her and drew her down, holding her as the big woman sobbed uncontrollably.

Sometime later, Blanche sat up. In a low voice she said, "I've got to deal with the bodies."

"And our dresses," Teresa added quietly.

"I'll burn them."

"The men. . . ."

"I'll take care of them." Blanche trembled visibly as she spoke. "There's a place over there," she said, and pointed to where she had been looking for chips. "I could take the bodies there . . . use the horses to get those rocks to roll over them. It should work. A grave is a grave." Grudgingly, she added, "I'll say some words over them."

Embittered, Teresa said, "They don't deserve them."

"I know, but I wasn't brought up that way." Blanche went off to take care of her gruesome task.

Teresa felt no remorse for the slain men. They had had murderous intent in their evil hearts. Damn that Lattimer for sending the devils after her! No doubt he'd send someone else when these two didn't return. But by then she and Blanche should be on a train to Chicago. Then it would be impossible to find them.

When Blanche returned a while later Teresa asked, "What are you going to do with their horses?"

Blanche tied them to a wagon wheel and immediately took off her dress. "Sell them in Preston. We'll be able to use the money."

"Lord knows we deserve every goddamned cent of it," was Teresa's only comment.

CHAPTER TEN

Teresa woke early, painfully sore and stiff.

"Do you want to rest again today?" Blanche asked. Yesterday, they had remained where they had stopped for noon break, too shocked and too injured to go on.

"No," Teresa said. "I'll feel better as soon as I start moving." She drew Blanche down to her side where she lay in her arms until she felt guilty enough to get up. "Thank God it's a new day," she said finally rising.

They tried to put yesterday out of their minds as they readied the wagon and horses for travel. Still badly shaken, they were unable to eat, and fearful about continuing to

151

travel alone. But they had at least six more days on the trail before reaching Preston. They had to go forward.

They had just settled themselves on the wagon seat to begin today's journey when Teresa pointed toward a cloud of dust coming from the north. "Blanche, look," she said in a near whisper.

Blanche shaded her eyes and studied the horizon. "It never rains but it pours. Those are Wichita."

"Lord, God," Teresa gasped. A tiny hand flew to her mouth.

Blanche said quickly, "They're not normally a warring tribe — but get your rifle anyway and get down between the team."

"We'll be crushed if they shoot the horses," Teresa argued.

"It would be better to be crushed than ravaged and scalped, if that's their intention," Blanche said flatly. "Let's go."

Teresa didn't argue further. The western-born and better-educated Blanche knew far more about Indians than she did.

They positioned themselves between the horses' backs. "I can't see anything," Teresa complained.

"Stand on the wagon tongue."

At least ten riders raced madly toward them, blood-curdling cries splitting the early morning air as the Indians charged, brandishing rifles, bows, and lances. As they came closer, the women could see paint on dark faces and lean bodies. The Wichita were almost upon them now and Teresa and Blanche prepared to defend themselves for the second time in two days. They rested their rifles across the backs of the horses and took aim.

"Don't shoot," Blanche repeated calmly. "Something's up. They should have started firing at us by now."

Without slowing their horses, the war party rode wildly around and around the wagon waving weapons decorated with eagle feathers hanging from the shaft or the barrel. Most of the riders had painted black or red rings around their eyes, stripes of brown on their cheeks. They wore printed shirts and fringed buckskin leggings tucked into moccasins reaching to the knee. Loincloths were worn over the leggings. Raven black hair in long braids or worn loose and decorated with one or two feathers whipped freely about their faces. Around their necks were several necklaces of large animal teeth. One warrior alone was without a shirt, showing tattoos in stripes and dots covering his arms and back and chest.

Horses of brown, black, roan, and white bulged with rippling muscles as they carried their riders bareback, faster and faster around the wagon, urged on by repeated kicks in their sides. The horses, too, had paint around their eyes and on their cheekbones and rumps.

Blanche followed the circle of raiders with her rifle as dust and dirt flew everywhere.

After several terrifying minutes the Indians came to an abrupt halt in front of the wagon in a billowing cloud of dust. Suddenly, the heavily tattooed brave raised his lance high in the air and let out an ear-splitting scream as he sent the lance toward the team of horses.

It landed quivering a foot away from Stormy. The horses reared and started to bolt but Blanche reached out a lightning-fast hand and grabbed Stormy's bridle. "Whoa, Stormy. Whoa, Night. Get out of here, Teresa. I don't think they're going to kill us, but by heavens, take one of the red devils with you if we have to go."

The women moved from between the horses. They stood watching the mounted braves holding their rifles, lances, and bows raised high above their heads as their horses pranced skittishly.

An Indian slid from his horse's back and walked over to Teresa. The Indian said something to his companions and

153

fingered her short hair. They laughed loudly, and slapped their thighs as he walked over to Blanche. He took the pins out of her hair and watched it fall down her back. He reached out and took a big handful, shaking it lightly. He said something else and again the party laughed.

The tattooed rider moved to Teresa's side and pushed his horse into her, jostling her a few feet before he stopped his frightening bullying.

"Not a word, Teresa," Blanche warned.

The warrior looked down at Blanche for several seconds, then spoke to her in his own language before returning to the group. He spoke again to another man who moved to his side and reached into a pouch tied to the blanket of his horse. He pulled out an intricately beaded belt, handing it to the tattooed man who let the belt fall open. About six inches across and at least four feet long, covered with red, blue, white, and yellow beads sewn onto a soft, thin hide, it was a complex, beautiful piece of work.

The tattooed man rode forward, his proud bearing evident in the way he sat his horse. Handing the belt to Blanche he said in English, "Chief." He pointed to himself. "I say, give to brave lady. You kill two —" The Indian displayed two fingers. "Bad men. Fight like wounded buffalo. Brave!" He struck his chest with a violent slap. The chief handed the belt to Blanche. "You pass safe. Sleep. We watch brave lady."

Blanche draped the belt carefully across her arm as she looked deep into black eyes. "I am grateful," she said in a strong voice. "I will give a gift in return."

"Whiskey," came the immediate and harsh reply.

"We have no whiskey," Blanche answered.

Scowling, the chief signaled to a brave who jumped into the back of the wagon and tore it apart in a rampant search, scattering the wagon's contents everywhere. He cut open the one remaining bag of grain and dumped it on the ground. Snatching the coffee and sugar, he grunted, "We take. Take horses."

154

"Blanche," Teresa whispered anxiously, grasping her arm. "We need the horses."

Blanche turned to the chief saying, "I will give you my hair if you leave the horses."

The air crackled with tension. Teresa watched Blanche's unwavering look, the chief glaring in return. Sweat poured down the sides of Blanche's face as she stood unmoving.

After an eternity, the chief nodded a barely discernible signal. Blanche spoke with urgency. "Quick, Teresa. Get into that wagon and find scissors or a knife I can cut with."

Teresa hesitated and Blanche said firmly, "Go. Keep your head and look them straight in the eye."

Still clutching her gun, Teresa searched frantically through their strewn belongings, finally finding a small pair of scissors.

Blanche stood unmoving, staring at the chief, as Teresa raised the scissors to Blanche's head. Forced to set her rifle aside, Teresa stood on tiptoes to cut away the long hair that she had treasured so briefly, that had lain across her naked body tickling her shoulders and face and nose when Blanche lay on top of her. She wanted to drive the blades deep into the hearts of every one of the savages.

"Give it to me as you cut it," Blanche said. "And hurry."

Leaving a ragged three-inch growth all over Blanche's head, Teresa handed her the thick wavy hair clump by clump. Blanche straightened the cut hair so that it fell neatly in a bunch. When Teresa had finished, Blanche bound it together at the top with a piece of string from a grain bag. Solemnly, she walked to the chief's side and handed the trussed hair to him. He took it and raised it above his head and let out a war whoop. Teresa could see Blanche barely manage to avoid flinching at the sudden outburst. Blanche returned to stand at Teresa's side.

A brave rode to the back of the wagon where he untied the dead men's horses and grunted, "We take." He retrieved his chief's lance and tossed it lightly through the air to him.

155

As suddenly as they had come, the Indians whirled their horses around and rode away, yelling and whooping until they were once again nothing more than a small dust cloud on the horizon.

When they were completely out of sight, Blanche leaned weakly against the wagon and put her hands to her temples. "Father told me the Wichita were farmers."

"When did he tell you that?" Teresa asked. Her voice shook uncontrollably.

"When I was a little girl. Before the railroad started moving west."

Teresa looked at the empty horizon and asked, "Will they be back?"

"No, I don't think so," Blanche said reflectively. "If they were going to kill us, we'd be dead by now. With the cavalry around, I thought this area was free of hostile Indians."

They held each other, drawing on one another's strength, trying not to cry over their possessions thrown all over the prairie along with the remainder of the precious grain. "I wouldn't have made a very good pioneer, Blanche," Teresa said through her barely controlled tears.

"You *are* a pioneer, Teresa, and we *will* make it. I promise."

"Your beautiful hair."

"It'll grow again."

They spent nearly two hours repacking everything and salvaging all the grain they could.

Teresa picked up the belt from the wagon wheel where Blanche had draped it earlier.

"It's a wampum belt," Blanche said. "It usually contains a message."

"Do you know what it says?" Teresa asked, fingering the beadwork.

"No, but I think it's our safe passage to Preston. At least I hope so. I think we'll be followed the rest of the way and

156

guarded by them. They think killing those men was an act of bravery."

"It was, Blanche," Teresa said sternly, grabbing her arm. "Those animals would have been shot in Starcross if they had done that to a woman."

"But not by me. I wouldn't have shot them." Blanche walked a few feet away. "I did out here, though."

Teresa walked to Blanche's side and put her arms around her. "Don't think about them. They're gone. They can't hurt us anymore."

"Lattimer could send others."

"He could, but don't worry about it unless it happens."

"I . . . need to pray, Teresa," Blanche said, embarrassed. "Do you mind?"

"There are some things I'd like to do in the wagon, anyway," Teresa said gently, and left Blanche alone. She herself didn't need to pray. She was damned glad those two bastards were dead.

The Indian who had torn the wagon apart in his wild search for whiskey had left the flour and bacon intact and hadn't gotten quite all the coffee and sugar. Teresa didn't know why, but fortunately he also hadn't touched the package she had last bought in Samson's Town. She didn't know what she would have done if Blanche had seen it before she had had time to explain.

Blanche returned. Teresa kissed her fiercely, happily. "Do you know that you don't swallow like you used to ?"

Blanche smiled and said, "I'd hoped you weren't aware of my little quirks."

"I'm very aware of you. All of you." Teresa felt herself turn crimson.

"Why, Teresa, darling," Blanche said. "I do believe you're blushing."

Teresa laughed. "I'm glad I still can. I guess there's hope, yet." She buried her face in the softness of Blanche's breasts.

157

"Don't be silly, Teresa," Blanche scolded lightly. "You're a good woman. You worry too much about Starcross."

"You're probably right, and as of now," Teresa declared firmly, "Starcross is no longer part of my life."

They kissed again and held each other for a long time as the heat built in their bodies. Teresa was the first to break away. "We'd better go."

Blanche said musingly, "Do you suppose we'd be having all these problems if one of us were a man?"

Teresa looked into Blanche's dark eyes. She rubbed a thoughtful finger across pursed lips and then wordlessly walked away, to disappear inside the wagon. "Blanche, would you consider wearing these?" she called out. She jumped down from the rear and stood holding her package. Opening it, she said, "I've got a shirt and pants in here. Here're some socks and boots and. . . ." She tore the wrapping paper away and removed the clothing piece by piece laying it out on the wagon as Blanche joined her. "Damn! And a bashed-in hat." She had tried to be so careful.

"These are men's clothes," Blanche said.

"I wanted to suggest the idea our first day out. But . . . I didn't want to offend you." Teresa's embarrassment was readily apparent.

"But they're men's clothes," Blanche said again.

"Are you upset?" Teresa asked nervously.

"I . . . I don't know. I've spent enough years envying men's comfortable attire, but to actually wear them myself. . . ." Blanche fingered the blue denim of the pants and gray flannel of the shirt. She picked up the boots and hat, looking them over carefully. "Are they the right size?"

"I had to guess but I'd say so," Teresa said. "Try them on."

"Pants," Blanche said smiling.

"To match your hair," Teresa said.

Blanche put a hand to her head. "What do I look like?"

Teresa quickly handed Blanche a small mirror. The big woman studied herself for a long time, turning her head this way and that. "Needs work," she said.

"I'll trim it so it looks better," Teresa promised.

Quickly, Blanche changed clothes. "They're very comfortable. Lots of leg room." Enthusiastically she said, "Fix my hair," and eagerly knelt in the dust so that Teresa could reach her easily.

Teresa shaped Blanche's hair into a reasonably decent cut. It was almost too short for success but when Blanche looked in the mirror she expressed satisfaction. She reshaped the crumpled hat and tried it on. "Not a bad fit," she said, pulling the wide brim low over her eyes, and looked again in the mirror.

Carefully, Teresa folded Blanche's dress and petticoat and put them in her suitcase. She noticed the envelope Matthew had delivered still lay unopened, and wondered when Blanche would finally read it.

Joining Blanche who was already on the wagon seat, Teresa stared at her lover, trying to adjust to the big woman's new look. Yes, she did look like a man, with even a mustache and sideburns of sorts. She thought Blanche had been bleaching her upper lip until just the last week or so. It hadn't shown too much before then. She wondered where Blanche hid the bleach.

"You look good, Blanche," she said. "Handsome. You're very tan, too. It's becoming on you."

"I'm not a man, Teresa," Blanche said, and blushed as she took up the reins to begin their day's travel.

"I know."

"Is that bad?"

"No," Teresa answered, scowling. "I don't want some damned fool man. Your dressing this way just helps us to be safer." Then she added, "I hope."

"I expect the Wichita know what I've done," Blanche

159

said, and propped a foot comfortably up on the front board. "I'll bet they're watching every move we make."

Teresa frowned. "Do you suppose they know we love each other?"

"That, I don't know," Blanche replied, and pulled Teresa close to her side. It was what Teresa would have done to Blanche, if Blanche hadn't done it first.

Daily, now, they watched everything with wary eyes, every perceptible movement, carrying their rifles under their arms with each step they took, each mile they drove, jumping at every little sound, unable to admire the sky and the birds and animals and changing land as they had before. They were nervous and edgy, not trusting the Indians watching them, not trusting that they wouldn't again come unexpectedly swooping down upon them. Even the Conestoga drawing closer and closer to Preston didn't lessen the women's alertness nor make them feel safer. They slept less, changing guard more often, always watching. Then, six days after their encounter with the Wichita, they crested a small hill in the late evening sun, and there below them lay Preston.

"That's the most beautiful city I've ever seen," Teresa said, and Blanche agreed wholeheartedly.

At the cattle pens, the reality of Preston sank into their tired minds. The air was rank with the smell of ammonia from hundreds of tightly packed cattle standing in their own dung and urine. The cattle dealer offered them an outrageously low price for their team and wagon.

"We'll take it," Teresa said, glaring at him. "Blanche, let's get out of here. It's the best we're going to do in this hole."

"Hotel's jes down the street," the dealer offered. "Stage leaves every three days. Next one's tomorrow."

Teresa knew he meant to say train but he was openly

160

leering at her through scraggly bearded lips as he paid her and she was anxious to get away.

She saw a look of sudden anger leap into Blanche's eyes as the big woman, too, observed his lecherous look. "Let's go," Teresa said firmly to her lover. "Now."

They hauled their suitcases out of the back of the wagon, took a moment to say a tearful goodbye to the faithful Stormy and Night, and began their walk to the hotel. Teresa squinted into the setting sun and said, "That man never mentioned a thing about your clothes. He didn't realize you're a woman."

"I can hardly imagine he didn't," Blanche answered, matching her steps with Teresa's smaller ones. Teresa could, but she wasn't going to say it.

"I'm glad we arrived when we did," Teresa said. "This place will be wild by tonight."

They walked down Preston's crowded main street. Its several small shops were closed by now but its countless saloons were already booming. There was no sidewalk and the women had to pick their way carefully through dung and ruts. The fading light of day made way for chandeliered illumination through the saloon's big windows and batwing doors, casting their artificial glow onto the dusty street. There were no townfolk to be seen; they had already tucked themselves safely away for the night, leaving Preston to the drovers and cowboys, some of whom stood in small groups talking and rolling cigarettes. Others rode by on big horses, or walked rapidly toward some unidentified destination.

Blanche reached down and took Teresa's suitcase from her hand. "Thanks," she said gratefully, and bumped into a man just coming through a pair of batwing doors.

The bearded cowboy staggered when he righted himself and said drunkenly, "Well, what have we got here?" Clumsily, he reached for Teresa.

Wanting only to lie down on a real bed and not move

161

until tomorrow, she pulled away angrily. "Lay off, cowboy."

"Hey," he growled. "Don't get so goddamn uppity."

"Lord, how trite," she said to Blanche. "I'll bet I've heard that line a thousand times."

Carefully, Blanche set down their suitcases. The cowboy again foolishly reached for Teresa and in a quiet deadly tone Blanche warned, "Let her go."

"Don't," Teresa said quickly to her protector. "Let me handle him."

"I'll handle him," Blanche roared, and stepped past Teresa to grab him.

Hardly recognizing the timid woman she had first met not three months ago, Teresa stepped back, frightened by the smoldering look on her lover's face. "Blanche, please," she uttered. She longed to escape with Blanche, somewhere to a place where they wouldn't have to keep dealing with situations like this, where they wouldn't have to constantly fight to be left alone, a place where they didn't have to keep worrying all the time. Whether it was a storm, bad men, or Indians, always there was something. Always!

"Blanche!" The cowboy roared with laughter. "What the hell kind of a name is Blanche for a man? What the hell are you, some kind of pantywaist or something?"

Blanche smiled a murderous smile and then struck him squarely in the chest, emptying his lungs of air. As he began to drop, she hit him a second time behind the ear to speed him on his way to the ground.

Looking down at the prostrate cowboy, she said through clenched teeth, "I like the name Blanche. It was my mother's."

She picked up the suitcases and, walking away with Teresa, said, "I've got to get another name."

Teresa couldn't help herself. She had to forcefully suppress the laugh threatening to burst from her lungs. She hurried wordlessly beside the scowling Blanche as they strode

162

toward the hotel. Her heart sang with love for the big lady. No man had ever cared for her the way Blanche did. Not one! The only thing men had ever wanted was a good roll in the sack. That was all she had ever been worth — until she met this marvelous woman. She remembered thinking how wonderful it had felt when she and Blanche had first started sleeping in each other's arms, how wonderful it had been not to be . . . used! She had no idea how she would ever repay even one small part of the love that Blanche gave her. But she intended to devote her life trying.

They took a small room and for the first time since outside of Samson's Town, they made love. They had teased each other all the time until the storm. They'd teased each other less after that and not at all after the drifters had shown up. By the time the Indians had forced them into twenty-four-hour-a-day total alertness, they hardly dared hug one another for fear of being taken by surprise. They were reduced to quick kisses, holding hands, linking arms, frightened away from each other and into the world around them.

Now that world was deliberately being shut out. The hungry lovers locked the door and rammed the room's only chair under the knob. Teresa pulled the shade and drew the flimsy curtains and then checked the window from all sides making sure it was impossible to see inside the darkened room. That done, they walked toward each other and held one another until their bodies screamed with heat.

Teresa unbuttoned the front of Blanche's shirt as Blanche unbuttoned the back of Teresa's dress. Trembling fingers of passion removed layers of clothing piece by piece, letting them fall unheeded to the bare wood floor until both women were nude.

Together, they moved to the double bed. Teresa gently pushed Blanche down and back so that her feet were still on the floor. She knelt to Blanche and began to kiss her, working her way up the insides of her thighs. Blanche seemed

163

agitated.

"What's wrong?" Teresa murmured, still kissing the prone woman.

"I . . . I'm concerned. It's been a long time since I've bathed."

Teresa silenced her by burying her face in the coarse black hair of her crotch. She drank in the odor of Blanche, intoxicated by her tangy and sweaty smells. It nearly drove her mad with longing and even as she licked Blanche, her own hips swayed unconsciously with each tongue stroke.

She groaned when she heard Blanche gasp loudly and then quickly mounted her, driving her hips against her until Blanche's back arched rigidly and she gasped again.

Blanche clung to Teresa, sweat pouring down the sides of her face, into her hair and ears. She spoke incoherent words of love and promise. Words that made Teresa pull at the bigger woman.

They readjusted their bodies so that they were lying full length on the bed. Blanche's feet hung off the end as she maneuvered her hips between Teresa's legs and a hand between her thighs.

Teresa wrapped an arm around Blanche's neck and grabbed her hand, helping to guide an exploring finger as she bent her knees and then raised her legs to wrap them around Blanche's waist. She strained her hips forward trying to get closer to Blanche. She felt watery inside, as if she were swimming in a great warm lake that caressed her entirely.

Blanche bent her head to take a tiny nipple into her mouth, sucking on the hardened bulb, chewing on the dark flesh.

Through Teresa's mind flashed the memory of the awesome strength of the lightning storm, and for a moment it was as if she had been struck by one of the bolts as she was hit with a powerful orgasm. As she strained for further release from pent-up desires so long denied on the trail, she was struck again, grinding against Blanche, fighting with her and against her, coming in repeated spasms until she thought her body would be split in two from where Blanche's hand clasped her to the top of her own skull. Then she lay still.

Slowly, she let her legs fall. Blanche still lay on top of her, her breathing heavy, labored. "Get up on your knees, darling," Teresa said. She would again love this woman who still desired her.

Without question Blanche raised herself to her hands and knees. Teresa slid beneath her and began to suck on one of the heavy breasts. With both hands she reached down and spread Blanche's lips apart. She heard a soft gasp and sucked harder on the willing nipple and then switched to the other. Her hands roamed up and down the insides of Blanche's moistness, sliding over every nuance of swollen flesh, moving in and out of Blanche, causing the raised woman's body to rock forward and backward rhythmically.

Teresa ran her hands through the hair on Blanche's mound and up her belly and then returned to the heat of her lover who dripped on her, wetting her hands.

"Now," Blanche said in a tight voice, and Teresa slid three fingers inside of Blanche with one hand and stroked her with the other. The smaller woman sucked wildly on Blanche's nipples, first one, then the other. She felt spasm after spasm strike her woman as Blanche rocked back and forth, back and forth, saying, "I love you. I love you. I love you," until her body slowed and then stopped.

Carefully, Blanche lowered herself on top of Teresa. "It's been too long."

Teresa buried her face in Blanche's neck as they whispered loving words to one another until their bodies cooled, until their minds were coherent.

They rested for a half-hour before they dressed, better prepared now to get on with their responsibilities, responsibilities made easier to face knowing that in a short time they would be back in the room again, and back in each other's arms.

A kiss of promise at the locked door made leaving the room an almost easy thing to do. They walked downstairs, Blanche dressed again in her men's attire, Teresa by her side. Together, they went to locate the train station.

After they had failed to see anything even remotely resembling a track, they consulted a thin seedy-looking clerk at the Wells Fargo Office. "Ain't no train, lady," he said to Teresa. "You take the stage direct to St. Louis, Missouri or go over to Jackson, Mississippi, and then take a steamboat to St. Louis. From there you catch a train to Chicago."

"Two tickets, direct to St. Louis, please," Teresa said. It would take them forever to reach Chicago. It was difficult for her to hide her disappointment.

"You'll be there in twelve days, ma'am."

Later that night as Teresa lay in Blanche's arms, after they had again torn each other apart with love, after their bodies had finally said, enough, more of life's realities set in. Teresa said, "We're running out of money. But we'll make it — barely."

"I know, it's bad," Blanche answered softly, and sighing, put a hand behind her head.

"We may have to stay in Chicago and work before going on."

"I know that, too," Blanche concurred.

Teresa reached up and ran a hand across Blanche's brow, brushing away the short hair from her forehead. "You can teach." Pensively, almost sadly she added, "I don't know what I could do."

"We'll figure things out, Teresa. Don't worry. Right now let's just love one another." Again, the women turned toward

166

each other. Their bodies had been wrong.

Teresa awoke hours later to a rustling in the room. Blanche stood by the window in the early morning light. Only half-awake she asked sleepily, "What are you doing, darling?"

"Reading my father's letter," Blanche answered quietly. "We leave Texas today. I wanted to read it while I was still in the same state he's in."

Teresa sat up and lit the lantern on the bedside table. She lit a cheroot and blew a thin line of smoke toward the ceiling. She hadn't yet been able to give them up, although she'd tried several different times since leaving Starcross.

"He sent my dowry," Blanche told her. "He'd told me he was going to give it to Steven on our wedding day but, he sent it along with Matthew instead."

"What else does he say?"

"Don't you want to know how much the dowry is?" Blanche asked.

"I don't think it's any of my business." Teresa killed the cheroot in an ashtray and walked over to Blanche's side.

"Of course it is, Teresa. Don't be silly." Blanche handed her a check.

"Good heavens, Blanche," Teresa exclaimed. "Five thousand dollars!"

Blanche said exultantly, "Our money worries are over — except I can't cash it until we reach Chicago. My father's made some kind of an arrangement with a man he deals with at a bank there. I'm sure he was worried I'd be robbed before I got there if he gave me cash."

"Yes, it certainly could have happened, couldn't it?" Teresa concurred.

"If I'd known what we were going to be facing, I probably wouldn't have come," Blanche admitted. "Big coward."

Teresa shook her head. "You're hardly a coward,

167

Blanche," she scoffed. "I don't know of anything that you once were before we left Starcross. You'e a very strong and courageous woman now. You used to sweat and break out in hives and swallow at every little thing. You don't anymore. And don't think I hadn't noticed how you powdered your thighs and bleached you upper lip. You've stopped doing that, too." She wouldn't mention Blanche's raging temper.

"My legs quit chafing a couple of weeks ago,"Blanche said. "And what am I going to do about my mustache, shave it? No thanks. Anyway, I'm out of bleach."

"I like it." Gently, Teresa ran a finger across Blanche's upper lip, caressing the downy hair. She pulled her lover's face to her own and kissed her. "You absolutely take my breath away, do you know that?"

Blanche smiled softly at her. "And you mine."

"Tell me what else your father says,"Teresa said breaking their spell. "Is he angry with you?" She looked deep into Blanche's eyes, fearing the answer.

Wordlessly, Blanche handed her the letter and went over to sit on the bed. Teresa drew closer to the light filtering through the dirt-encrusted window. She read:

June 23, 1869

My dearest daughter,

I'm sure Matthew has caught up with you somewhere in Samson's Town. I trust that you and Teresa are fine and I anxiously await your brother's return to reassure me. I want first to tell you that even though your leaving was a tremendous shock to your mother and Mable and Matthew, they all still love you as do I.

I, myself, knew you would be leaving Starcross eventually. I think I first realized it that morning you took your first ride with Teresa. I knew that's where you had gone. There was a different look in your eyes

168

when you returned — and from that day forth. I've seen that look before, Blanche. It was long ago when I was a young man still living with my family in New York City. You've heard me speak, off and on, of your Aunt Irene. You are much like her in ideals and temperament and I think if you go to her she can explain to you things I only half understand. She has lived for years and years with a lovely woman named Marie Atwater. I've enclosed Irene's address if you should decide to visit her.

The dowry which was for your wedding is still yours to use as you wish. You'll see that the check can only be cashed by James Hathaway, a trusted friend of mine. Enclosed, too, is his bank's address. I took this precautionary measure knowing you had enough cash with you (your gift to Teresa), and also knowing what Teresa had in her own account — an advantage of being a banker.

I'd better hasten, as Matthew awaits angry and impatient in the outer bank while I hide in my office.

Write to us, Blanche. Let us know how you are and where you decide to settle. But never forget where you came from. My best to both you and Teresa. Please be careful. I love you very much.

The letter was simply signed, *Father.* Tears glistened on Teresa's cheeks as she dropped the letter and gazed out the window through dingy curtains.

It was impossible for her to believe a father could be so understanding. But there it was on paper. He knew before they themselves knew that this was how she and Blanche would end up — she in love with his daughter and his daughter with her — as his letter suggested. He must have been keeping track of them for weeks. Strange that Blanche had never mentioned it. She probably hadn't realized. What if

169

Blanche had read this letter the night it had been delivered? Blanche probably wouldn't have understood what he was talking about. And neither would she. But it would have put her mind to work, given her some idea of why she wanted to see Blanche all the time, to be with her more than any other person. It would have explained the intense longing to be held by her again, after that first memorable day they had held each other beneath the mesquite trees. She smiled, remembering.

Teresa looked at Blanche who had lain back down and was gazing up at the ceiling, hands propped behind her head. She walked over and sat beside her, leaning against her side. "Do you want to visit your aunt?"

"I'd like to," Blanche responded, still looking at the ceiling. "I'd like to meet someone else like me in temperament."

Teresa said, "I had no idea. I hope to goodness we're not the only ones on earth."

"If what Father's letter is suggesting is true. . . ."

"Do you definitely want to leave this morning?" Teresa asked. "Or do you want to wait until the next stage?"

"I'm tired," Blanche answered honestly. "But I'd like to go."

They dressed leisurely and packed their few belongings. Blanche was once again in her only remaining dress.

CHAPTER ELEVEN

Teresa and Blanche and several other passengers were first ferried by flatboat across the wide Red River before boarding the stage. The large red coach, smartly trimmed with gold lettering and ornate striping with gold wheels trimmed in black, boasted of three richly padded leather seats and thorough braces that drastically cut down on sharp bumps, but caused severe motion sickness from the coach's substituted rocking movement.

For the next twelve days, the eight-foot-tall vehicle became a home for Teresa and Blanche. The six-horse-teamed vehicle passed through Oklahoma's flat lands and into

Kansas, where they saw prairie grass nine feet high, and hostile Indians on distant bluffs who watched them drive by, and acres of buffalo bones bleaching in the sun, the bones left by white hunters and waiting to be gathered and shipped to the east to be processed as fertilizer.

The coach stopped in small nondescript towns letting off and picking up passengers. The dusty travelers, tired and worn, a few of them sick from travel motion, stopped to spend their nights in adobe or log dwellings, to sleep in bunks less than clean, grateful to stretch out no matter what the conditions. More often than not, despite the cool temperatures, the men took their blankets and slept outdoors under a tree. The passengers ate monotonous meals of fried salt pork, corn dodgers, dried fruit, and bitter coffee which only rarely saw sugar and even more rarely, milk.

Finally, the coach finished its dreadfully long ride across Missouri and reached St. Louis. Drunk with fatigue, Teresa and Blanche thanked their friendly driver, too travel-weary to inquire about the next leg of their seemingly endless journey.

They could only barely manage to admire St. Louis' bustling life, its tall brick and stone buildings and even taller beautiful church steeples, as they walked toward a modest hotel to which the Wells, Fargo stationmaster had directed them. Finally in their room, they dropped their suitcases, stripped off their dusty sweaty clothing, lay down nude side by side, and slept without moving from early evening to the following mid-morning.

They hired a tub to be brought to their room where they leisurely soaked away days of dusty travel. Refreshed, they went first to the train station where they bought two second-class seats on tomorrow's train. They went next in search of a dress shop and came back with new undergarments and stockings and hats and plain dresses — and with their stomachs tied in knots at having spent all but their last twenty dollars. There was a dress of green trimmed in white for Teresa and one of pale blue trimmed in an even paler blue for Blanche, and small hats covered with flowers that tied under their chins with white satin bows.

Early the next morning, they crossed the Mississippi on their first steamboat, to the Illinois shore. The great river teemed with other steamboats, their huge paddles churning, carrying passengers north and south who yelled and waved at each other in friendly fashion as they passed by. There were countless cargo boats carrying covered wagons, horses, mules, chickens, goats, dogs, and, of course, scores of river men and husbands cursing and poling the small crafts, with pale mothers protectively holding crying infants in their arms, and older children scrambling over boxes, crates, and each other.

"I can't believe my eyes," Blanche kept saying over and over again, and Teresa, too, gawked from their second-story view on the large boat at the industrious life around them. An unexpected resounding blast from the steamboat's whistle warning smaller craft aside caused the inexperienced passengers to clutch each other with fear. The more seasoned travelers laughed at their fright, and after a second or two of their own dismay, Teresa and Blanche laughed with them.

Docking on the Illinois shore, they walked down the gangplank and into East St. Louis, and then the short distance to the train station to board their car. They found seats near the rear and tucked their suitcases away on overhead racks. Having ridden on a train before, Teresa insisted that Blanche take the inside seat, but the upright, lightly padded wood benches afforded little comfort. Windows were constructed in two sections with one side designed to slide behind the other allowing fresh air into the car. At the rear of the car was a crude comfort station for both men and women with a single commode and simple wash basin.

With eyes bright as pennies, Blanche slid next to the wall and opened a window. "Trains are big, aren't they?" she said with a look of awe, and Teresa just grinned.

173

Passengers filled the car to capacity. People spoke in languages that Teresa and Blanche didn't recognize, and wore clothing neither had ever seen before. Mothers and fathers cradled sleeping infants in their arms, and tried unsuccessfully to keep the older ones from hanging too far out the windows. There were no cowboys with wide-brimmed hats and holsters on their hips; instead, men wore dark business suits and read newspapers and smoked long black cigars.

A choking belch of black smoke from the engine's stack blew in the car's windows. A loud hiss of steam, wheels screaming on iron rails, a sudden jerking motion, told the passengers that they were on their way. Everyone settled down to watch East St. Louis pass from view as the train headed for its first of many whistle stops before reaching Chicago.

The train passed through parts of Illinois thick with forests and dense vegetation, pleasing to Teresa who hungered for the greener sights of her upbringing. Blanche, on the other hand, was overwhelmed, and said on one occasion that it almost made her feel penned in after living on the spacious flat plains of Texas. And yet, there were also miles of open space with fields of corn and wheat and pasture-land to ease Blanche's sense of entrapment.

At stations along the way they got off the train at a run to beat the crowds into lunch rooms for meager tasteless sandwiches and weak coffee before boarding again. Their spirits remained high as new sights appeared and disappeared rapidly through their window. The dirt and dust, constant companions, even seemed friendly as they drew closer and closer to Chicago.

And then, after what had seemed to be surely an impossible feat fifteen hundred miles and six weeks ago, their train pulled into the depot at ten o'clock at night depositing them in the luminous city.

As excited as a child, Teresa exclaimed, "We made it! We honest to God made it!"

"That day you asked me to go with you," Blanche confessed, "I never thought we could do it. What did I know about traveling or money? Or anything, for that matter."

"Now you see how," Teresa advised simply. "One exhausting day at a time."

They shouldered their way through the crowded depot amid masses of other exiting passengers who were coming and going at a rapid pace with no apparent direction. The noise and confusion soon affected Blanche. "This may sound insane, Teresa, but I've got to sit down and rest. I've never seen so many people."

"Over here," Teresa directed. They sat down on one of the many benches in the large depot, and straightened their dresses around them. "We have four dollars and seventy-three cents," Teresa said, carefully fingering the change she had taken from her purse.

Without further discussion they settled back to wait out the night. They would go to the bank the very first thing in the morning.

They kept their suitcases close to them as they studied the massive structure of the depot, marveling at the gas lights brightly illuminating the building. It was a tall structure of ornate design with frescos of wild horses and muscular men riding across the high ceiling. Behind the women was a long row of counters offering tickets to dozens of destinations. Even at this hour a few people were standing in line.

The weary travelers watched the passersby. Women of distinction wore brightly colored dresses of satin and silk and matching wide-brimmed hats trimmed with gorgeous downy feathers, some two feet long, and dyed lovely colors of green and blue and pink, or an undyed snowy white. In contrast to this virtual parade of fashion were women wearing plain

175

brown or black or dull white dresses of rough linen, their head scarves triangular and tied in large practical knots under their chins. The lowest of the unescorted women, with heavily painted faces and gaudy colored dresses not quite reaching to the knee, were searching for their own type of gentlemen.

The men who escorted the ladies of class wore well-pressed business suits of navy or black or brown, with gold chains draped across their chests and attached to pocket watches tucked in small pockets on silk vests. Men who walked with the women wearing the drab linen spoke to them in foreign tongues and wore narrow-brimmed hats and rumpled suits that looked like they had never seen a good cleaning.

Unexpectedly disrupted from their sightseeing by a voice directly addressing them, Teresa and Blanche glanced up to see a tall well-dressed man in a gray business suit, his beard flecked with silver. He looked to be in his fifties. The man politely removed his hat to show more silver on a thinning head of brown hair. He had an air of exceeding prosperity.

Immediately, Teresa thought of Lattimer. It would be like him to keep looking for her and then hire some fancy dude like this to fool her and then harm her somehow. Lattimer was the damnedest poorest loser she ever knew. Four men that she knew of were dead because they had beaten the saloon owner out of something that he had wanted — a woman, a good horse, winning at a card game. Stupid things! Stupid reasons to die! She wondered if he himself would have to be dead before she would ever be completely free of him.

"Are you Blanche Bartholomew and Teresa Stark?" the man asked.

Teresa saw a warning light leap into Blanche's eye and knew the same idea had occurred to her. "Who wants to know?" Blanche questioned in a threatening tone. She stood quickly, matching the man's own height.

176

"Did Lattimer send you?" Teresa asked bluntly. She would kill the bastard with her bare hands right where he stood. Neither she nor Blanche had ever discussed it, but ever since the drifters had come up on them so unexpectedly, both women had looked suspiciously at every man who breathed. Without ever having to say it, neither woman was going to let that happen again.

"Lattimer? No," the man answered. "I am James Hathaway."

Hathaway! What an incredible stroke of luck. Teresa felt the tension drain from her body.

"I've been meeting this train for several nights now, expecting you," he said. "That is, if you're Blanche Bartholomew."

Blanche stammered. "I . . . I am. But how did you know?"

"Your father wired me the day you left. I estimated the time you would arrive. But just to be on the safe side, I've come each evening for the last week."

Blanche nodded, speechless at Hathaway's words.

"You and Teresa are to be the guests of my wife and me until you decide what you want to do next. It would be much more comfortable than a hotel."

Teresa fought an overwhelming lump in her throat when Blanche said, "Thank you. Thank you very much, Mr. Hathaway. We would be honored."

Instantly, Teresa noticed a change in Blanche. She had become . . . quiet. And demure. A perfect lady with perfect manners. Teresa knew that she would have to watch her own mouth and quit the cheroots for good now. She was determined not to make any social slips and embarrass them both. Lord, she'd been such a tramp for so long, she hoped she'd remember how to do and say everything right.

Hathaway picked up their suitcases and guided his guests out of the depot. "My carriage is this way," he said leading them down a busy street almost as bright as day with its dozens of gas street lamps lighting the way. Towering buildings of brick, stone, and wood solidly lined the streets. They passed stores of every imaginable type, closed for the night, displaying wares from all parts of the world. Restaurants were still open and serving dozens of couples. Even at this hour people strolled the wooden sidewalks as they leisurely window-shopped. Carriages driven by uniformed drivers sitting on high front seats carried snuggling couples in the rear to and fro over cobbled streets. Fringed surreys hastened by.

"There are so many people here," Blanche said.

"The theater let out just a short time ago," Hathaway explained. "It's usually very busy at this time of night."

They climbed into Hathaway's carriage and drove north for several blocks until they had reached Chicago's residential section.

"What do I smell?" Blanche asked. "It almost smells like . . . like. . . ."

"That's fish," Hathaway finished. "You smell Lake Michigan. You'll see it tomorrow."

Windows from one-, two-, and three-story homes cast distorted rectangles of light onto large spacious lawns decorated with the shadowy shapes of trees and shrubs as the horse's iron shoes clip-clopped over the cobbles.

"It's a lovely city, Mr.Hathaway," Blanche commented.

"It is," he agreed. Pulling into his drive, he said, "I'll take you inside and then tend to the horse." He helped each woman from the carriage and, picking up their bags, guided them into his home.

They climbed a stone stairway of a three-story brick structure and entered the large main hall of the Hathaway home, passing several rooms to their left and right before entering the drawing room. A magnificent crystal chandelier, suspended from a plaster ceiling embossed with an intricate design, dominated the room. On the floor was a thick carpet of gold design. On one side of the room a large fireplace with a glossy black marble mantle took up a good portion of the wall. On each end of the mantle sat candelabra tall and large enough to hold six candles each. Over the mantle hung a large oil of a beautiful young woman with sparkling eyes and just the suggestion of a smile on her generous mouth. In one corner between tall windows curtained in gold silk stood a grandfather's clock of black cherry; its pendulum swung noiselessly, its ticking silent. On the walls around the room gas lamps flooded the room with light. Comfortable over-stuffed chairs and a couch with mahogany and cherry end tables shared the room's remaining space.

Teresa longed to sit down on the big couch but a musical voice called from the hallway interrupting her thoughts. "Bring them in here, James. I'm sure they're famished."

"My wife," Hathaway said, and smiled. He left their baggage at the foot of a gently winding staircase and showed them to the kitchen. There, they met an older version of the lady in the portrait. "Please call me Victoria," she said, and extended a slender hand. The sparkle in the painting was still in her eyes.

Victoria Hathaway was a small woman with a slight build. A pair of thick glasses were perched on her nose. Snow white hair circled her head in thick braids. Her round cheeks were rosy, made rosier still by her billowing pink dress. Her tiny mouth appeared to have a permanent smile. "Forgive me for not meeting you at the door. I wanted to have something ready for you as soon as you walked in."

"We were that sure you would show up tonight," Hathaway said. "And no doubt hungry. I've traveled on a few trains, myself."

"The kitchen is so much more cozy than the dining room," Victoria said. "I thought you needed more pampering tonight than you needed elegance."

The tired travelers smiled. How realistic Victoria is,

179

thought Teresa, in spite of her wealth.

Teresa and Blanche sat at a large heavy oak work table in the big kitchen and ate their first full meal in days — thin slices of roast beef, parsley potatoes, fresh salad, and hot rolls. When seconds were offered, they politely refused once before allowing Victoria to fill their plates a second time. It was hard for them not to gulp their food as they forced themselves to take small bites and tiny sips of the delicious hot coffee.

Later, Victoria showed Teresa and Blanche to their rooms. A quick look from Teresa told Blanche not to say a word. They could survive a few nights' separation.

On the floor of Teresa's room a thick rug of mixed blues set off the blue in the silk curtains and flowered wallpaper. A white down-filled quilt covered the mattress of the canopied bed from head to foot, hiding two fat goose-feather pillows. To one side of the bed, a small maple table held a handsome hurricane lamp with an unidentifiable blossom painted on each globe. Against the left wall stood a Chippendale chest-on-chest; on the opposite wall, a Chippendale-type mirror. There were two straight-backed chairs and a single rocker. The room had about it a strong feeling of comfort and warmth.

Blanche's room contained a walnut pencil-post canopied bed covered with lace and curtains in an elaborate floral pattern. The rug, a rich red of oriental design, completely hid the floor. Long red velvet curtains hung from the windows. There was also a chest-on-chest in Blanche's room with a large mirror hanging next to it, along with two small oil paintings of lakes and mountains. A single rocking chair sat in one corner.

Victoria asked, "Would you care to sleep late in the morning?"

Blanche walked to Teresa's door. "It would certainly be a luxury. I very seldom have had the opportunity."

180

"I've slept late —" Teresa began and flushed, instantly realizing her error. "But only rarely." No self-respecting woman slept late in the morning unless she was sick. Damned sick! From over Victoria's shoulder Teresa saw Blanche suppress a tiny smile and look innocently toward the ceiling.

"You each have your own small toilette," Victoria said, popping in and out of each room, throwing back the covers of their beds. "Well, I'll leave you, then."

Teresa glanced at the stairwell and the disappearing back of their hostess, and asking in a conspiring whisper, "Would it look funny if we closed my door for a few minutes?"

Blanche answered with a smile.

Teresa quietly closed the door. She checked to be sure the window shades were completely pulled down and an instant later was in her great lover's arms. "It's been a century," she whispered. But she was somehow disturbed at the different feel of Blanche, Blanche's noticeably diminished size. She didn't want anything about her lover to change.

And yet, this change, good as it was for Blanche, had already taken place. Other changes, too, had occurred. Some good, some frightening. The good ones needed no words; the frightening had been necessary.

Teresa hoped there would be no further use for her and Blanche to be so brave. Like tonight at the depot when both of them had been ready to fly into Hathaway.

Their trip had made them suspicious of everyone. It had depleted them and pulled them away from each other. Now, though, for at least the next few minutes, Teresa didn't have to think about danger and threats and cruel men. Now she was in her lady's strong arms, arms that had defended her, saved her, soothed her, loved her. What Teresa did with words, Blanche did with action. They were perfectly matched.

She melted into Blanche's softness. Pressing her body against Blanche, Teresa inhaled the intoxicating odor of her and longed to be touched by her gentle hand. Their breathing became ragged as they kissed. Unable to stand it any longer, Teresa finally said, "I must go, Blanche."

"Stay," Blanche answered simply, holding her tight.

"We don't dare," Teresa whispered. "We don't know these people. Or how they would react if they knew about us."

"Or what they would do," Blanche added with a heavy sigh. Prudently, she stepped back. "I do need to cash that check."

"Your father is a very cautious man, isn't he?" Teresa observed.

"That's what made him rich. I'm glad now. It never mattered before. It's a godsend for us."

"That's your money, Blanche. Remember that."

"It's a dowry, Teresa," Blanche answered, and walked over to the window making sure a second time the shade was securely shut against prying night eyes.

Teresa spoke sadly. "We're not married. Never will be."

Blanche turned quickly and stalked over to Teresa. She grabbed her firmly by the arms and drew her close to her and said fiercely, "The hell we're not, Teresa. I'm married. I'm damned married. To you. And I intend to stay that way."

Teresa looked into the blazing eyes, unable to speak, able only to stare at the angry woman holding her in a grip as strong as any man's, loving the scolding she was receiving, trying not to cry out with joy.

Blanche continued strongly, "You'll be my wife — or my husband — or whatever you are to me. Mate, maybe. Yes, you'll be my mate. For all eternity."

She let go of Teresa, flailing her arms to emphasize her forceful words. "You'll be my mate with or without benefit of clergy. Damn!" she expostulated, and turned abruptly away. She turned back immediately to face the smaller woman, who tried to look severely reprimanded. "That makes that money yours as well as mine, understand?"

She took Teresa's cheeks in her hands. But tenderly, now. Blanche tipped Teresa's face to her own and gazed into her eyes.

Mate? Teresa's word exactly. Weeks ago. "I understand, Blanche," Teresa demurely answered. "It's our money."

"That's right, darling. Ours." Blanche enfolded Teresa against her. "I love you, Teresa. I would fight and die for you."

Yes, Teresa knew for a certainty, Blanche would fight and die for her. She closed her eyes and buried her face in Blanche's great breasts. Tears stung her eyelids as she wondered if Blanche would ever again mention the dead men. She hadn't so far, other than that one brief time after their brush with Indians.

Unable to think anymore, Teresa desired nothing more than to fall into bed and not get up until next year. She pulled herself together. Her suddenly welling tears were only from being so tired. Lightly, she scolded, "Don't swear, Blanche. It doesn't sound as good on you as it does on me."

Blanche smiled down on her, saying, "I'm sorry, Teresa. I shouldn't be using such language. I've changed lately."

"Don't change too much," Teresa whispered softly.

"Never."

Teresa returned to her room after a final goodnight kiss which left them both almost out of their minds with longing. As she climbed into her large, empty bed she wondered how long Blanche planned for them to stay in Chicago.

Neither woman arose before one the next afternoon but Blanche was already downstairs, eating a midday lunch when Teresa finally came in swollen-eyed and a little hoarse.

"Are you all right, dear?" Victoria asked.

"I'm just tired, Victoria," Teresa replied, smiling weakly.

Victoria said, "I understand perfectly. I know what it is to travel for days, never able to get comfortable, and always wondering what the next mile will bring."

"You do?" Teresa questioned. Again, as she had last night, Teresa glanced at the opulent surroundings. Even the kitchen displayed the best money could buy. Hand-hammered copper kettles gleaming with the light of day hung from black wrought iron hooks overhead. Again, as last night, the table was set for two with thin delicate china dishes and cups and highly polished silver utensils. The walls were covered with red oak shelves displaying a wonderful array of canned jams, jellies, and vegetables in fancy jars, too lovely to hide in a pantry. The large cast iron stove could cook for ten easily.

"Oh, yes," Victoria responded, urged on by Teresa's tone. She launched into a long and colorful account of how she and dear James had come to Chicago from the south over barely passable roads along with five other wagons of settlers. "It was very rough in those days," she said, flying about the kitchen, preparing lunch for Teresa.

Teresa looked at Blanche who gazed back with amusement over a steaming cup of coffee. Teresa raised her eyebrows and settled back in a cane-bottomed chair to listen to their hostess and enjoy the excellent food placed before her.

After lunch, Victoria had their manservant drive them about town. She showed off her favorite stores where Teresa and Blanche openly stared at hats with brims large enough to cover two people and dresses with enough material to clothe three women. Dazzling pastels and deep purples and blues and reds stunned their eyes. They stopped at a confectionary where Blanche experienced her first ice cream. Victoria and Teresa laughed when Blanche said, "My chest aches."

"Don't eat it so fast, dear," Victoria advised, putting a motherly hand on Blanche's arm.

But Blanche's greatest thrill was yet to come. "Good heavens!" she exclaimed when her eyes first sighted the massive body of water being whipped into three foot high waves by strong gusty winds. "Why doesn't it spill out?"

Teresa, who had once seen the Atlantic Ocean, and

184

Victoria, quite used to Lake Michigan, laughed at Blanche's amazement.

The women kept a firm hand on their hats as they continued their stroll, as sudden gusts of wind off the lake whipped their long dresses around their legs and threatened to tear their bonnets from their heads. Gulls screamed overhead as tall-masted ships moved in and out of port and dark-skinned men from countries all over the world worked shirtless with bulging muscles to load and unload the great vessels. Boys jumped off wharves and into the water, laughing and splashing each other. Old men leaned against railings and fished while gulls stole what they had already caught and left carelessly lying unprotected on the dock behind them.

Teresa and Blanche politely declined the opportunity to see Chicago's great stock pens with their thousands of head of cattle waiting to be shipped by rail to New England. Even over Lake Michigan's strong sea odors, the pens could still be detected. The western women had had their fill of cows.

That evening after dinner, Hathaway led Blanche into his study. Blanche signaled Teresa to follow and she did so, half-expecting Hathaway to ask her to stay behind.

The study's walls were lined with hundreds of leather-bound books. A mahogany desk was littered with stacks of papers. Hathaway sat in a heavily padded leather chair and signaled to the women to be seated in smaller versions of the one he had settled into.

"Ah, here it is," Hathaway said to himself, and pulled a small piece of paper from one of the desk's many piles. "I've got to get caught up soon." He looked up and smiled at Blanche. "Your father's telegram. He says here," Hathaway began, "that you have a check to be cashed."

"Yes," she concurred.

"May I ask how much it is for?"

"Five thousand dollars," Blanche answered.

Hathaway thoughtfully rubbed his eyes with thumb and

forefinger, apparently lost in thought. Then he said,"Do you know what the state of the economy is right now, ladies? No, no, of course not," Hathaway said, answering his own question. "How could you know such a thing? Men control business, don't they? Very few women have as large a sum as you have." Again, a smile.

The two women waited for Hathaway to continue.

"May I ask what your plans are, Blanche?" he asked. "What you've got is a great deal of money as I'm sure you realize. Nearly a fortune for one woman to have."

"Some new clothing is needed, of course," Blanche said. "Tickets to New York State. Or further."

"Save what you can," Hathaway advised. "Save all you can." He stood and walked to a window. With his back to them he said, "I enjoy a rich full life, ladies. And I've worked like a mule for it. But, if I'm not careful, and I mean very, very careful. . . ." Slowly, he turned to face them. "If I'm not careful I'll lose it all in the next two, perhaps three, years."

Blanche asked, "Why are you telling us this, Mr. Hathaway?"

"I'm afraid," he told her, "that post-war problems are almost upon us. I would dare say that before 1874, this country will fall into a depression. We've over-extended ourselves almost to the limit in reconstruction. Farmers . . . businesses . . . It won't be long before the United States falls off the edge."

"You're frightening me, Mr. Hathaway," Blanche admitted.

"I hope you *are* frightened, Blanche. Only a fool wouldn't be. As a banker I can see the signs. That's almost all that's discussed these days at our business luncheons. The men sit around, eating, growing fat, smoking long cigars, and asking themselves, 'What can we do?' " Hathaway sat back down and continued, "Some of us know what to do. Advise against long-term borrowing, sell what you don't need. Save

186

the rest. And don't buy a thing unless you have to."

"What does this mean to me?" Blanche asked. "I want to buy a place. I'll need to furnish it."

"I understand," Hathaway said. "And this is my advice to you: property is beginning to drop in price in some areas even now. You could buy yourself a decent spot. But, if you buy, buy in the country, not in the city. Cities will be places in which only the very rich or the very poor will live. There will be no middle ground. And if you buy in the country, Blanche. . . ." Hathaway's voice dropped. He sounded almost sad as he said, "Get yourself a good gun. More than one, in fact, because those city folk who are put out of work and into the streets are going to drift to the country. And anything that's edible will be fair game. People will be desperate with hunger and need. Those who don't take precautions against these wanderers may find themselves in more trouble than they can handle. Believe me, ladies," he said, pointing a wagging finger at them. "Hungry people have no conscience."

Teresa rubbed a hand across a cheek. She sat numbly in her chair staring at Hathaway. She didn't want a lot. Wasn't asking for a lot. All she desired was to live a peaceful existence with Blanche. And a place they could call their own. Without guns. A place where weapons weren't needed.

"Don't spend a lot on a big wardrobe," Hathaway was saying as Teresa again turned her attention to his advice. "Don't buy the biggest house you can find or the most expensive furnishings."

"What will you do?" Teresa asked him, willing herself into the conversation.

"Hopefully, I can keep what we've got. But people know me as a wealthy man. I'll buy a good gun or two, myself. I'll try to feed as many of the poor as I can for however long I'm able. Hopefully, the depression won't last long."

"I'll seriously consider your advice," Blanche promised.

187

"Please do," Hathaway encouraged, and quickly switching to a lighter subject said, "By the way, I took the liberty of telegraphing your father to let him know you and Teresa have arrived safely."

"Thank you very much," Blanche said, smiling.

"Then if business is over, shall we have dinner?" Hathaway offered, rising from his comfortable chair. "Victoria has prepared a delicious rump roast tonight."

The Hathaway bedroom was on the same floor as Teresa's and Blanche's, but tonight Teresa didn't care. She wanted to sleep with Blanche, to lie beside her, to feel her body next to her own, to feel her strong comforting presence. When she was sure her hosts were asleep she would go to Blanche and later steal back to her own bed before morning.

Listening to the clock downstairs signal its long awaited stroke of two, Teresa arose from the chair where she had waited, and gave her head a little shake to clear the grittiness from her eyes and the heaviness from her mind. She had put up the shades earlier to allow the gas lantern on the opposite side of the street to cast its friendly light into her room, and to watch couples stroll by walking hand in hand and listen to their soft laughter.

Suddenly, she thought she saw someone standing just inside the shadow of the lamp's glow. She looked again, squinting for better focus, wondering who would be out at this late hour. Deciding it had been her tired eyes playing tricks, she dismissed the shadow. But then it moved slightly and caught her attention again. Yes, there was someone there. A man. Why wasn't he moving on?

She watched as the man stepped even further back into the shadows to lean carelessly against a fence surrounding the opposite house. She peered more intently at him as she felt her heartbeat increase. A thread of fear began to worm its way into her mind; he looked familiar. She watched for a few seconds more. He appeared to be staring at this house. Studying it. After watching another five minutes, Teresa was convinced. She saw him look up into her window. He was staring at her, looking right into her eyes! She swallowed in terror, ready to run. Then, realizing that the room was too dark for him to see into the room or to know she was there, some of the fear left her. But not much.

Her only thought was to get to Blanche's room.

CHAPTER TWELVE

As quietly and as quickly as possible, Teresa entered Blanche's room and crossed to her bedside. "Blanche," she whispered loudly, shaking her awake.

"What is it?" Blanche sat up, confused.

"It's me. Get up. Quick. Look out the window."

Blanche rose immediately and followed her to the window.

"Don't move the curtain," Teresa warned. "Look down there. Next to the fence. See that man? He's been there quite a while — watching this place."

"He has?" Blanche squinted her eyes for a better look.

"You know him. At least you've seen him before."
Teresa sure as hell recognized him. She'd slept with him
enough times.

"Where's he from? He looks like a drover."

"He's the cowboy you first saw me with in front of the
Blackjack. His name's Gene something-or-other."

"Damn!" Blanche exclaimed. "How in hell did he ever
find us?"

"He must have picked up our trail back in Preston."
Teresa's voice shook as she spoke. "Two lone women asking
about St. Louis? You get that far, you know the next logical
step is checking the train station. Easy tracking." She said
unnecessarily, "I know Lattimer sent him."

"Time to move on."

"When?"

"Tomorrow. I'll get my banking done right away and
then we'll go straight to the train station."

Teresa said, "I'm staying with you tonight."

Blanche nodded. "Damn!" she said again. "Don't say
anything to Victoria or Hathaway. We'll just say we were
anxious to get going. There's no sense in worrying them."

"Lattimer's not ever going to give up," Teresa said. "He'll
hound me to my grave."

"You're never going back, Teresa," Blanche vowed. "So
don't worry about it."

Not worry? Not worry? With two men already dead? A
third sent? How was she not to worry?

"Come to bed. Let me hold you."

Woodenly, Teresa climbed in and cuddled close to
Blanche who spoke reassuringly, and softly stroked her hair.
"We're going to be all right, darling. We'll be out of here way
before noon."

Teresa had to believe her lover. Had to! To believe
anything else would surely give way to the panic she only
barely had under control. "I'm so sorry I've brought all this

191

grief on you, my beloved lady." She wrapped an arm around Blanche's neck, burying her face against her.

"What grief?"

"Don't pretend it isn't there." Teresa sat up slowly and wiped away tears.

"I'm asking you, what grief?" Blanche leaned on an elbow.

Teresa shook her head. "There are two dead men out there. We are being followed by a third. You haven't been to church in God knows how long."

"That's right, Teresa," Blanche interrupted. "God knows how long. He knows why, too. When I can go again, I will."

She took the small woman in her arms. "I'm very sorry that I killed those drifters. But they were going to kill us. Listen, my little one, my sin is not that I killed them. My sin is that after they were dead, I kept shooting them and shooting them and . . . and . . . shooting them." Blanche burst into sudden tears. "How will I ever be forgiven for that?" she cried softly.

Teresa held Blanche tightly. "You were out of your head. You can't be held responsible for that. How can you?"

"Everyone is responsible for their actions, Teresa. Don't you remember me telling you that back in Starcross? But darling, when you're in danger I can't stand it. I can't think straight. I never even knew I could get so angry. I never did before that day. Never. I was always in control. I . . . I don't even recognize myself anymore. And now someone else is following us. He's in worse danger than we are and he doesn't even know it. I'm actually afraid for him."

"It's not him I'm worried about," Teresa said, leaning against Blanche. "It's you. I feel so . . . so responsible. Maybe you should have stuck to your first decision and stayed in Texas."

"And married Steven? That's a laugh."

"You would have been safe. You're not safe now. You

192

haven't been since we left Starcross."

"I gave up security for love, Teresa. I'm sure it's a question that comes up occasionally in love affairs. Does the princess want to live in a castle with a prince or does she want to live with her lover and be happy the rest of her life? It's an old story. You've probably heard it in a hundred different ways. You know the princess always chooses her lover."

"But the lover always has a beautiful home to take her to," Teresa informed her. "Where are we going? In fact, where are we running to?"

"Let's see," Blanche said thoughtfully. "First we'll run over to the bank. Then we'll run to the train station. Next we'll run to catch the train if, by chance we're late. Then we'll run to New York —"

"Blanche, will you be serious?" Teresa scolded angrily. "We're in trouble. Big trouble."

"I realize that, Teresa. But I have two choices about that. I can either be in big trouble and make light of it so that I'm not nearly so scared, or I can be in the same big trouble and panic. I choose to make light of the whole thing."

Teresa expelled a heavy sigh. "Why don't I have your sense of humor?"

"Too bright, darling. You're far too bright."

The following morning, Teresa and Blanche sat on the edge of Blanche's bed listening for Hathaway's steps to pass by their door. "There he goes," Teresa whispered. "Wait till he goes downstairs."

A few seconds later they followed him into the kitchen where Victoria already had breakfast going. "Suitcases?" he questioned with upraised eyebrows as they stood in the doorway, bags in hand.

Clearing her throat, Blanche began. "We've decided to leave, Mr. Hathaway. We'd like to ride to the bank with you and cash my check if you don't mind, and then go directly to

193

the train station."

"Well," he said, unable to conceal his surprise. "I didn't expect you to leave this soon."

"Don't you want to shop, ladies?" Victoria asked. "To see more of Chicago? I so looked forward to showing off our great city."

"We'd love to, Victoria," Teresa assured her. "But we feel we should get on. Summer isn't that long in the north and we want to get settled as soon as possible." At least that much was true. She was so damned tired of deceit.

"But there's plenty of time," Hathaway protested.

"We really must," Blanche insisted.

"I'm very sorry we won't be spending more time together." Hathaway spoke with evident sincerity. "Why don't you wait until my telegram reaches your father? He may want to reply."

Blanche stood firm. "I'll give you an address you can forward it to, Mr. Hathaway. We wish to go."

Their abrupt departure looked strange, Teresa knew. But it couldn't be helped. They might even now be endangering this household. And she alone was responsible. She wanted to get moving. Today!

"All right," he reluctantly agreed. "But you must let me see you off. And," he added firmly, "don't forget to give me the address of where you're going."

"I will," Blanche promised.

"Things have certainly changed since I was a young girl," Victoria said, setting a steaming hot coffeepot on the table. "I'd be scared to death to travel without a man along."

A man, thought Teresa. That's exactly why they were leaving today. They didn't want a man with them. They wanted to lose one, the one who was chasing her!

After Blanche had completed her banking, Hathaway took the anxious women to the station. And every foot of the way they kept a wary eye out for the cowboy.

Hathaway stayed until it was time for their train to depart. Blanche and Teresa thanked their host as the sound of "All aboooard!" carried up and down the rail line. "Let me carry your bags," he offered.

They walked to the train and quickly and shyly Blanche and Teresa gave him a brief hug. "Tell your wife thank you again for us," Blanche said. 'We wish we could have stayed longer."

"You're a wonderful man, Mr. Hathaway." Teresa spoke with deep conviction. She wanted him to know how she felt about him. It was terribly important that she tell him. She had met so few truly good men during the last few years.

He looked at her and smiled warmly. "Why, thank you, Teresa. My wife is the only other woman who has ever told me that."

The women boarded quickly and waved to him through a window as the train gave a jerk, beginning its eastern journey.

When they had found their compartment and were leaning comfortably against the back of the leather seat, Teresa said, "I had to say that to him, Blanche."

Blanche smiled and said, "I understand."

Traveling first class, they found the trip restful and exciting. They enjoyed sleeping in berths at night and eating regular meals that one might find in a fine restaurant, with fancy lamb and steak dishes delighting their sense of grandeur. Cities, small towns, bountiful fields of corn and wheat and oats and hay, grazing animals — all slid by their windows, and when they reached New York they viewed orchards of apples and cherries and arbors of grapes. Occasionally, they caught glimpses off to their left of the incredible Lake Erie, and the following morning, Lake Ontario, leaving them staring in wonder at the lakes' vastness. In two short days they found themselves stepping off the train and into the Rochester depot.

"We did it!" Teresa squealed. "We honestly did it! We're in the East. Look at those hills. Look at all the trees. They're eastern trees, Blanche. And look at those clouds. They were formed right here in the East!"

Blanche laughed at her. "I think they're northern clouds."

"Doesn't matter," Teresa said happily. "They're not in the West."

"Well, let's admire the eastern clouds, then."

In the beautiful late afternoon sun, the modest city of Rochester radiated. The women gazed at the tall structures lining its busy main street. Surreys drove by, drawn by smart looking horses, their tack jingling in the crisp air. Ladies and gentlemen and children, followed by dogs, walked along the wood sidewalks. Unlike Chicago, Rochester's streets were still dirt, and strollers carefully avoided puddles of mud as they crossed the wide street.

They had scarcely begun to enjoy the spectacle before them when suddenly a voice roared, "There she is, by God. My niece! I know that's Blanche Irene."

They whirled toward the booming voice. Stomping toward them down the wooden sidewalk came a woman almost as tall as Blanche and only slightly heavier. Her silver hair was swept on top of her head, giving her an extra three inches of height. Her eyes were chocolate brown. The lines in her face suggested a perpetual smile. She wore a light brown blouse tucked into a darker brown skirt. She looked robust and healthy.

"You are Blanche Irene Bartholomew, aren't you?" she demanded, grabbing Blanche by the arm.

"I am," Blanche answered quietly.

"Listen to her, Marie," Irene called over her shoulder to a woman waiting in a two-seated buggy. " 'I am.' Quite a lady, isn't she? She looks just like Alex, doesn't she? Honey, I'm

196

your Aunt Irene Bartholomew." She brought her face close to Blanche's, smiling widely.

Teresa stood back watching the two women. If Blanche didn't burst into tears in the next five seconds, Teresa knew she would herself.

"How do you do?" Blanche said politely.

"Oh, hell," Irene said, and clasped Blanche solidly against her chest. Blanche threw her arms around her aunt.

Pulling away, Blanche wiped away the tears Teresa had expected and said, "I'd like you to meet Teresa Stark."

"How are you, Teresa?" Irene shook hands like a man.

"Fine, thank you," Teresa said, overwhelmed by this boisterous woman.

"Come on." She grabbed their bags from their hands and led them over to Marie.

Marie Atwater wore a comfortable white linen dress, belted at the waist. Her slightly graying hair, carefully combed into waves, surrounded her face and was gathered in a bun at the nape of her neck. In her mid-fifties, she had hardly a noticeable line in her face. Her skin was perfectly clear and she had exceptionally rosy cheeks. Her eyes, the most unusual either Teresa or Blanche had ever seen, were one blue, the other brown. It was difficult not to stare at her natural beauty.

Carefully putting the bags in the back of the carriage, Irene said, "Climb in, girls. We're going home!" making it sound like a grand event. As if they were all going to a circus. "This is Marie Atwater," she said introducing their driver. "She and I share a house together. Marie, this is my niece, Blanche Irene Bartholomew. Named after me." She spoke with great pride. "And this is her friend, Teresa Stark."

"How did you know we were coming?" Blanche asked.

"Alex telegraphed weeks ago. So did a man named Hathaway. Just yesterday. He said you'd be on this train."

Settling themselves behind Irene and Marie, Teresa leaned

197

toward Blanche and said with a smile, "Lots of help."

Marie drove skillfully down the busy street and out of town. "Irene has talked of nothing else but your expected arrival since she got Alex's telegram."

"That's right," Irene boomed. "I couldn't wait. We've got a million things to chat about. I haven't seen Alex since we were practically children."

"Is that what you call my father?" Blanche asked. "Alex?"

"Ever since the day he was born," Irene replied. "He was such a little tiny baby. Much too small for a big name like Alexander. So I shortened it for him."

Teresa exchanged smiles with Blanche. She intended to give Blanche and her aunt all the time alone together that they needed. She needed time with Blanche, too. Hours and hours of peaceful, uninterrupted time. But she could wait. All she and Blanche had left to take care of was deciding where to live — and making sure that Gene hadn't followed them. After those two things were completed she and Blanche would have all the time together they had ever dreamed of and wished for.

They rode for an hour and a half before reaching their destination. They passed both large and small farms separated by thick woods of pine or maple or indestructible stone fences built three and four feet high, flat as an anvil on top and straight as a rod, works of art crafted by the sturdy men and women who had cleared their fields with muscle and sweat to construct them.

The land was a gentle rolling thing. There were no severe hills and when they came to several farms strung in a row, Blanche said, "It reminds me of home — somewhat." The near-flat land apparently fulfilled a needed sense of space for the Texas-bred woman, while Teresa was in love with the greeness of it all.

Passing through an opening in a stone fence, Marie turned

into a long drive and pulled the horse to a halt in front of a moderately sized two-story house. Barn-red clapboards were set off by black shutters at every window. Beneath the windows were window boxes filled with blooming flowers. A large porch extended the length of the house and contained several reclining chairs; suspended from the ceiling by two chains hung a swing. On each side of the front door sat small tables built of thick branches crudely trimmed into short poles and fashioned into legs teepee style; short rough boards nailed to the ends of the legs served as tabletops. On the rustic furniture sat geranium plants loaded with blossoms.

The house was surrounded by tall stately sugar maple trees, while shrubs and herbs grew around the edge of the house. A giant lilac bush stood proudly alone in the middle of the small yard. Off to the left of the house, a hundred yards or so away, stood a single small red barn, the weather vane on top of its steep gabled roof turning with a lonesome squeak back and forth in the quiet evening breeze of the dying day.

"Go on inside, ladies," Irene told them. "Marie and I will take care of the horse and buggy first and then be in. Take this with you." She reached down at her feet and picked up a chimney lantern. Lighting it, she handed it to Blanche. Marie fished from her purse the door key and gave it to Teresa.

The cozy setting made Teresa feel right at home. When she and Blanche finally owned a house, it too would have much the same type of shrubbery — a welcome reprieve from mesquite trees and dead-looking bushes with lawns that sprouted grass tough enough to spike a bare foot.

The two women entered the house and left their suitcases by a staircase near the entrance. Just inside the parlor to their left was a table with a tall chimney lantern. Blanche lit it while Teresa lit two more hurricane lanterns on small oak tables at each end of an overstuffed couch. Then both women looked around. There were three chairs, two of them

199

overstuffed like the couch, and a single upright cane-bottomed chair placed next to a brick fireplace. In the center of the fireplace's stone mantle was a vase of fresh flowers.

"I want our house to be this delightful," Teresa said, gazing at the walls of the parlor which were papered with rows of tiny light tan flowers extending from floor to ceiling with perhaps a foot of flat tan color in between. A few small prints hung on the walls. The wide pine plank floor was covered by a large braided oval rug.

"It will be," Blanche promised and kissed Teresa briefly.

Soon after, Marie and Irene sat on the couch across from their guests who had claimed the comfortable chairs. Settling herself, Irene boldly announced, "I want to know everything that's happened to Alex and his family for the last thirty years."

"Not all in one night, dear." Marie reached for Irene's hand and gave it a brief squeeze.

"No, not all in one night, Marie," Irene laughingly agreed. "I don't think they could stay awake that long. We'll just cover some of the high points tonight. If that's all right, Blanche." Irene looked at her niece.

"Teresa?" Blanche asked.

"I can stand it if you can," she quipped.

As Blanche related her family's history, Irene interjected experiences of her own when she was a girl. Marie and Teresa listened quietly while aunt and niece talked, and laughed with them at funny family anecdotes. Eventually the conversation turned to Blanche and Teresa's long northern journey and Blanche said, "I think we should tell them about Chicago first, Teresa."

"I agree." If she and Blanche were going to be staying here for a day or two, Irene and Marie did have the right to know about the trailing cowboy — in order to be on their guard. Just as she and Blanche were now.

Teresa began, "We're being followed by someone."

"Who?" Irene asked sharply.

"A man named Gene," Teresa replied. "A cowboy I once knew."

"It should take him a while to catch up with us," Blanche said. "But we'll be leaving in a couple of days so it shouldn't become a problem for you."

"Now, just hold it, girls," Irene bellowed.

"Irene, please speak quietly," Marie suggested softly.

"Sorry," she said briefly to her wide-eyed guests.

Turning to them, Irene spoke firmly. "By God, ladies, you're staying. You tell me what's going on and we'll deal with it. Men!" she expostulated, forgetting Marie's request, and stood and stomped around the room waving her arms.

Teresa's eyes followed her. It was amazing how much Irene and Blanche resembled each other. She thought back to the night Blanche had told her the dowry belonged to them both.

"They've given me no end of grief throughout my life," Irene was saying. "Have they you?" she demanded, whirling on Blanche.

Startled, Blanche jumped and replied quickly, "No, not bad."

"You?" She looked accusingly at Teresa.

"Some," Teresa answered meekly.

"Irene, you're frightening our guests. Please sit and calm down." Marie linked her arm through Irene's and led her back to the sofa. "She gets very excited at times," she explained to Teresa with a small smile.

'But I'm harmless," Irene assured her. "Tell us, then. What about this man following you?"

"Why don't we just tell how it all happened?" Blanche suggested to Teresa. "You know. From when I first met you."

Teresa's heart began to pound. "Are you sure?" Her hands twisted nervously in her lap. My God! To tell someone *that* about themselves? Mr. Bartholomew's letter had only suggested these two women were in love — not that they were. She and Blanche could make a terrible mistake by saying anything. Let Irene or Marie tell *them* first.

"From the very beginning," Blanche encouraged.

Good Lord, to take such a chance! But the worst that could happen, Teresa supposed, was that they'd be booted out. She took a deep breath and looked at her confident lover. She had told herself the day they had left Samson's Town that as long as she was with Blanche, she was home. The front porch for one night would be all right.

"Well, I, uh. . . . You see, back in Texas. . . ." The others waited patiently for Teresa to find a starting point. "You see. . . ." Her voice began to shake badly. "Blanche and I. . . ." She didn't see how she could possibly get through this. Stammering badly, she said, "Blanche and I are . . . uh. . . ."

"Yes, yes, I understand," Irene said. "You're in love. Go on. Go on." A hand waved impatiently.

Marie nudged Irene in the side and said, "Let her tell it, dear," and snuggled comfortably against her.

Teresa burst into sobs. Blanche went to her and knelt beside her. Rocking her gently, she said. "It's all right, Teresa. Everything's all right, now."

Irene asked, "What is it? Did I frighten her?"

'No," Blanche answered, cradling Teresa in her arms. "She thought the two of us were the only ones . . . that we were alone."

"Alone?" Marie asked, her face puzzled.

"There's only been just us," Blanche explained. "And a letter from my father suggesting strongly that you and Irene are . . . sweethearts. Who can ever be sure unless they ask or are told?"

"Well," Marie said brightly, "now you know there are more of us."

"The Lord said, Go forth and multiply," offered Irene.

"I don't think that's what He meant, dear," Marie told her.

"I'm all right now," Teresa said to them, brushing away her tears. "Let me go on."

Blanche released her but stayed seated on the floor by her side as Teresa talked. Occasionally, Blanche would add a comment, or chuckle at something Teresa said; she kept a reassuring hand in Teresa's lap.

Teresa and Blanche talked long into the night with their hostesses, describing their wagon trip, the violent thunder and lightning storm, their encounter with the drifters — and the deadly results, which their hostesses firmly supported much to the surprise — and relief — of Teresa and Blanche. They went on to describe their brush with the Wichita — accounting for the loss of Blanche's hair, still too short for a lady of style — and their stagecoach and train rides, the wonders of the big cities and large lakes and the vast changing country itself. Lastly, they talked of what they tentatively planned to do with their lives.

Finally, around two o'clock, Blanche said, "I can't think anymore, Aunt Irene. If you don't mind, I'd like to go to bed."

"Good idea," Marie agreed, yawning wide behind a polite hand.

"We'll talk again tomorrow," Irene said. "You'll both be better rested then. Come on. I'll show you your room."

Not rooms Teresa noted, but room. No need to pretend. Not here.

"Sleep late if you like, ladies," Marie said, and gave each of them a warm hug before they left for bed.

Irene led the way to a small bedroom tucked snugly into a first floor corner of the house. She lit chimney lanterns sitting on small doily-covered tables on either side of a double bed which displayed a colorful patchwork quilt intricately sewn into a large floral pattern. Irene threw open a window to let in gentle breezes; the lightweight white curtains billowed. "The room is absolutely beautiful," Teresa said.

"Like home," Blanche remarked.

"We sleep upstairs," Irene told her guests. "On the opposite end of the house. So make all the noise you want. You won't bother us." She, too, hugged the weary travelers before leaving.

In that brief moment in Irene's arms, Teresa noted interestingly how much like her niece Irene felt. Their voices were even similar — except for the volume. She'd have to get used to Irene's loudness.

After Irene left, Teresa said, "Your aunt loves you very much. Do you realize that, darling?"

"I do," Blanche answered. "And I love her. But right now, I want to love only you."

Teresa went to her lady's waiting arms and kissed her until neither was aware of time nor of being tired nor of danger. They were aware of nothing at all — except each other.

CHAPTER THIRTEEN

The four women sat around the breakfast table, the early morning sun shining pleasantly through gingham curtains and splashing onto the checkered tablecloth. They ate eggs and bacon off thick clay-fired plates and drank coffee from heavy mugs. Marie got up once and walked over to the cast-iron stove to turn a second helping of bacon in a spider, the grease in the hot skillet snapping loudly. Briefly she lifted the stove lid to be sure enough wood burned to finish frying the pork. "Biscuits?" she asked, peeking into the warming oven above the grill. Muttered sounds of assent were heard from the table and Marie set a second dish of the white fluffy rolls on the table.

Teresa and Blanche had been here three weeks and were still prudently staying out of sight. They still maintained a watchful guard and took no unnecessary chances.

Right now, however, their thoughts were not of the stalking cowboy, if indeed he still followed them, but of America's dim future and how conditions had already begun to affect Marie and Irene.

Marie spoke knowingly of the coming depression. "Hathaway is right. People aren't buying like they used to." She was referring to the drop in sales in their own little mercantile store that she and Irene had run for years in Albert, a small town only a mile to the east of them. "It's beginning to affect little things like candy for the youngsters, cloth for dresses that women have been buying in abundance since the War."

"Men don't buy tobacco as much as they did even six months ago," Irene said.

"It's amazing how they realize something's coming," Teresa commented.

"If they don't sell whatever it is they have to offer, then they have to cut back," Irene said informatively. "Then, we have to cut back. Then, the distributors have to cut back."

Marie got up from the table to pour a second round of coffee. "It's a mad cycle," she said. "We've already started cutting back, ourselves. When the depression hits, it will touch everybody."

"Maybe not too badly," Irene said to Blanche. "That is, if you play it right."

Teresa asked, "Won't everyone be affected in some way or another? No matter what?"

"Not the rich," Marie answered. "But they don't count."

"Buy land. Just like Hathaway told you," Irene advised. "Don't bother teaching, Blanche. Children will be working as hard as their parents just so the whole family can get by.

206

And, Teresa, people won't be able to afford to have someone do their sewing for them."

Teresa had suggested this idea a couple of days ago as something she might be able to do to earn money but neither Irene nor Marie had commented on its feasibility. Now Teresa knew why.

"What then?" Blanche asked. "Buy land and do what with it? The only thing I know how to do is teach. I can play the organ but there's no way to make a living doing that."

"What about raising vegetables?" Teresa offered.

"Vegetables?" Blanche turned to her.

"That's what I was going to suggest," Irene concurred. "Very good, Teresa. You have a very intelligent lady, Blanche. You should be proud of her."

"I am," Blanche admitted. Teresa blushed.

"Everyone needs to eat," Irene said getting back to her subject.

Marie added her own ideas. "Start a vegetable farm next spring. For now, learn what you need to learn. Make your mistakes now. Before the depression gets here. There's time. And, luckily for you, you have the money to do it."

"That's right," Irene agreed heartily. "Get your farm going, haul your wares into Rochester every week or every few days. Build up your clientele. When the bad times hit, those people will still buy from you."

"You'll have to lower your prices then, of course," Marie said. "And that will certainly cut into your profits."

"But it shouldn't hurt you that much," Irene put in. "You'll still have food to eat whereas those city folk won't unless you sell to them. They'll be very dependent on you. Keep your prices as low as possible during that time without bankrupting yourselves and you'll be able to ride out the bad times."

"How in the world do you know so much about all of this?" asked Teresa, a little awed by the rapidly flowing

207

advice.

"Oh, I don't know, Teresa," Marie answered. "Years of experience with the public can teach you a lot. When people have money, they pay more. When they're broke you should be willing to make allowances for them. I've seen several businesses lose everything to competitors just because they didn't know how to handle prices."

"That's what it all comes down to," Irene contended. "How you handle your prices."

"It all sounds very simple, Aunt Irene," Blanche said. "But how do we even begin? We don't know anything about buying land or raising vegetables."

"Irene can take you and Teresa around to look for decent land," Marie said. "And she knows quite a bit about gardening. She does most of ours."

Carefully, Irene placed her fork down beside her plate. "I'm going to suggest something else to you, Blanche. I hope you won't take offense. Years ago when Marie and I came here looking for a permanent place to stay, we were given no end of trouble by men who tried to take advantage of two single women. Financially, emotionally. . . ."

"Physically," Marie put in.

Irene nodded. "Had one of us been a man none of it would have happened. Men just normally do not prey on women who have another man with them."

Teresa knew what was coming. She didn't think it was a bad idea. It had worked once before for them. It might again.

"You're going to suggest that I wear men's clothing, aren't you?" Blanche said.

Teresa suppressed a smile.

Irene nodded.

"Do you really think anyone would be fooled?"

"Yes," Teresa said quickly. "Look what happened in Preston."

"He was drunk, Teresa," Blanche said in reference to the

208

intoxicated cowboy she had struck to the sidewalk.

"The hotel clerk wasn't," Teresa countered. "He never even batted an eye. And neither did the dealer who bought our wagon and team."

"It might work, Blanche," Irene said. "It could be to your advantage. You might not save any money buying land by successfully covering your identity, but you're not so likely to be overcharged, either. And, you'll cut down on harrassment of other types. It would be worth trying."

"The reason we came East," Teresa reminded her lover, "was to be able to live the way we want." She leaned toward the big woman and put a hand on her arm. "To buy a place, to earn a living. . . ."

"I'd be made a fool of if I were discovered."

"It worked on the trail," Teresa repeated. "I think you ought to try it. Besides, you look good."

Blanche gave her a dubious glance.

Teresa looked back at her levelly. Blanche *had* looked good. Damned good.

"What about Gene?"

Teresa scowled angrily. "We can't keep living in a cocoon. We've got to get on with our plans and quit allowing him to dictate our every step. Do you realize that the only place we've gone since we've been here is to the backhouse? There's a whole world out there for us, for Lord's sake. We'll just carry a gun." As Blanche continued to look hesitant, Teresa said sternly, "Let's do it, damn it. I'm sick of hiding."

It was Marie's strong voice that finally convinced Blanche. "Teresa's right. You two are trying to begin a new life. Do stop hiding, do carry a gun, and do look at land as a man and woman together. If I had thought about it, I would have had your Aunt Irene do the same thing. She's big, loud. . . ."

"What do you mean, loud?" Irene bellowed.

"Just that, dear," Marie said. "You speak loudly.

209

Forcefully. It's an asset. In a man, it usually indicates he's sure of himself — even if he isn't."

"And in a woman?" Irene said, raising her eyebrows.

"Later, dear," Marie answered, putting her off. "Let me finish my thought. As I was saying, Blanche, it's easier to look for a place as a married couple."

Briefly, Teresa and Blanche glanced at each other in an exchange of smiles.

"It makes you look stable. If you're looking for land then apparently you want to settle down. Communities like that in a young couple."

"What happens then, Marie?" Blanche countered. "When after I buy the land, they learn that I'm a woman?"

"Explain that you were concerned you would be bothered by the wrong kind of men and were just looking out for your best interests. They'd most likely understand. Most folks here are good people, Blanche."

"All right," Blanche reluctantly agreed. "I'll try it."

Later that night as Teresa and Blanche lay in each other's arms Blanche said, "Thank you for forcing me to think. Living comfortably like we are lately, with enough money, enough to eat, and so on and so on, has lulled me into my old ways of taking the easy way out. I was like that in Starcross. Like the way I felt about myself, my weight, and my looks. Being with you, meeting Irene and recognizing that her beauty and strength comes from her size and her good feelings about herself has caused me to know how foolish I was."

"I'll keep you on track, darling," Teresa whispered into her ear. "I promise."

The night disappeared from their consciousness.

CHAPTER FOURTEEN

Teresa and Blanche had decided that New York State was where they would permanently settle. That firm decision made, they had ahead of them the search for their new home. They felt an urgent necessity to find a place immediately so that they could begin to break ground promptly after spring's final frost struck. Throughout the remainder of August, all of September, and into the cool days of October and the cold, sometimes snowy days of early November, Irene hitched the horse and buggy. Armed with a rifle, the three of them traveled the countryside looking at farms and fields, talking to people, writing letters to the land agents in Rochester with

211

whom they preferred not to deal directly, searching for exactly what the newcomers could both agree upon. Finally in mid-November, they looked at a place and knew at a glance that this was what they wanted. Even before they had explored the house, inspected the barns, walked the fields. Silently, their eyes met and simultaneously they nodded their agreement.

They were home.

The farm was set several hundred feet back off the main road. Tall sugar maples lined both sides of the drive, planted in rigid straight rows decades ago; perhaps, the women speculated, when the place had first been homesteaded. Stone fences in good repair separated several fields. There were two big barns, one nearby the farm house itself, the other out in a field a good half mile away.

Irene pulled the buggy up to the front door of a two-story dwelling. Built square and sturdy, its clapboard exterior looked durable but the white building and its green window shutters needed fresh paint. There were shrubs around the outside of the house, bare of leaves now as they rested for the winter. More mammoth maples sheltered the building.

Together, the women dismounted from the buggy and walked to the front door through a fresh three-inch layer of snow. A knock on the thick oak was answered by a tiny woman with piercing blue eyes. She was shockingly wrinkled and old. Completely toothless, her lips sank into her face seemingly trying to pull her nose in, too. A scarf tied in a tight knot beneath her chin covered thin gray hair. Gnarled hands held a pale yellow woolen sweater drawn tightly across her chest, over a brown linsey-woolsey dress reaching to the floor.

Teresa looked at the ancient woman, apparently bent from the toil of her years on this land, and thought of the loving care that must have been given to this place by her and

212

her loved ones over the decades. What better way, she questioned silently, to become bent and old with age than by working the earth from which you came, and the earth to which you'd eventually return?

"Are you Mrs. Bowne?" Irene asked respectfully.

"Grace Bowne, I am. My son send you?" asked the old woman in a strong voice.

"He did," Irene answered. Briefly, she introduced them. She said, "We received a letter from him yesterday. He had heard we were looking for a farm and suggested we come here."

"Why the men's duds?" Grace Bowne gruffly asked Blanche who had stuck to Marie and Irene's plan and had daily worn pants. Other sellers had recognized that Blanche was a woman, too. If she hadn't gotten away with trying to pass herself off as a man, they hadn't been offered unreasonable prices either, just because of Blanche's pants. And neither had she been asked why she was dressed this way. Until now.

Blanche replied, "It protects my interests."

Bless Blanche for her honesty, thought Teresa. Herself, she'd have stood there for ten minutes trying to rationalize an answer.

"Good idea," Grace Bowne grunted, and with shuffling footsteps led the three women into the big kitchen. They secretly smiled to each other behind her back. Bless Grace Bowne, too, Teresa said to herself, for her understanding.

Invited to hang their wraps on pegs on the back of the door, they were given a thorough tour of a house dating back to the seventeen hundreds. Surprisingly, the kitchen still contained a brick-lined bee-hive oven that extended back into the wall five feet in a half-sphere shape, and was large enough to bake twenty pies at a time. On the opposite wall was a stone fireplace large enough to sit in, although right now it roared with a welcome blaze. Leaning against an inside wall were several small soapstones to be used later in bed to drive the chill from the covers and keep the old woman's feet warm all night. A dry sink took up one corner of the room, a long rickety table took up the center space, surrounded by six worn chairs, handmade years ago but still serviceable. A tall three-drawer hutch displayed dishes, cups, saucers, and bowls. Built against the walls were several crude shelves holding candles in pewter holders, four lanterns, knickknacks, and a few small boxes of drygoods. Overhead from low rafters hung dried herbs, and onions braided together in long rows.

In the living room white lace curtains hung limply from the windows. A large faded oval rug lay on the wide plank floor. The frugal furniture consisted of a worn couch, one small maple leaf table graced with a tall chimney lantern, and three ladder-backed chairs. A moderate fireplace was devoid of a fire. On the mantle and enclosed in small brass oval frames were four photographs of prosperous-looking men standing behind seated women holding small children in their laps.

The women were led up steep narrow stairs to view four small bedrooms, two on each end of the house and separated by a tiny hallway. The first three rooms were identical, each with a double bed blanketed with a colorful patchwork quilt, a small dresser covered with linen and containing wash bowls and pitchers and cloudy mirrors.

It was the last bedroom that fully conveyed the love that had once abounded in this home. On the double bed, capturing and holding the eye, was a magnificent quilt depicting life on this farm over the years. It lay exposed like an open picture book, colors leaping out, life leaping out, to touch the heart of anyone who looked upon it. In the upper left hand corner was a picture of a church. A wide road led from the church to a rising sun behind the building. Tiny blue birds flew in the sky. In the upper right hand corner a young man and woman were reaping grain; several stacks already stood in neat rows. The lower left hand corner of the quilt depicted four children, two boys, two girls. They stood in a row looking at tall trees. Opposite, the farm itself was pictured, the nearby barn showing hay bulging from its upper windows and door, the fields full of tall grass, the house surrounded by people. In the very center of the quilt, bringing the entire mural together, was a big yellow sun, the rays of the sun acting as dividers between scenes.

Teresa, Blanche, and Irene stood spellbound by the beauty of the quilt, which had been carefully fashioned from tiny scraps of cloth, its countless colors cleverly shaped into realistic patterns, and from fine thread depicting smiling faces. It was intricate in design yet stunning in its simplicity.

"Our life," the old woman said quietly, and gazed lovingly at it.

"Did you make this?" Blanche asked incredulously.

"Over the years," answered the old woman. "I finished it this past winter. After my man died. Didn't seem fittin' to finish it before. Didn't have time."

Why, Teresa wondered, was this old woman alone now? She vowed deeply that no harm would ever come to this treasured place.

By lantern light, they were taken downstairs to a shallow cellar beneath the kitchen. The glow from the lantern reflected dully off rows and rows of canned goods in dusty glass jars lining the walls on neat shelves.

"Watch yer feet," their guide warned.

Looking down they saw, with some surprise, a small stream, frozen now, and unmistakably designed to run through the center of the dirt floor.

"Used it to keep the milk cool in the summer when we had cows," the old woman explained. "Lost my last cow this spring. Now I jes use the ice this winter to suck on. There ain't nothin' like crushed sweet ice in the winter."

"Sweet ice?" Blanche questioned.

"It's maple syrup poured over ice," Teresa explained.

"I pour it over snow," remarked Irene. "Let's have some when we get back home."

"Let's have some right now," cackled the old woman, her toothless mouth a black cavern in her face. With the lantern, she walked to a darkened side of the cellar and picked up a thick clay jug. Carrying the heavy container with her, she guided them back upstairs to the kitchen. Setting it down on the table with a thud she said, "Get some snow will you, honey?" and handed Irene a big bowl from the hutch. In no time Irene was back with the fresh snow which Grace quickly divided equally into smaller bowls. She pried the seal off the jug and deftly poured thick golden maple syrup over the white powder nearly filling the bowls to overflowing. "Eat it fast," she urged, glancing at the blazing fireplace.

They sat at the table and ate wordlessly, savoring the unexpected treat. Blanche, who had never tasted maple syrup before, ate hers hungrily.

Breaking their silence, Irene asked, "Where will you go if you sell your farm?"

"Got a son in Rochester," the old woman answered. "I'll go there. Can't do the work alone here anymore. Too goddamn old."

The three younger women wheezed a laugh and smacked their lips on frosty, sticky golden liquid.

Teresa started to say something, then stopped abruptly at the rheumy look in their hostess's eyes. Old people often looked rheumy-eyed, it was part of being old. Was that what this was? A display of age? "Grace," she said very gently, suspecting that the woman's thoughts on her long life were not all that was causing her eyes to suddenly fill.

Quickly, Grace Bowne glanced down at her bowl.

216

"Blanche." Teresa looked pleadingly at her lover who was also staring intensely at the thin gray hair and scarf covering the small head, all that Grace Bowne would let any of them see right now.

Softly, Blanche asked, "Would you care to stay on, Mrs. Bowne?" She reached out and put a hand over gnarled fingers to stop the old woman from stirring her syrup and snow into mush. "Would you teach us what you know? We know nothing about farming. You could help us. This would still be your home. Your dishes would still be your dishes. Your bedroom with your beautiful quilt would still be yours. This . . ." Blanche gestured with a graceful sweep of her hand. ". . . is your home. Keep it . . . and teach us."

Teresa fought a growing lump in her throat. She dropped her eyes to her own bowl as Irene reached over to squeeze her niece's arm.

The ancient woman looked up. A certain arrogance seemed to come into her eyes clearing them, invading the tilt of her chin, the lift of her head. "I know more about farmin' than anyone around here. Know more 'bout medicine herbs, too. Saved my chilln 'n my man mor'n once. An' sometimes the neighbors."

She stood and carefully set her bowl on the table. "Place needs work. Needs new curtains. Ought to paint the house, too. Looks ratty. First thing this spring, I got to clear my man's grave. Get's growed over. Can't hardly keep up with it. Damn lotta work to do." She walked over and poked at the fire with a black poker, sending sparks cascading up the chimney. "Can't write," she muttered.

"We'll write your son," Teresa said. "Your family could come and visit you anytime they wished. For as long as they wish."

"Big city folk now," the old woman said, her back still toward them.

"They'll come," Irene said, going over to her and leading

217

her back to the table. "I promise."

Teresa was sure Grace Bowne's sons and daughters would visit this treasure of a woman who had nearly been displaced from where she belonged. They would come if Irene had anything to do with it. Teresa smiled to herself and wondered if she could survive the loving ache in her chest.

CHAPTER FIFTEEN

The weeks piled up into December, then January, and February was half way behind them with two feet of snow on the ground. The new homeowners had decided to stay with Irene and Marie until spring — more at the outright suggestion of Grace Bowne than any plan on their part. The old woman wanted to spend time alone with her farm and her memories before strangers moved in and began changing things — even though she had been the first to suggest changes. Teresa and Blanche would have preferred to move right away but they respected the old woman's wishes.

Frequently, they rode into Albert with Irene and Marie in

a surrey with runners which was drawn over silvery hardpacked snow by a strong horse, his breath coming in big billowing puffs as the surrey glided silently except for the musical jingling of the harness bells and the dull thud of his shoes. The women bundled up tightly against the cold, protecting their lungs with woolen scarves wrapped across chilly faces.

Albert was a small town. Much like Blanche's Starcross in some ways. It, too, had its dress shop, a cobbler's shop, a smithy, a jail, a restaurant, one or two saloons — not nearly as rowdy as those Teresa was used to — and homes within the town itself, spreading further and further out from its boundaries. And, of course, there was Irene and Marie's mercantile store.

Like Johnson's Drygoods and Honest Scales, and Samson's Town's drygoods store, the shelves of this mercantile were also filled from floor to ceiling with every imaginable item one could need: tins of food, barrels of crackers and pickles, flour, dried peas, dried beans, spices, bolts of cloth, guns, ammunition, hats, boots, gloves. The items were endless. The pleasant odors of mingling dyes, spices, tobacco, and leather filled the air. And even here, the standard pot-bellied stove was surrounded by the same spindle-backed chairs. "Things are alike all over, aren't they?" Blanche commented upon entering the store for the first time.

Teresa and Blanche offered what little help they might in the store, but more often than not they just sat around and talked.

On this late and sunny afternoon, with the store quiet for the moment, the four women pulled chairs up to the roaring stove. The jingling of the bell over the door sounded. "I'll take care of it," Marie offered, and left to wait on the customer.

Suddenly, there was a loud crash. Irene jumped up. "What the hell —"

Teresa and Blanche looked toward the door to see an

220

entire shelf of goods come crashing down over the countertop to spill dozens of items all over the floor.

"No one moves," an angry voice ordered sharply. A single shot exploding toward the ceiling froze them in their tracks.

"Gene!" gasped Teresa. She hardly recognized him with his hat pulled down low concealing his eyes in shadow, and the heavy sheepskin coat cloaking his tall thin frame.

"You got it, Teresa, honey," he answered. An ugly sneer crossed his face. "Lattimer wants you. Now!" He grabbed Marie and pulled her against him in a vice-like grip. He pointed his revolver directly at her head.

Teresa cursed herself for her stupidity. Along with the rest of them, she had been lulled into carelessness over the snowy months. Never in her wildest imagination did she suspect he would have come this far north in the winter. If anything, he would have given up in Chicago if he couldn't figure out right away which train they had taken — and where they had gotten off. She had thought they were safe; safe because only a fool traveled any distance at this time of year. But if there was one thing a cowboy could do and do well, it was track. Normally, he looked for lost doggies. Not this time. Teresa's mind blazed with impotent rage.

Irene leaped at Gene. Without hesitating, he turned his gun from Marie's head and fired. Wordlessly, Irene slumped face down to the floor.

"No," Marie screamed, and struggled to break loose from his grasp.

"Yer next, goddamn it," he hissed viciously as she struggled uselessly against him, "if you don't quit yer foolin' around." Brutally, he rammed the gun against her head.

Blanche dropped to her aunt's side and slowly turned her over. Irene moaned from the movement. She was bleeding heavily from the upper chest.

"How the hell did you find us?" Teresa asked vehemently.

221

But she already knew. He'd hunted her like he'd hunt an animal — with skill and determination, ignoring no possibility in his search. But what had turned Gene into such a beast?

"Shit, lady," Gene swore, and answered her question: "There ain't no place I won't go fer enough money. Now get yer ass over here an' git ready to move. Yer goin' back to Texas."

"Like hell I am," she said determinedly, and moved to help Irene.

He shot at her feet. She leaped in panic. "Goddamn you," she screamed. "I'll get you for this, you bowlegged son of a bitch."

He shot again, this time winging her arm. She spun around from the blow and staggered against a chair, falling into it.

Blanche rose slowly from her aunt's side, staring first at Teresa who nodded that she was all right. Then she glared fiercely at the cowboy.

"Hey, I recognize you," he said. "Yer that fat old pig that used to hang around the Blackjack. I wondered who went with Teresa."

Blanche looked at Gene and smiled a deadly smile, her face smoldering as she said to him, "You remember me, I see. I may or may not be as fat. But I'm not as slow. And I never was a pig."

The tone of Blanche's voice terrified Teresa. "Blanche," she pleaded. "Don't."

"Don't?" Gene growled contemptuously. "What the hell is she gonna do? The fat pig." He pointed his gun directly at Blanche's head.

"Gene, for the love of God, please," Teresa begged, ignoring the searing pain in her arm. She knew *exactly* what Blanche would do.

The cowboy laughed harshly. Teresa knew he had gone absolutely mad.

"Don't hurt them," she cried. "Let the rest go. I'll go with you." She would not let Blanche be killed. Not over her. She would not let the one good thing in her life die because of what she had once been. She stood to go, painfully cradling her injured arm.

Blanche walked over to her and forcibly made Teresa sit down again. "You're not going anywhere, Teresa."

"Let's go, sweetheart," the cowboy roared. "I ain't got all day." He pulled the hammer back on the gun and the deadly sound filled the small room.

"Blanche, you must let me go," Teresa insisted strongly. "He'll kill you if you try anything."

"Life's meaningless without you."

"What the hell. . . ." Gene's eyes were full of questions.

"What'd he pay you?" Blanche asked. "I'll double it. Just leave."

Gene's eyes flickered as if considering the offer. But then he muttered, "Lattimer'd find me, he'd -" He shouted, "Let's go, whore!" Again, the gun was pressed tightly against Marie's head.

"I'm leaving, Blanche. You don't own me. Please step aside." Teresa spoke firmly, her eyes drilling into Blanche's.

Blanche shook her head. "I'm not letting you do this, Teresa."

"You don't, an' this bitch is dead," Gene raged, and gave Marie such a violent shake that she groaned in pain.

Teresa stepped around Blanche and went to get her coat, holding her injured arm to her side. Blood had soaked her blouse sleeve; it dripped a bright crimson onto the floor. Carefully pulling on her coat, she avoided looking at Blanche. She walked over to the tall cowboy. "Let go of Marie or none of us will get out of here alive. I mean it, Gene."

Blanche would come down on him like the wrath of God. She'd be shot in the process, and so would the rest of them. But Blanche would make sure Gene died, too. Of them all,

223

herself included, Teresa did not want Blanche harmed.

Gene threw back his head and roared his laughter at Teresa's words. Taking advantage of his momentary distraction, Marie seized the opportunity to escape his grasp and squatted down, then quickly twisted away from him.

Cursing, he reached for her but Teresa stepped closer to him, blocking his way, pushing him back. She said, "You wanted me, Gene. You've got me. Now let's leave."

He sneered at her and drew her roughly to his chest. "Watch, Blanchey," he said, and grabbed Teresa by the back of her hair forcing his mouth over hers. Teresa made no move to resist him, but Blanche took a threatening step toward them. He looked up at her and warned, "Don't you move, or your little darlin' is dead."

So Gene knew. Teresa felt sick with fear.

He gripped her cruelly by her injured arm causing her to cry out in pain, and backed to the door pulling her with him. "If I even *think* one of you is after me, I'll kill 'er. You understand?" he growled. The others stood as if frozen while he continued to back out of the store, dragging Teresa with him. "You better hope they take my advice, bitch," he said, and kicked the door shut.

He dragged her to his horse. Mounting, he pulled her up in front of him, the saddle horn digging painfully into her pelvis. Holding his arms tightly around her waist, he rammed his heels viciously into the horse's sides, kicking the bolting animal savagely. They rode out of Albert at a deadly pace toward Rochester.

Her mind filled with fear, blocking out even her own safety, she thought of Irene lying shot — perhaps dead — back in Albert. Thank God, at least Blanche and Marie were safe, and that she had been able to get Gene away from them.

It would be dark within minutes. And terribly, terribly cold. Teresa wondered where Gene was taking her and what the crazed cowboy's next step would be.

As if reading her thoughts, he leaned forward and shouted into her ear as the evening wind whistled by. The words were jolted from his mouth but she understood clearly every word. "Oh, I got a good plan, honey. A real good one. An' yer part of it. I got a fancy hotel in Rochester where I been stayin' for weeks trying to find you. You were real hard to track down after you left Chicago. Yer makin' me a world traveler an' I don't like it. I don't like leavin' Texas and travelin' all over hell. But Lattimer pays good. Even the hotel bill. An' that's where you an' me are gonna stay nice and warm tonight. Jes the two of us."

"I always thought you were a friend of mine, Gene," Teresa shouted back. "We always got along good."

"That's a joke," he yelled, and laughed cruelly. "I never thought you were anything but a little whore."

She bitterly fought back tears at his harsh words. What he said probably echoed what the other men who had slept with her thought: no matter how good a time they'd had with her, no matter how friendly some had become, in their minds she was only one thing — a whore. But not anymore, goddamit. She'd die first!

For fifteen minutes Gene drove the horse at a killing gallop. Slowing, he turned off into the woods where a second horse stood saddled and waiting.

"Get down," he growled, dismounting. She fell as he yanked her roughly from the saddle. He mounted the fresh horse and again brutally pulled her up in front of him.

"We're goin' to Rochester and get good and lost, Teresa honey," he said through clenched teeth. "Why the hell Lattimer wants a wasted bitch like you, I'll never know. Goddamn! To screw around with women. I got a cock that'll straighten you out, pronto!"

As they rode, Teresa's teeth chattered from the cold and

225

her entire body ached unmercifully. Fighting him was useless. He stood well over a foot taller than she and was as strong as a bull. Her only hope lay in outwitting him. One thing she knew for sure: one of them would be dead before he ever laid another hand on her.

They rode rapidly, never slowing to allow the horse to rest. Teresa's arm was now so stiff it was nearly useless and she was weak from loss of blood. The endless ride became an endless nightmare. She was without a hat and her coat wasn't nearly heavy enough to protect her. Exposed skin on her face and hands began to feel numb. She wondered if she would ever see Blanche again.

An expert rider, Gene guided the horse and held the weakened woman around the waist with one hand while brutishly grabbing her breasts with the other, squeezing them painfully until she thought she would faint. She was only able to brush at him ineffectively in protest.

As they rode into the falling darkness, he continued to talk of what he would do to her once they reached his room. His words excited him and his breath became short and ragged. Pulling her tighter to him he ran a hand down her thigh and moaned.

"Don't Gene," she begged pitifully. He ignored her and continued mauling her as they drew closer and closer to Rochester, his breathing increasing to near gasps.

Without warning, she was wrenched violently out of the saddle and thrown on the ground, knocked breathless. Her head struck a chunk of hardpacked snow as lights exploded in front of her eyes. Gene's passion had at last taken over his reasoning and Teresa wondered how she was ever going to stop him now. She moaned once, reached up a hand to ward him off, and then, mercifully, a velvet night closed in around her and she lay still.

CHAPTER SIXTEEN

"She'll be all right now." A voice from miles away floated in and out of her consciousness.

Another voice said, "The son-of-a-bitch ought to be strung up."

"Maybe he will be," replied the first.

Teresa could feel a blanket both under and over her. As she began to stir, someone knelt by her side. "You all right, ma'am? I'm sorry you had to take such a hard knock. It was the only way to stop this fool."

She opened her eyes to see a bearded man in a wide-brimmed hat and heavy coat silhouetted by a full moon. She rolled her head slowly to her left and saw Gene sitting in a snowbank. Another man stood nearby pointing a gun at him, the moonlight reflecting off a badge pinned to his heavy coat.

"How . . . how. . . ." Teresa murmured.

"We got a telegram from Albert about him," the young deputy by her side explained. "We rode out to meet him. When we heard his horse we moved off the side of the road. William here is an expert with the rope. He was just supposed to lasso this crazy jackass." The deputy gestured toward Gene.

"I ain't too good in the dark, ma'am," the deputy guarding Gene said apologetically. "I'm real sorry."

"It's all right," Teresa said. "I don't know what I would have done without you."

"Bah," Gene sneered. "You fellas know what that tramp is?"

Teresa's heart leaped to her throat. If he told the deputies about her love for Blanche, what might they do to her?

A resounding slap of the gun barrel across Gene's cheek knocked him backwards. "We know what *you* are, fella, and we don't like it. So shut up."

Gene pulled himself upright saying nothing more.

Inwardly, Teresa collapsed in relief.

The deputy helped Teresa to her feet and kept a blanket held snugly around her. "There's a doctor not too far from here ma'am," he said. "You need to get your arm tended."

Teresa was put on her own horse. She ached agonizingly and wished desperately that she could lie down and sleep. But even more she wanted to get back to Blanche. She fought to keep a clear head. She pulled the blanket tighter around herself and nudged the horse into a highly unpleasant trot.

They returned to Albert by midnight and as they pulled up before the sheriff's office, Blanche and Marie came running out. Behind them came Albert's Sheriff Roberts, a no-nonsense man with a wide drooping mustache on a face weathered by age but by no means beaten by it. He stood lean and tall, made taller still by his high hat. The heavy coat he wore against the night's bitter cold hid the ever-present gun on his hip tied with a thong to a long thin leg.

"Teresa," Blanche cried. She ran to the half-frozen woman and tenderly helped her from the saddle.

Safe in Blanche's arms, Teresa's next thoughts were of Blanche's aunt. "Irene," she asked, "how is she?" Please God, she begged silently, let her be all right.

"Sleeping — but recovering," Blanche told her. "Let's take care of you now."

Teresa's knees sagged; she leaned heavily against Blanche. If she had been responsible for that woman's death she couldn't have lived with herself. She said another short prayer: this one of thanks.

A deputy hauled Gene unceremoniously from the saddle, dumping him in the street lit only by the light from the sheriff's office. "There's your man, Sheriff. He got a little chilly on the way back. But we figured as long as he was complaining, he was still alive." Gene's hands were tied behind him and he was shivering badly.

Without warning, Gene said through clattering teeth, "Them two women over there, they're perverts, they screw each —"

With a quick and mighty arm, Sheriff Roberts grabbed Gene by his coat collar, cutting off his words, and hauled him roughly to his feet. He dragged the astonished cowboy away from the others. They couldn't hear what was said, so softly did the sheriff speak, his face only an inch away from the outlaw's. Then, returning with the outlaw, Roberts said gruffly, "Well, I guess that's it, then," and roughly pushed the badly shaken and deflated cowboy before him toward the jail.

Teresa stared at Blanche, seeing her own amazement reflected in Blanche's face.

"I'll put you men up at my house tonight," Roberts said to the deputies. "Marie, you and Blanche stay with Doc Adams. His wife will expect you. Teresa shouldn't go any further tonight, anyway. If the doc doesn't tell you that, I will."

Teresa insisted on seeing Irene before she would let Blanche put her to bed. Marie and Blanche stood back while Teresa walked to the prostrate woman's bedside and gingerly sat down in a chair next to Irene, wincing from her own bandaged gunshot wound. Thank God, she had only been winged.

Irene lay very still, looking pale and weak in the subdued light of the lantern by her bedside. She stirred and turned her head to the woman seated beside her. "Teresa?"

"I'm back," Teresa said softly and gave her hand a reassuring squeeze.

"Well, I'm glad," Irene whispered tiredly.

"I'm sorry, Irene. I'm so very sorry." Teresa burst into silent tears, her shoulders shaking with grief.

"Don't worry, dear. We've survived other crises. We'll make it through this one just fine." Irene closed her eyes and fell into a restful sleep.

Teresa stood and Marie took her place beside the bed to watch over Irene.

"Lattimer will just send others," Teresa said tearfully, looking down on the woman who had filled their lives with so much goodness and hope these last few months.

"No, he won't, Teresa," Blanche said, holding her close. "Gene was the last man who will bother you."

Teresa looked questioningly into Blanche's eyes.

"I told Sheriff Roberts what Lattimer was up to, the savages he had sent after us. . . ."

"The drifters?" A new fear gripped Teresa, and she had to

230

grab onto Blanche for support. Blanche would go to jail. There'd be a trial. She'd be hung! There was no end to this. None!

"Don't worry," Blanche whispered soothingly. "The only thing Roberts did was nod and spit tobacco into his spittoon. He wired Sheriff Maynard in Starcross and gave me his word that Lattimer would be in jail by morning. He told me this is a free and law-abiding country we live in, no one can just hunt people down like animals and get away with it."

"Are you sure?" Teresa looked at Blanche with questioning eyes, pleading eyes, eyes that begged for a halt to this madness.

"He pledged me his word."

"I don't understand about Sheriff Roberts," Teresa said. "The way he's helped us, the way he was with Gene, acting like he'd tear his head off —"

"There's a simple reason," Marie said with a smile. "His sister Emma. She's a nurse up at the almshouse — and one of us."

"Then, it's all over."

"Yes," her lover answered, smiling. "It's all over — except for the plowing, the planting, the harvesting . . . which Grace Bowne must yet teach us to do."

The three of them laughed quietly together while Irene snored gently.

"It's been a long trail," Teresa said looking into her lover's eyes.

"Yes," Blanche agreed. "It's been a long trail. But we made it. Through it all. We made it."

Teresa sighed and leaned contentedly against Blanche, thinking of all that had brought them here, to this point in their lives, to a place where they could finally stop moving, stop running. There was a coming depression to face, there was no denying that — and a necessity for buying more guns. But they'd be able to handle it. They'd conquered everything

231

else the trail had thrown at them — and won. Compared to what they'd been through, the depression would be a mere pebble in their path.

Overwhelmed with emotion, with a burning love for the woman in her arms she said, "If we were alone. . . ."

"Yes?" Blanche looked down at the trembling woman in her arms, a playful half-smile on her lips.

"If we were alone. . . ."

"Go ahead, Teresa," Marie suggested quietly. "Doctor Adams and his wife are in bed. As for the rest of us, well, we're all friends, here."

Blushing deeply, Teresa said, "I never have in front of another woman before, Marie."

"Have what?" Marie asked innocently.

Blanche just shook her head and kissed Teresa, silencing her silly words.

A few of the publications of
THE NAIAD PRESS, INC.
P.O. Box 10543 • Tallahassee, Florida 32302
Mail orders welcome. Please include 15% postage.

The Long Trail by Penny Hayes. A western novel. 248 pp.
ISBN 0-930044-76-2 $8.95

Horizon of the Heart by Shelley Smith. A novel. 192 pp.
ISBN 0-930044-75-4 $7.95

An Emergence of Green by Katherine V. Forrest. A novel.
288 pp. ISBN 0-930044-69-X $8.95

The Lesbian Periodical Index edited by Clare Potter. 432 pp.
ISBN 0-930044-74-6 $24.95

Desert of the Heart by Jane Rule. A novel. 224 pp.
ISBN 0-930044-73-8 $7.95

Spring Forward/Fall Back by Sheila Ortiz Taylor. A novel.
288 pp. ISBN 0-930044-70-3 $7.95

For Keeps by Elisabeth C. Nonas. A novel. 144 pp.
ISBN 0-930044-71-1 $7.95

Torchlight to Valhalla by Gail Wilhelm. A novel. 128 pp.
ISBN 0-930044-68-1 $7.95

Lesbian Nuns: Breaking Silence edited by Rosemary Curb and
Nancy Manahan. Autobiographies. 432 pp.
ISBN 0-930044-62-2 $9.95
ISBN 0-930044-63-0 $16.95

The Swashbuckler by Lee Lynch. A novel. 288 pp.
ISBN 0-930044-66-5 $7.95

Misfortune's Friend by Sarah Aldridge. A novel. 320 pp.
ISBN 0-930044-67-3 $7.95

A Studio of One's Own by Ann Stokes. Edited by Dolores
Klaich. Autobiography. 128 pp. ISBN 0-930044-64-9 $7.95

Sex Variant Women in Literature by Jeannette Howard Foster.
Literary history. 448 pp. ISBN 0-930044-65-7 $8.95

A Hot-Eyed Moderate by Jane Rule. Essays. 252 pp.
ISBN 0-930044-57-6 $7.95
ISBN 0-930044-59-2 $13.95

Inland Passage and Other Stories by Jane Rule. 288 pp.
ISBN 0-930044-56-8 $7.95
ISBN 0-930044-58-4 $13.95

We Too Are Drifting by Gale Wilhelm. A novel. 128 pp.
ISBN 0-930044-61-4 $6.95

Amateur City by Katherine V. Forrest. A mystery novel. 224 pp.
ISBN 0-930044-55-X $7.95

The Sophie Horowitz Story by Sarah Schulman. A novel. 176 pp.
ISBN 0-930044-54-1 $7.95

The Young in One Another's Arms by Jane Rule. A novel.
224 pp. ISBN 0-930044-53-3 $7.95

The Burnton Widows by Vicki P. McConnell. A mystery novel.
272 pp. ISBN 0-930044-52-5 $7.95

Old Dyke Tales by Lee Lynch. Short stories. 224 pp.
ISBN 0-930044-51-7 $7.95

Daughters of a Coral Dawn by Katherine V. Forrest. Science
fiction. 240 pp. ISBN 0-930044-50-9 $7.95

The Price of Salt by Claire Morgan. A novel. 288 pp.
ISBN 0-930044-49-5 $7.95

Against the Season by Jane Rule. A novel. 224 pp.
ISBN 0-930044-48-7 $7.95

Lovers in the Present Afternoon by Kathleen Fleming. A novel.
288 pp. ISBN 0-930044-46-0 $8.50

Toothpick House by Lee Lynch. A novel. 264 pp.
ISBN 0-930044-45-2 $7.95

Madame Aurora by Sarah Aldridge. A novel. 256 pp.
ISBN 0-930044-44-4 $7.95

Curious Wine by Katherine V. Forrest. A novel. 176 pp.
ISBN 0-930044-43-6 $7.50

Black Lesbian in White America by Anita Cornwell. Short stories,
essays, autobiography. 144 pp. ISBN 0-930044-41-X $7.50

Contract with the World by Jane Rule. A novel. 340 pp.
ISBN 0-930044-28-2 $7.95

Yantras of Womanlove by Tee A. Corinne. Photographs.
64 pp. ISBN 0-930044-30-4 $6.95

Mrs. Porter's Letter by Vicki P. McConnell. A mystery novel.
224 pp. ISBN 0-930044-29-0 $6.95

To the Cleveland Station by Carol Anne Douglas. A novel.
192 pp. ISBN 0-930044-27-4 $6.95

The Nesting Place by Sarah Aldridge. A novel. 224 pp.
ISBN 0-930044-26-6 $6.95

This Is Not for You by Jane Rule. A novel. 284 pp.
   ISBN 0-930044-25-8 $7.95

Faultline by Sheila Ortiz Taylor. A novel. 140 pp.
   ISBN 0-930044-24-X $6.95

The Lesbian in Literature by Barbara Grier. 3d ed. Foreword by
   Maida Tilchen. A comprehensive bibliography. 240 pp.
   ISBN 0-930044-23-1 $7.95

Anna's Country by Elizabeth Lang. A novel. 208 pp.
   ISBN 0-930044-19-3 $6.95

Prism by Valerie Taylor. A novel. 158 pp.
   ISBN 0-930044-18-5 $6.95

Black Lesbians: An Annotated Bibliography compiled by
   J. R. Roberts. Foreword by Barbara Smith. 112 pp.
   ISBN 0-930044-21-5 $5.95

The Marquise and the Novice by Victoria Ramstetter. A novel.
   108 pp. ISBN 0-930044-16-9 $4.95

Labiaflowers by Tee A. Corinne. 40 pp.
   ISBN 0-930044-20-7 $3.95

Outlander by Jane Rule. Short stories, essays. 207 pp.
   ISBN 0-930044-17-7 $6.95

Sapphistry: The Book of Lesbian Sexuality by Pat Califia. 2nd
   edition, revised. 195 pp. ISBN 0-930044-47-9 $7.95

All True Lovers by Sarah Aldridge. A novel. 292 pp.
   ISBN 0-930044-10-X $6.95

A Woman Appeared to Me by Renee Vivien. Translated by
   Jeannette H. Foster. A novel. xxxi, 65 pp.
   ISBN 0-930044-06-1 $5.00

Cytherea's Breath by Sarah Aldridge. A novel. 240 pp.
   ISBN 0-930044-02-9 $6.95

Tottie by Sarah Aldridge. A novel. 181 pp.
   ISBN 0-930044-01-0 $6.95

The Latecomer by Sarah Aldridge. A novel. 107 pp.
   ISBN 0-930044-00-2 $5.00

VOLUTE BOOKS

Journey to Fulfillment	by Valerie Taylor	$3.95
A World without Men	by Valerie Taylor	$3.95
Return to Lesbos	by Valerie Taylor	$3.95
Odd Girl Out	by Ann Bannon	$3.95

I Am a Woman	by Ann Bannon	$3.95
Women in the Shadows	by Ann Bannon	$3.95
Journey to a Woman	by Ann Bannon	$3.95
Beebo Brinker	by Ann Bannon	$3.95

These are just a few of the many Naiad Press titles. Please request a complete catalog! We encourage and welcome direct mail orders from individuals who have limited access to bookstores carrying our publications.